# SECRETS BEYOND SECRETS

I had kept putting off and putting off telling Delia of my origins. To her, I was a savage clansman, with a strange underspirit that did not come from the plains of Segesthes. But—Earth! How could I tell her I came from a star in the sky she could barely make out? How could she possibly believe in a world which possessed only one sun? What sense was there in a world with only one moon! And, how could any sensible person of Kregen believe in a world that contained only apims as men and women, where diffs were unknown? My story would be taken as the ravings of a madman. I ploughed on somehow:

"You will find it hard to believe me. But I shall tell you the truth. I swear it. I swear it by Zair."

"There arose a flying steed of remarkable appearance."

# SAVAGE SCORPIO

by
*Alan Burt Akers*

Illustrated by
Josh Kirby

DAW BOOKS, INC.
DONALD A. WOLLHEIM, PUBLISHER

1301 Avenue of the Americas
New York, N. Y.     10019

Published by
THE NEW AMERICAN LIBRARY
OF CANADA LIMITED

Copyright ©, 1978, by DAW BOOKS, INC.

All Rights Reserved.

Cover art by Josh Kirby.

SAVAGE SCORPIO is the 16th novel in the Saga of Dray Prescot and the 2nd novel in the Vallian Cycle.

First Printing, April 1978

1 2 3 4 5 6 7 8 9

PRINTED IN CANADA
COVER PRINTED IN U.S.A.

# Table of Contents

| | | |
|---|---|---|
| | A Note on Dray Prescot | 7 |
| 1 | The Brotherhood Rides Out | 9 |
| 2 | Kroveres of Iztar | 31 |
| 3 | Of Processions and Mercenary Guards | 39 |
| 4 | Ashti Melekhi, the Vadnicha of Venga | 50 |
| 5 | Of a Ruffianly Meeting at *The Rose of Valka* | 61 |
| 6 | We Pay a Duty Call on the Emperor of Vallia | 68 |
| 7 | Hamun ham Farthytu Asks Questions | 77 |
| 8 | A Brush with Flutsmen | 83 |
| 9 | In the Akhram of Bet-Aqsa | 89 |
| 10 | "In Aphrasöe You Will Find Only Death!" | 99 |
| 11 | Of Weapons, Colors—and the Scorpion | 104 |
| 12 | Strife Among the Star Lords | 111 |
| 13 | How Fimi Obtained Her Wedding Portion | 120 |
| 14 | The Fight with the Leem | 129 |
| 15 | Shadow | 139 |
| 16 | A Draught to Mother Zinzu the Blessed | 148 |
| 17 | Gifts from a Savanti nal Aphrasöe | 157 |
| 18 | The King of Djanduin Flies to Vallia | 165 |
| 19 | "There Stands the Notorious Dray Prescot!" | 176 |
| 20 | Savage Kregen | 185 |

## List of Illustrations

"There arose a flying steed of remarkable appearance."  ii

"They charge! See, the Shanks attack!"  29

"I lifted the sword and faced the advancing Khirrs."  145

"The stranded vessel was surrounded by an army of shrilling Katakis."  163

# DRAY PRESCOT

## *A Note on Dray Prescot*

*Savage Scorpio* chronicles the headlong adventures of Dray Prescot on the marvelous and mystical beautiful and terrible world of Kregen, beneath the Suns of Scorpio, four hundred light years from Earth.

Dray Prescot himself is an enigmatic figure. Reared in the inhumanly harsh conditions of Nelson's Navy, he has been transported to Kregen many times through the agencies of the Star Lords and also of the Savanti nal Aphrasöe, mortal but superhuman men and women of the Swinging City. There is a discernible pattern underlying all his breathtaking adventures, he is sure of that; but the pattern and its meanings remain veiled and unguessable.

His appearance as described by one who has seen him is of a man above middle height, with brown hair and level brown eyes, brooding and dominating, with enormously broad shoulders and powerful physique. There is about him an abrasive honesty and an indomitable courage and he moves like a savage hunting cat, quiet and deadly. On the dangerous and exotic world of Kregen he has at various times and for various reasons become a Vovedeer and Zorcander of his wild Clansmen of Segesthes, the Lord of Strombor, Strom of Valka, Prince Majister of Vallia, King of Djanduin—and a member of the Order of Krozairs of Zy, a plethora of titles to which he confesses with a wryness and an irony I am sure masks much deeper feelings at which we can only guess.

The volumes chronicling his life are arranged to be read as individual books. Now Dray Prescot is plunged headlong into fresh adventures beneath the hurtling Moons of Kregen, in the streaming mingled lights of Antares, under the Suns of Scorpio.

*Alan Burt Akers.*

# *Chapter One*

## The Brotherhood Rides Out

Shrill laughter broke excitedly over the Fair of Arial. The deep hum of many voices bartering, chaffering, driving hard bargains mingled with the roars and snarls from the wild-beast cages, the yells of barkers fronting their gaudily striped stalls, the tinkling of bells, the braying of calsanys. The exotic smells of a myriad different foods being cooked and served, the pervasive aromas of wines, the pungent fumes of dopa, coiled above the sweating happy throngs among the stalls and booths in the broad open space cresting Arial's Mound. A living breathing tapestry of noise and movement and color proclaimed the holiday atmosphere of the Fair.

The two half-naked ragamuffins, scratched by briars and panting from a long run, who ran fleetly from the forest into the outskirts of the throngs where hundreds of people haggled and drank and sweated and enjoyed themselves attracted no attention.

The boys were shouting. Above the din only a few grizzled zorcahandlers near them heard much, and these men, anxious about selling to a credulous fop a zorca whose single spiral horn had cracked and been expertly pinned and varnished over, shooed the boys away impatiently.

Quickly the boys ran on and tried to attract the attention of others; but everyone was too intent about the business of the pleasures of the Day, too self-engrossed to pay any heed to two dirty ragged lads, acting up a mischief. A group of men who by their equipment and rugged looks were tazll mercenaries, men at the moment without employment, gawped and joked before a brilliant tent where feather-clad maidens swayed and danced, clinking silver bells, flashing white teeth, kohled eyes very inviting as their puce-faced barker waved his arms and shouted hoarsely, jingling silver coins, wheedling the tazll mercenaries to enter and enjoy the dancing. The mercenaries sent the boys off with fleas in their ears.

Along the rows of stalls where all the varied produce of the Czarin Sea was displayed for sale the boys rushed, grabbing tunics, pulling decorated sleeves, shouting, and being cuffed and pushed away. Through the packed throngs and the noise moved vendors carrying heaped trays of delicacies, steaming mouth-wateringly. Cutpurses were active and a man must lief keep his eyes open and a hand closed over his purse. A few late Elders, solemn and grave with the importance of the coming ceremony, moved toward the central dais, Priests of many cults and religions walked sedately in the blended gorgeous suns shine of Antares, moving in spaces that opened magically for them and closed as magically after they had passed by. Mostly they were priests of Opaz. There was not one priest of the Great Chyyan, for the last apostle of the Black Feathers had been hanged, very high and very thoroughly from the tallest tree on the island of Nikzm, two of the months of the Maiden with the Many Smiles ago.

The Fair of Arial on the island of Nikzm in the Czarin Sea was, in this guise, only a recent institution. Previously it had been the marketplace for the pirates who thronged the busy sea lanes. From the island of Zamra just over the horizon to the north through the islands fringing Vallia to the west, from past the twin islands of Arlton and Meltzer to the south and Vetal to the east, the people sailed for this seasonal event. Now most of the renders had been destroyed, the pirates rendered harmless. Now the hullabaloo of commerce and pleasure gave joy and holidays to the good folk of the Czarin Sea.

Even from south of Arlton and Meltzer, from Veliadrin and from Valka, the people would sail in a grotesque variety of ships and unseaworthy boats to the Fair of Arial.

Then, when this fair was over for the season, the folk who followed the Fairs would pack up and travel to the next venue, hoping for richer pickings, perhaps, for more adventure, for a fresh zest and spice to life. For not all of Kregen, that mysterious and ominous planet four hundred light years from Earth is grim and cruel; among the beauty and the splendor there is room and more for fun and frolic and the enjoyment of living.

The two boys, bare of foot, scratched of legs and arms, red of face, continually tried to attract attention and were as continually rejected. A fat woman in a red skirt and black bodice, all wobbling chins and bust and stomach, dropped a wicker basket of loloo's eggs, well packed with straw and moss. Her hands flew up in horror as the two boys caught at her red skirt, shrieking in her ear, dragging her forcibly to make her listen.

The straw and moss proved woefully insufficient. Loloo's eggs rolled and cracked and splashed under the feet of the crowds. The woman threw her apron over her head, concealing her glistening face, and although her face was thus hidden and her screams lost in the merry uproar, by her lurching movements it was clear the boys had caused her the utmost terror. She staggered away. The corner tent pole into which she blundered supported an awning giving welcome shade from the twin suns. The awning collapsed. It billowed inward upon rows of men, dedicated drinkers all assiduously practicing their craft, quaffing good Vallian ale from glazed ceramic jugs.

Through all the bedlam of the Fair, belching out like an erupting volcano, the furious uproar from the devotees of Beng Dikkane, the patron saint of all the ale drinkers of Paz, bellowed and burst with the impassioned fervor of men interrupted at their worship. Flushed-faced men fought the tangles of cloth. Billows and humps of the gaudy material disgorged men raging with fury. Ale jugs flew, cascading their foaming contents over the drinkers, over passersby, over the trampled grass indiscriminately, in a wanton paroxysm of involuntary libations. The two boys, who made no attempt to run away and who—amazingly—did not laugh, would be chastised now for a certainty.

Seg nudged me.

"Brassud, my old dom! Here comes the Chief Elder." Seg shot me a wary glance from those fey blue eyes of his, his strong tanned face beneath the mop of dark hair very merry as he prepared to mock me in his usual way. "Where are your wits wandering? This is the islanders' great moment, and here you are, gawping into the air like a loon."

"I was watching those two lads, Seg. They've disappeared in the confusion—but they're in for a bit of stick, I fancy. Anyone who gets between an ale-drinker's ale and his stomach has only himself to blame."

"I'll allow that," said Inch, standing up so that his full seven feet of height gave him some advantage in peering over the heads of the jostling thousands. "They're having themselves a good time down there. The tent's right over now and there are ale barrels a-rolling every which way."

The confusion really was rather splendid. But my attention had to be directed to the portly, stiff, embarrassed form of doughty old Dolan Pyvorr. The Chief Elder, caparisoned in a blaze of finery, glistening and glittering in the mingled rays of the twin suns, advanced ponderously upon the steps leading up to the dais. He carried his Balass Rod with great ceremony. The Rod was all of two feet in length, banded by nine silver rings, and topped by a silver hirvel head, all fashioned superbly in Vandayha, the city of silversmiths in Valka.

Seg and Inch and the others of my friends and comrades upon the dais stood up to welcome the Chief Elder of Nikzm. I, too, stood up, for the protocol of princes means less than nothing beside the simple virtues of good manners.

A little scuffle of shoe leather at my rear took my attention. Turko the Shield used always to stand solidly at my back, in peace as in war. Now I heard his voice, low, saying: "By Morro the Muscle, Tarek, tread with care—"

And Tarek Dredd Pyvorr's answering voice, low, passionate: "You think I seek to harm the prince, Turko the Shield? Are you mad? Have you lost your senses? I, who owe everything to him? He meets my father, and he has asked that I stand with him at that time."

I took no notice. Turko might be overly officious about caring for my person—that is a great comfort on Kregen, believe me.

A little more shuffling and arrangements went on, and Balass the Hawk and Oby would have to shift along, I guessed. I killed my smile. Yes, we were a real bunch of tearaways, right villains all, comrades in arms, and here we were, dressed up like popinjays and standing on an overly-ornately decorated dais beneath a pavilion of cloth of silver, the focus of attention and—as they say—the cynosure of all eyes, waiting for the great moment, a great inaugural moment, in the Fair of Arial.

Among that group on the dais were others of my friends, some of whom you have met before in my narrative, others who, comrades in arms, have not yet found a personal mention. We were here expressly at the invitation of the Elders and People of Nikzm to take part in the ceremony about to begin. That was the official explanation for our presence. The true reason we were here was to meet in privacy, away from the prying eyes and ears of the capital—from which, anyway, I was banished—and all other teeming cities, to take further steps in the formation of the new Brotherhood.

Dredd Pyvorr stood a half-pace to the rear and to my left. He was garbed resplendently, as we all were, out of honor to the Elders and People of this tiny island of Nikzm. Now as his father climbed the steps to the dais, Dredd Pyvorr whispered his thanks anew to me.

"You have made me a Tarek, my prince. My father has been raised to become an Elder of our island, and to be Chief Elder—"

"I did not make him Chief Elder, Dredd. That he achieved himself, elected by his peers, out of his honesty and courage."

The Pyvorrs were hard-working, simple folk, the salt of the Earth—or of Kregen—and once the pirates had been cleared away and their markets closed to make way for the Fair of Arial, the island needed to be handled afresh. Situated just south of the island of Zamra, of which I am kov, Nikzm needed a council of Elders. Also, because he had fought well for us, and because he pleased me in his forthrightness and gallantry, Dredd Pyvorr had been made a Tarek, a rank of the minor nobility and within the gifting of a kov. Seg had made his Tareks in his kovnate of Falinur, and Inch his in his kovnate of the Black Mountains, both in Vallia.

"My loyalty to you is unshakable, my prince. And my gratitude eternal." In some mouths these words would have raised my hackles, made me think, created suspicion. They did nothing of the kind when spoken by Dredd Pyvorr.

His father climbed up the last few steps, puffing, broad and scarlet, and he bowed. He knew enough of my ways not to go into the incline or the full incline. I bowed in return and held out my hand.

"Well met, Elder Pyvorr. The Fair is a great success." We could hear ourselves speak, up here on the dais, with the bumblebee murmuring of the crowds around us. The fun over at the upset ale tent continued, and I fancied two small ragged forms would be eel-like squirming to avoid capture and chastisement.

"Lahal, my prince! Lahal and Lahal! Indeed—" and here Pyvorr turned himself ponderously around to survey the magnitude of the Fair with the noise and color and jollity. "Indeed this is an auspicious day."

I did not know why the invitation to attend this Fair had been sent me in the form it had. But Seg and Inch and the others seemed to know, and had prevailed upon me to attend. Anyway, I wanted to know how the island was prospering, now that it no longer had piracy to depend on for a living. The economy ran well, and the crops grew and the fishermen reported bumper catches, and copper had been discovered in the rolling hills that centered the tiny island. A tiny breeze licked in and flicked lazily at the banners and guidons, at the standards and flags. My old scarlet and yellow flag flew up there, and the red and white of Valka, and the red and yellow Vallia, and the blue and yellow of Zamra. And, surrounded by panoply, we stood like peacocks in our glittering clothes.

Pyvorr gestured to his Council of Elders, all standing gravely to one side, waiting for the proceedings to open. The few guards needed to keep the more importunate of the crowds away from the railed off space at the foot of the dais had no trouble. They were Pachaks, and they were every one a picked man, and they were the first bodyguard of the Brotherhood, not as yet fully inducted into the secrets of the Order; but devoted and loyal and soon to become acolytes. They were not mercenaries, having homes and steadings on Zamra.

The Council Elders all lifted their right hands.

Pyvorr turned heavily back to face me and lifted his own right hand. He glanced across at the rank of nine Womox trumpeters. Their horns were gilded and garlanded with roses above the fierce bull-like faces. Their tabards shone with silver thread. They lifted the long straight silver trumpets.

Each massive chest expanded with air sucked into powerful lungs. The trumpets caught the streaming mingled lights of the suns and glittered with silver starpoints.

The trumpeters pealed their fanfare. High and ringing, shrill, imperative, demanding, the silver notes pierced above the hubbub.

Silence did not fall at once. Rather, gradually and with ebbing and flowing disturbances, the uproar slowly faded. People ceased what they were doing—bargaining, buying, selling, eating, drinking, skylarking, testing their strength, having their fortunes told—and drifted out from the booths and tents into the open spaces and alleyways where they might see and hear what went on upon the high dais. The noise persisted as the people settled down in the suns shine for the ceremony.

Two dirty, raggedy figures darted out from the mass, pushing and shoving to make their way through to the front where the Pachaks stood on guard with the steel winking in their tail hands, upflung past their shoulders.

The boys shouted; but their shouts were lost in the bellows of outraged anger from some of the crowd. Others in the crowd began to shout, but in a different key, and to push and shove away, trying to escape the pressing throngs.

The boys burst out into the little cleared space at the foot of the dais. The Pachaks, veterans all, eyed them cautiously.

Amid the confusion of shout and counter shout some words jumped up from those in the crowd trying to push away:

". . . all riding sleeths!" and ". . . leaving us defenseless, open to massacre or enslavement!"

And, coinciding with the two boys' impassioned shrieks as they darted past the Pachaks and halfway up the steps, a word that grew and rolled about the Fairground and drew into itself much of the dark evil that festers on Kregen—

"Katakis! *Katakis!*"

"Slavers! *Slavers!*"

Somehow, my sword was in my fist.

Not all slavers are Katakis, that tailed race of devils, but almost all Katakis are slavers—given half a chance.

I swung about to face that band of brothers there on the high dais. Resplendent nincompoops we looked, decked out in all our finery. But each man wore a sword—except Turko—and each man was a comrade in arms, a bonny fighter, a veteran.

"Brothers!" I bellowed. I lifted the sword in a deliberately theatrical gesture, the long slender rapier blade glittering high. "This is work for the Order! For this we are created." I yelled at Turko direct. "Turko—fetch me up those two lads—and treat them gently. Oby—the zorcas. Seg, Inch, Balass—"

But my friends were already running, leaping down the steps four at a time, pouring out to belt across the flattened grass to the zorca lines. And Young Oby raced ahead of them all.

Turko appeared with a squirming tattered figure under each arm.

"And keep silent until the prince speaks to you, you Imps of Sicce!"

They slammed onto their feet, and Turko held a scruff of the neck in each ferociously powerful fist. I bent down.

"You have done well," I said. I spoke evenly but firmly, well knowing the kind of impression I could make if I was clumsy. "Where away are these Opaz-forsaken Katakis? You will lead us?"

"Yes, koter—"

Turko shook them.

Koter is the equivalent of gentleman, mister, and it was clear these two ragamuffins had encountered koters as the highest form of life. Not that I put store by ranks and titles, as you know, except as artifices to get things done.

"Address the prince as prince, famblys!"

"Yes, prince—"

As useful to ask these two if they could ride a zorca as ask them if they had a pocket full of golden talens.

"You take one, Turko. I'll take this rascal."

Seizing up my lad, who had a shock of brown hair that was probably more alive than many a languid noble of the court, I leaped off down the steps. Turko followed. Tom Tomor ti Vulheim reined past on his zorca, kicking dust as he slewed around and so pushed back the crowd. Vangar ti Valkanium did the same on the other side. Dredd Pyvorr appeared leading a zorca and Turko would have given her to me; but I waved him on and caught at the reins Oby flung at me. Up went my urchin across the saddle, my left boot went into the stirrup, and with a flick of my hand I was seated. My lad squirmed around, for the zorca may be the most beautiful of mounts, with four tall spindly legs, a marvel of grace and stamina; but the zorca is remarkably close-coupled and there is barely room for two.

"Your name, lad?"

"Tim, if it please you, ko—prince."

"Right, Tim. Which way?"

He pointed.

The wide expanse of Arial's Mound covered with the booths and stalls and wild-beast pens and stabling lines, with the now more than a little ludicrous high dais at the center, was rapidly clearing of people. They were running off in all directions. Some, at least, must be heading straight for the viciously-waiting arms of the Kataki slavers.

Tim pointed to the east, a direction that paralleled the coast, distant some two ulms.

Dredd Pyvorr reined across, his face furious, highly colored, intense.

"Briar's Cove, lad? Am I right?"

"Yes, prince, you are right!" sang out the lad with Turko.

"Fambly!" said Turko, incensed. "Only the prince is the prince."

"For the Order!" I bellowed. As of its own volition, it seemed, my rapier had appeared in a twinkling at the first mention of the Katakis, and had scabbarded itself when the lads had run up, so now, once more, the glittering blade snapped out. I waved it high and pointed forward. *"Ride!"*

As a group we rode out, past the last scattering fugitives, screaming and wailing, out along the narrow track that led through this neck of the forest, to curve down to Briar's Cove.

It appeared to me the Katakis, with the Fair as cover, had struck inland to take the chief town of Nikzm by surprise. Once they had possession of that, they could sweep up the people as they arrived. Long memories of pirate raids, of slavers and aragorn snatching away whole families, dictated that only those villages that needs must, say by reason of the fishing, would be built on the coast. In this, this section of the Outer Oceans resembled the Inner Sea, the Eye of the World of Kregen.

As we rode furiously along a fresh thought rose to torment me. The Katakis are a race strong and powerful, with a tail that, equipped with bladed steel, makes of them formidable opponents. They are also low-browed, dark, with thick black hair, oiled and curled, with gape-jawed mouths fanged with snaggly teeth, and generally of an evil, pestiferous nature. But we had met and bested them before. The thought that occasioned me some agony was simply this; no force of Kataki slavers would raid here, in the very shadow of the puissant empire of Vallia, for all the empire's internal problems, unless they raided in strength. They must be a strong and determined band.

And we were few.

I led my men into a battle that could easily end with us all dead or enslaved.

Yet no one had thought to count the cost. No one had thought to reck the consequences. Katakis had had the nerve to land on one of my islands to raid and enslave; therefore my band of brothers followed me into headlong action.

Through the coldness of these thoughts the warmth flowed that we were a band of brothers, we fought together as comrades in arms. This would be the first real test of the Order, for every man who rode with me had been invited to become a member, and had joyfully accepted. He had accepted the strictures laid on him, the demands that membership of the Order would entail. The simple, pure-minded and naive chivalry of the first rules of the Order may make me smile now; but they remain as true as ever, despite all that has happened since. We were idealistic, believing that too much violence on Kregen was being used by the wrong people, that we should do what we could to redress the balance. And these Opaz-forsaken Kataki slavers had turned up, right on our doorstep, to present us with our first challenge, our first test.

Certainly, as we thundered along the forest trail, kicking dust and twigs, a bright and colorful company, I did not count the discomfiture of the Black Feathers of the Great Chyyan. That evil creed had been bested in Vallia, for the time being, and the beating of it had not been at the hands of the Order as an Order. If I am a credulous man that is understandable, seeing the marvels I have witnessed in my life. But I detected a fundamental and powerful current of fate in this meeting between slavers and the Brotherhood.

Ahead the track twisted around a giant lenk, the oak-like tree growing to an enormous girth and shedding a deep and somber shadow upon the trail. We roared around the angle and beyond a sharp declivity the trees ended and a long greensward opened up. I reined in, my hand upflung, my zorca skidding and sliding.

Slowly, I cantered out into the open.

The others followed.

We stared.

The ground was littered with color, with steel, with bodies and with blood.

Slowly, we walked our zorcas through the shambles, the animals restive, not liking the stink of fresh-spilled blood, but obedient and going on, well-trained to the stark realities of war.

"So here are your Katakis, Tim."

Tim was being sick.

The ground was littered with bodies and with blood—Kataki bodies and Kataki blood.

I dismounted. As I looked up I saw for the first time that Young Oby had snatched up the scarlet flag with the great yellow cross upon it, my flag, the battle flag that fighting men call Old Superb. It shone in the mingled sunslight.

"These devils have been killed handsomely," observed Seg. He bent over a corpse, kicking the limp tail away so that the bladed steel strapped to the tip clinked against a fallen helmet. He picked up a bow. Oh, it was not a great Lohvian long bow; being of a compound reflex construction; but in Seg Segutorio's hands any bow is a deadly weapon par excellence. He smiled up at me. "I feel only half naked now."

The Katakis had fought hard. They lay in windrows at the end, piled high. Their wounds were all in front. But they were all dead, methodically butchered.

"Who could have done this?" said Dredd Pyvorr. He looked pinched of face. "Katakis are notorious. Chuliks?"

Chuliks and Pachaks command the highest fees as mercenaries, for different reasons. Our small guard of Pachaks remained mounted, instinctively carrying out soldier's work, scouting ahead, sniffing out the devils who had slain devils.

The body of one Kataki intrigued me. He was a big fellow, although Katakis are as a rule not overly tall. His helmet had fallen off. His face reminded me of that of Rukker. The arrow had punched through his bronze-studded scaled corselet.

At my side, Seg whistled.

"A goodly shaft...."

He bent to pull it out.

I said: "You'll find it will come hard. As a wager, I'll venture there are six or seven barbs a side. That's no Lohvian shaft, Seg."

"But it is as long—what bow is there that—oh!"

"Yes," I said. And I nodded and felt the anger in me, and the despair, the sorrow, and the vengeful fury.

"I have never met an archer who can best a Bowman of Loh," said Seg Segutorio, speaking softly. "But you have told me of these devils, and it seems we are to meet them, now."

"They must be devils indeed to destroy these Katakis, who are devils spawned from Cottmer's Caverns," said Dredd Pyvorr, feelingly.

"From around the curve of the world," I said. "From whence no man knows. They sail in their swift, magical ships, raiding, destroying, looting, burning. They are diffs unlike any in the whole of Paz. They are not men like us. They are the Shanks, the Shants, the Shtarkins, Leem Lovers, vile, to be destroyed, vermin—and yet, and yet, I know they are courageous to sail their ships all those untold dwaburs across the open seas. They are not men like us; but they are men."

"And they'll slay us all as soon as look," said Inch, sourly.

Dredd Pyvorr gripped onto the hilt of his rapier. His pinched mouth shook; then he had control of himself.

"I know of whom you speak, prince. We call them Shkanes—they have many names, all vile. Fish-Heads—yes, their horror goes before them."

I turned to young Tim, who had recovered and was now busily plundering the dead bodies, a most sensible occupation.

"You said they rode sleeths, Tim."

"So they did, prince." Tim looked up, his hands full of rings and chains and brooches, with a wicked-looking dagger stuck into his breechclout. I winced. He could do himself a permanent and most unfortunate injury if he were injudicious.

"There are no sleeths here, you imp of Sicce!" roared Balass the Hawk. He was prowling about looking for a sword more to his liking than a rapier, and hoping vainly to come across a shield. "Sleeths are stupid reptiles, at best, but they'd stick to their dead masters."

"That means, brothers, that the Shanks have ridden off on the Katakis' sleeths."

Oby ran off.

The sleeth is a saddle dinosaur, variously scaled and marked, which runs on two legs, the fore claws stunted and in a way pathetically stupid, and with the long thick tail outstretched to the rear to provide balance. They are an uncomfortable ride and I have nothing to do with them. I am a Zorca and a Vove man. I ride a Nikvove when I cannot saddle a Vove, and I like the superb joats of my Djangs, and I have some time for a few other of the riding mounts of Kregen. But sleeths—no, I do not fancy them.

From just over the brow of the slope Oby screeched and waved his arms, so we trotted over there. He pointed down.

The unmistakable tracks of sleeth claws showed in a muddy patch where water trickled past the grasses. The tracks pointed downslope and to the farther side of the greensward where the forest closed in again. The forest did not, at that moment, look in the least inviting.

"Find yourselves battle weapons more suitable than rapiers," I shouted. "Then we ride to deal with the Fish-Heads."

No one passed a comment on our riding to deal with men who had already dealt with the Katakis for us. For all their horrific reputation, the Katakis were small beer beside the Shanks, the Fish-Heads, from over the curve of the world.

Our Pachaks trotted in from their scouting duty and dismounted to search for weapons. The choices were plentiful. If the Shanks had taken any weapons from the shambles of the battlefield it made little impression on the numbers remaining. I selected a good stout cut and thruster, a version of the Havilfarese thraxter or the Vallian clanxer, and buckled it on scabbarded to its own belt. Its owner no longer possessed a face, besides now losing his sword.

Because I had steeled myself to go through with the ceremony at the Fair of Arial, a function whose purpose appeared to be known to all my friends and not to myself, I had donned the bright foppish clothes and had forced myself to ignore them, to grow accustomed to them. Now, and, I confess, with some relief and also somewhat pettishly, I stripped off the belts and ripped away the gaudy silks and sensils, threw down the brocaded pelisse and the feathered mazilla—the thing had been irritating and itching at me all day—and so stood forth clad only in the old scarlet breechclout.

In a battle a man needs protection from the blow he does not see. With resignation, then, I found pieces of armor that would fit and so donned a semblance of a breast and back, finding a reasonable fit over a padded vest. The scaled armor was flexible enough, the bronze studs barbaric against the black. Also, I took up a bow and four quivers, filling them from other, half-emptied quivers. As for the helmets of the Katakis, these are small and round and completely without embellishment, save for what may be painted on or engraved. The Pachaks are the same about their helmets. No fighting man who uses a bladed tail wants gaudy ornaments in his helmet to interfere with the lean lethal sweep of that deadly tail.

Finding one that fit I strapped it up. At the least, it might save my old vosk-skull from a terminal crack.

Inch appeared in high delight, tempered only by the fact that the axe he had found was not a true danheim axe, being double-bitted and short in the haft; but, as he said, it would serve to lop a few Fish-Heads' heads, it would serve....

There were no shields, for, as you know, the fighting men of this part of Kregen regarded the shield as a coward's accoutrement, a stupidity that Balass and I had been doing something to rectify. So Balass had to content himself with a good cut and thruster, and a powerful main-gauche built to mammoth proportions. As for Turko, the Khamster who could rip a warrior apart with his bare hands, the Khamorro who disdained all edged and pointed weapons, he still had his balass and steel parrying stick, a decadence of belief shocking and yet reassuring to me, for he, too, Turko the Shield, could not carry his great shield into battle at my back.

Oby took up Old Superb, and with the old battle flag floating above us, we rode from that scene of destruction and plunged into the gloomy defiles of the forest.

Turning in my saddle I saw the two lads, Tim and his friend, still hard at work. I sighed. Children learn the facts of life hard on Kregen—a phenomenon not unfamiliar to children on this Earth—but the facts they learn on Kregen are altogether more harsh and lurid. Turned in my saddle I noticed the tall whipcord tough body of the tazll mercenary who had been the only one to ride with us when we'd galloped from the Fair. He was a diff, a Khibil, with the hard, sharp, fox-like face of that people, with bristling whiskers and proud dark eyes. He had not dismounted to collect weapons. He carried a long lance, a rapier and main gauche and a cut and thruster. I had not failed to notice the silver mortil-head looped on its silver silken cord at his throat. He was a Paktun, a famed mercenary. He was not of the Order, not one of the Brotherhood, and so I had been wrong when I had so enthusiastically enjoined on us all as a band of brothers that we rode about the Order's business. But, all the same, he looked competent and tough and a useful man to have in such a fight as we would soon encounter.

Just ahead of him rode half a dozen of the minor nobility created by Seg and Inch, Tareks all, young men devoted to their lords and to the ideals of the Order.

Foleanor Arc, the young Strom of Meltzer, rode next ahead, brilliant, laughing, his guitar slung to his saddle bow and, I knew, causing him great anguish that he could not strum the strings and then give us a rousing song to help us on our way. With him rode Kenli ti Valkanium, straight and lean and grim.

They followed Nath Dangorn, called Totrix, who rode a zorca and would have preferred an ugly, six-legged totrix as a mount, and with him Nev ti Drakanium, who owed his loyalty to the Lady of Delphond.

Oh, yes, we were a goodly company, for there were others who rode with us along the forest trails in the somber shadows of the trees, with only the occasional chink of sunlight falling through, burning red when the ruby sun Zim shone down and lambent green when the emerald sun Genodras caught shafts of viridian light through the tracery of leaves. But we were few, pitifully few. Inch and Seg had counted at least a hundred and seventy-five Kataki corpses.

Truly, I had never before been of two minds over the numbers of dead Katakis there might be scattered about. Well, by Zair, to be honest, perhaps only when Rukker had been involved.

The way ahead showed a streaming mass of golden light as the commingled shafts from the suns drenched the end of the trail in radiance. We rode out from the forest onto a broad sweep of greensward. Small white flowers grew in clumps among the green. The little breeze tufted the grasses. Away before us the trail, which was in truth only a narrow beaten way where the grass struggled to cling to life, trended through a copse and then rose to skirt a hillside and so round the bend and, presumably, descend to Briar's Cove. The sound of the sea reached us in long murmured susurrations. Birds wheeled above, but their wheelings soon ceased as they set course for the shambles in our rear. At this sign we all knew the Shanks could not be far off.

I held up my right hand and made chopping motions

left and right. The column formed out and we rode abreast. The flowers and the grasses and the breeze, the high blue sky and, over all, the streaming mingled radiance of Zim and Genodras, created an unforgettable picture. We rode on.

The long swelling sound of the sea reached us from the right and on our left the small hill was crowned by a ruin from the olden time. White columns leaned, splotched with lichen. The corner of an architrave hung perilously over nothing. Insects murmured among the tall grasses and flowers bowering the ruin. We rode on.

The greenness of the grass was a greenness that held nothing of menace, lush and bright and soothing. Clumps of red flowers grew here and there, mingled with the white star-like blooms. Blue flowers, perfumed, delicate, drifted above tall stems in the little breeze. A few clouds, white against the blue, drifted in counterpoint to the blue flowers starring the grasses.

Truly, there are times and places on Kregen that are heartbreakingly beautiful. But we grim men, panoplied for war, rode on.

The Shanks rode out from the copse fronting us, a dense columns that debouched like a dark river in flood, formed a thickly ranked line that extended to flank us left and right, and sat, waiting, their weapons all a-glitter in the light of the Suns of Scorpio.

We had no trumpeter.

There was no need to sound the charge.

If men exist who prey on other men, looting and destroying and killing, then the victims must either perish or resist. To perish is not always easy, if nonresistance is part of a creed. To resist is sometimes the easier course, even if it does, in the end, lead to total destruction. Then, perhaps, it were better not to have resisted at all.

Who could say that these Fish-Heads did not have the right to sail over the curve of the world from their own lands, and burn and loot and destroy our lands?

These questions are imponderables, particularly when you are pounding along at full gallop, the sword in your fist, the suns light of Scorpio beating on your helmet, feeling the jolting lunge of your zorca, seeing the onrushing blur of Fish-Faces, the glitter of hostile weapons, readying yourself for the scarlet moment of impact.

The Brotherhood hit the thick ranks of Shanks and burst through in a welter of flashing blades and spurting blood, of screaming sleeths and zorcas, of men going down and of Fish-Heads being ridden into the turf.

It was all a blur of action. The sword thrust and cut, parried, leaped, slicked with the greasy green ichor of the Shanks, a live brand in my hand.

We were surrounded. The Shanks closed in. Seg's arrows cut them down as fast as he could draw the string and let fly. Inch's axe slashed with metronomic regularity, cutting swathes through the fishy bodies. Icy eyes glared at us, the abominable stink of fishy bodies clammied in with a foul miasma. We fought. Balass showed all the skill of the hyrkaidur, fighting with professional skill tempered now with the berserk rage of the warrior. Oby, using men's weapons, hewed and hacked and drove down his opponents. The clangor of sword against sword beat across that pleasant grassy sward. Blood dropped upon the flowers, the red blood of Paz and the green ichor of the Fish-Heads.

The Shanks wore bronzen armor, fashioned into fish scales. They possessed man-like bodies; but their heads were the heads of fish. Many varieties of fish, there were, I suppose. But we slew those we could and did not stop to reck the differences. In their fishy eyes no doubt we looked alike, although a Pachak and a Khibil do not look much alike, and diffs differ from apims like me. And apims differ, too, as Inch's seven foot of height marks him out from Oby's lithe youth.

The crowds of stinking Fish-Heads pressed in. Our zorcas reared as we fought, struggling to find space. We were hard pressed. Swords cut and slashed. Over and over again a man would be saved in the last moment by a comrade's blade. Our brands ran thick with green ichor. Soon our arms would tire. We were all fighting men, warriors of Kregen, men who were inured to hardship and suffering and the clangor of war.

But humanity is frail. Muscles and blood, sinews and breath, can only sustain a man for so long. Then strength will fail and breath come hard. Then muscles will fail to bring the sword up in time, to deliver the terminal blow. And there were many Fish-Heads, over twice as many as in the Brotherhood.

We fought magnificently.

But we were pressed in and back. The Pachaks found a weak link in the circle and we smashed our way through. I lifted in the stirrups and waved the dripping sword.

"To the trees!" I yelled. I took the responsibility. I ordered the retreat. I, it was, who took my men away from that death trap.

We galloped hard for the trees and we passed the little ruin atop its hill. There were fewer of us who thus retreated than there had been who so valiantly charged.

At the tree line we reformed. Our zorcas were tiring. We were all panting. Most of us were wounded. Blood shone red upon our armor. And, over all, the sticky green ichor clung, stinking, foul, like a vomit to revolt us all and remind us of the inevitable end.

The dark mass of the Shanks with those evil glittering points of light from point and edge of weapons waited at the far end of the greensward slope. Banners fluttered above them, a multi-colored display that meant much to them and nothing save as targets for destruction to us. I looked at the Brotherhood, panting but determined still. We were few.

"We will chew them up piecemeal and spit them out as one spits out gregarian pips," I shouted. "We hit the left flank and break clean through and retire. Understood?"

"Aye, prince. Understood." The cries came bluffly, strong, confident despite wounds and tiredness. I shook my zorca's reins and led out.

We hit them like a rapier lunge, chopping off the left flank. We lost men, yes, we lost good men; but we trampled down and slew more of them than they of us.

The Shanks—the Shkanes as Pyvorr called them— handled their tridents with superb efficiency. The wicked barbs would degut a man as neatly as a fishmonger deguts a cod. But the wicked tridents had their disadvantages. Seg deflected one with the bowstave in his left hand, his sword blurred down and sliced away an icy Fish-Face, and Inch, the barbs of a trident caught in his saddle, slashed his axe in a merciless horizontal sweep that sprayed bits of fish everywhere.

We reformed back upslope and turned, and hit them again.

Four, five, six times we regrouped and charged.

At each charge we were less. The zorca, as we all believed then, was not the animal for the solid shoulder-to-shoulder, knee-to-knee charge, bodyweight and mass of metal counting more than fleetness and agility. Times change—but that is for later.

Seven times we raced fleetly over the slope, angling the

direction of our lunge, trying to chew and chop at the mass of Fish-Heads as a man hews and cuts at a stubborn log of wood to shape it to his satisfaction. The fight was of great intensity during the action; the compass might be small but of individual prowess the battle was of epic proportions.

The arrow storm I had expected to greet us from the Shanks' asymmetrical bows stormed only once. We lost men; but I shouted and lifted my sword and beat away the glancing shafts, and others bent their heads into the sleet. We charged through that ordeal, losing men—the Pachaks suffered here—and so came to hand strokes, again. After that the arrows fell sparingly and I guessed the Shanks were running low.

If ever the relative merits of the reptilian two-legged sleeth and the close-coupled four-legged zorca could be proved, then this battle matched them and proved decisively the zorca as the master. Pirouetting, dancing nimbly sideways, circling, the zorcas outran and outmaneuvered the clumsy sleeths. This gave us one tremendous advantage. We could drive in, deliver our blows and spin away before the sleethriders could form front to receive our onslaught.

The grasses stained red and green with dropped blood. Men and Fish-Heads lay upon the stained grass, some howling, some screeching, most dead.

Eight times we roared in, and on the eighth time we were fractionally slow through tiredness and so were nearly surrounded and trapped. We fought free. Sword against serrated sword and trident, we hewed and savaged our way through the pressing ranks, rode with bent heads for the tree line past the white columns of the ancient ruin. We were nearly exhausted. All were wounded. We gasped for breath. Our superb zorcas were near the end.

I rode a few paces before the brothers of the Order—with the Pachaks and the Khibil there in the line with us—and I lifted in the stirrups. I surveyed my men from under the helmet rim.

"If any man wishes to withdraw through the forest, he is free to do so. I shall not think any the worse of him for that. If any one of you wishes to go, then go now, and may Opaz guide your footsteps."

There were gaps in the ranks, and the gaps closed up.

No man moved back.

The zorcas shifted on their polished hooves. Oby held the scarlet and yellow banner high.

I let out my breath.

"Then let us all go forward, together, as a band of brothers."

"They fight hard, by Erthyr the Bow," said Seg. He shook his bow at the dark ranks of Shanks, speckled with the cruel glitter from their weapons. "But we'll have 'em!"

"We'll take a few with us to the Ice Floes of Sicce," said Inch. "By Ngrangi, this old axe will lop a few fishy heads."

"By Xurrhuk of the Curved Sword," spat out Balass the Hawk. "We can lick them yet."

"Aye!" sang out Oby. He used an oath of the jikhorkdun, in remembrance of other days. "You speak sooth, Balass, by the glass eye and brass sword of Beng Thrax!"

Other oaths rose as men swore on their honor. These men would fight to death, however nonsensical that might be. And yet—and yet? Could I detect a wavering among some of those with us? A very slight, an almost imperceptible, reluctance? Some of the shouts and cries carried overtones of hysteria. Some of these men might waver. They could see quite plainly that this affair could end only in their deaths. Where was the sense in that? Yet these men were brothers, of the Order—yet the Order was new, unfledged, with no long-rooted traditions to inspire and uplift and enable men to act beyond their own resources. Could I blame them?

"The island of Nikzm is small," I shouted. "Since we dispersed the pirates there has been no fighting. There is no garrison to speak of. All that lies between these Fish-Heads and the defenseless people—is us—the Order." I did not wave my sword. I sat hard and upright and glared upon these, my men, the brothers of the Order I hoped would achieve so much. "But that is not the whole reason why we fight on. Yes, it is the ultimate reason for our being. For the people of Nikzm represent all the peoples of Paz. All the continents and islands here. But we fight for our own honor. We fight in our own eyes, we are our own judges. It is to us, and us alone, that this jikai belongs. And in honor we must redeem our pledges so freely given."

The line, so shrunken now, quivered. Zorcas began to sidle. The men were dispirited, despite their words. In only

"They charge! See, the Shanks attack!"

moments one man might break, and with his desertion the whole line could crumble. Was this how my own vaunting ambitions were to end? On a tiny island, destroyed by stinking Fish-Heads? Was my own pride so vainglorious that I would condemn to death this fine company of men, young and proud in their strength, laughing and merry, send them remorselessly to destruction? For myself? For my overweening pride and ambition?

In that dark moment, I, too, I, Dray Prescot, of Earth and of Kregen, came very close to despair.

A voice, an anonymous voice, rose from the ranks.

"Let us ride from hence and gather reinforcements. Let us save ourselves so that we may fight another day."

I looked.

I confess it, I looked to mark the man.

It was Dredd Pyvorr, Tarek, created by me, given honor and rank, his father uplifted, an Elder, the Chief Elder of this island we fought to save.

"If this is your will—" I started to say, not thinking, not even savage, but resigned. I, Dray Prescot, the Lord of Strombor, Krozair of Zy, resigned to running from my foes!

Another voice bellowed, hard and fierce.

"They charge! See, the Shanks attack!"

I swung about, lowering, hating, filled with anger and remorse and fury and shame.

The Fish-Heads bore down on us, a long dark breaking wave of beasts and mounts, tipped with steel, riding knee to knee, hard and savage and utterly without mercy, riding to crush us and smash us into utter destruction.

"Now are we doomed!" The shriek rose and shattered in despair.

The line began to break.

# Chapter Two

## Kroveres of Iztar

As that dark and glittering onrushing mass bore down on us I cursed my own stupidity and pig-headed vanity and folly. I, Dray Prescot, had led these men to their deaths. The horrid clicking and scratching of many sleeth claws reached us with hypnotic intensity. The tridents glittered red in the light of the Suns of Scorpio—glittered red with our blood.

The line at my back moved and snaked, restively. The zorcas were tired. The men were exhausted. Fool! Onker! I should have retreated at the first, sought what assistance there was in Nikzm; small though it was, it would have made the difference. All the mercenaries at the Fair, the stout country-folk, the fishermen—with what weapons we could have gathered up for them, we would have fought—and I realized even as I thus castigated myself that no simple countryman, no fisherman, was going to meet and best in battle these supremely warlike Shanks. The Shanks lived for battle. It was a creed with them, some divine right given to them by their own dark and fishy gods, driving them on, egging them on to plunder and conquest and eternal battle.

The truth was the Brotherhood had achieved against the Shanks what few groups of men of Paz had ever achieved before. And the cost was high, the payment dear, the final reckoning written in blood and spelling death.

"Brotherhood of Paz!" I bellowed, turning in the saddle, glaring back at the shuffling line. "Those of you who will, go! Flee! Save yourselves. Raise the island, carry word to Zamra, rouse the garrisons. And those that will—follow me!"

Lumpily turning in the saddle and ready to clap in

heels—no man who is a rider uses spurs to a zorca—I hesitated, and turned back. My face must have borne that old intolerant, savage, devil's look. I bellowed.

"Seg! Inch! Balass! Turko! Oby!" I shouted, loud, intemperately, viciously. "Tom! Vangar! Nath! Kenli! Naghan! You do not ride with me. Your duty lies in other places closer to your hearts! I order you to ride and seek succour! *Ride!*"

They left it to Seg to speak for them all.

Seg Segutorio lifted his bow. He smiled that raffish, fey grin of his, his blue eyes very bright and merry in that tanned face beneath the shock of black hair.

"Oh, aye, my old dom. We'll ride. We'll obey your damned high-handed orders. Only it happens that the quickest way for us to ride to do your bidding—*prince*—is to ride straight ahead. Straight ahead!"

"And if any lumpen Fish-Face happens to get in the way, let him look out," Inch finished.

"Famblys!" I shouted, feeling the gush of warmth, the anger, the pride at their folly, the agony and the shame. "Idiots! Onkers! It is my duty and mine alone—it falls to me—"

"Sometimes you take too much on your shoulders," said Turko. His magnificent muscles bulged. I blinked. In Turko's left hand a green-dripping sword caught the lights of the twin suns. "Turko? A sword?"

He laughed. "They broke my parrying stick. This serves in its stead. Had I my great shield, now, then—"

The clicking scrape of the advancing sleeths bore down on us.

The line shifted and yet, and yet they would not ride off. For a space the tension hung. Now I knew that they must ride. I had been wrong, criminally wrong, in thus dragging these men to their deaths. In my own folly and pride I thought I had been doing the right, the noble, thing. But nobility can be bought at too high a price. It was folly to have these men slain to no purpose now. If we all died here—as we would, as we would!—how would that help this tiny island of Nikzm, let alone the mighty empire of Vallia?

No thoughts of my Delia must be allowed to enter my stubborn old vosk-skull of a head. None.

"Go!" I bellowed. "Save yourselves!"

A few men shook out their reins, they would not look at me. But I did not blame them as they began to turn their zorcas' heads, ready to ride back through the dark defiles of the forest.

So this was how all my brave dreams for a great Brotherhood had foundered! The Order was finished. It had never even begun.

I turned back to face the oncoming mass of Shkanes, and I wished I could have had my old Krozair longsword with me, and I kicked in my heels and the zorca lunged forward for the last time.

Headlong I belted for the black and silver glittering mass of Fish-Heads.

A shrill and shocked shrieking began—began to my rear.

I did not look back. The zorca flew fleetly over the grass where the blue and red and white flowers starred the green, where drops of red blood stained across the flowers. The shouting at my back increased and voices mingled in shocked disbelief. I looked up to my left, toward the white ruins.

I stared, disbelieving.

A light glowed among the white tumbled columns.

A golden yellow light, lambent, blazing, growing in color and luminosity, swelling. And at the heart of that refulgent radiance the figure of a woman astride a zorca. A woman wearing golden armor, astride a white zorca whose single spiral horn blazed with golden light. I stared and the mount beneath me ran loose. I stared at the apparition. She wore golden armor and carried a great banner which flowed freely outspread in a breeze no one else could feel, an unearthly breeze from a land beyond the senses of normal men.

"Zena Iztar!" I screamed it out, shaken, dazed, wondering. *"Zena Iztar!"*

This was the supernatural woman who had visited me on Earth when I had been banished there for twenty-one miserable years. Then she had used the fashionable name of Madam Ivanovna. She had appeared to me before, using supernatural means, and I believed she had helped me. She was not, as far as I then knew, aligned either with the Savanti or with the Star Lords. I gaped and the zorca eased up, and slowed down. Zena Iztar lifted the great banner so that all could see the device coruscating upon the crimson surface.

Outlined in white upon the glowing crimson banner the deep royal blue of her cogwheel device forced itself upon my own senses, yet I had never grasped the significance of that emblem. Always before Zena Iztar had appeared to me alone, with those around us frozen in a timeless sleep. Yet now—now from the shouts and excited and shocked exclamations that broke from the brothers of the Order, she could be seen by us all.

Her voice reached us. Golden, ringing, full-bodied, her voice floated above all the sounds of coming battle, over the shouts and yells of the men, over the clicking scraping advance of the sleeths and the hissing malevolence of the Fish-Heads, over the mingled jingling of war harness.

"Men of Paz! Brothers of the Order! Comrades in blood! Those you call Fish-Heads must be shown the error of their ways. The Order demands sacrifice, loyalty, utter devotion, unswerving purpose, obedience." She lifted the banner in her left hand and golden coruscating sparks shot from her armor. In her right hand a sword—a sword! A sword like unto a Savanti sword—lifted high and pointed. The brand pointed at the Shanks. "Death is a small price to pay for honor! Brothers of the Order! Your duty in honor is to be true to yourselves and to Paz and to the Order."

The light began to fade.

I shook my head. There was much she had said with which I would not, could not, agree. But a great deal summed up something of what I struggled for.

But, in the name of Zair! How did she know the Order existed at all?

But, then, she was no mortal woman. She understood many secrets I longed to know, could see into the hearts of men, must surely comprehend the doings of Kregen and attempt to mold them to her own ends.

The Shanks pressed nearer. They were confident now. They had withstood all we could throw at them. They had suffered and had lost a goodly number from their ranks. But they could see how we had suffered. They shrilled their hideous screeching war cries and they came on, fishy, stinking, scaly, repulsive, deadly.

They had not seen the golden glowing apparition of Zena Iztar.

Her chiming voice rang out for one last time before the vision disappeared.

"Fight for what you believe to be true, Men of Paz. And, remember, never speak to anyone not of the Order of my presence, for I am sacrosanct. This is a stricture laid on you as members of the Order—and a privilege. Follow Dray Prescot. *Jikai!*"

The first man to move was Dredd Pyvorr.

With a high lifting shriek he set his zorca in a straight dead run at the oncoming Shanks.

We saw him galloping madly into the thickest of them. We saw his sword swirling and smiting left and right, saw him engulfed as a stone is engulfed in a pool. In the same instant we were all once more in motion, roaring down, headlong belting down into the repulsively stinking mass of Fish-Heads.

Dredd Pyvorr had shouted as he charged for the last time.

Over and over he had shouted as he roared to his death.

"For the Brotherhood of Iztar! For the Order! For Dray Prescot! Iztar! Iztar!"

I felt the coldness running through me.

There were manipulations here, superhuman twistings of normal human men to supernatural ends.

Then we hit.

The red roaring madness of battle descended on us. I am contemptuous of that notorious red curtain that falls before the fighting man's eyes—so it is said—but it is a thing that transcends humanity and must be used and manipulated in its turn so far as a man may. We fought. We fought.

I think, now, as I thought then, that Zena Iztar brought some of her magical powers to our assistance. Nothing else, in all sanity, serves to explain what happened.

The few of us, the few Brothers of the Order of Iztar, smashed and beat and routed the confident might of the Shanks from around the curve of the world. We destroyed them. The survivors ran. The sleeths poured blood as the Shkanes poured blood. Green ichor fuming onto the grass, smoking under the suns.

We pursued them.

Down the long slope and through the copse and so down the last curve of the trail into Briar's Cove we pursued them, slaying all the way.

Memories are scarlet and monstrous and do not pass.

Our arms did not tire. We were possessed of superhuman strength. Tireless, we smote and slew and drove them down to the beach where we slew them in the water as they tried to reach their ships. Those ships with their clumsy square upperworks and the sleek fishlike lines below water, with the tall banded aerodynamic sails, pushed off with the last few remnants. The black and amber sails slid up the tall masts, curving to the breeze. The ships pulled away, sliding easily through the water, and we stood on the beach and shook our fists at the Shanks, and cursed them, and jeered them, and felt, perhaps, as no men of Paz had ever felt before.

We did not attempt to sail the ships in which the Katakis had landed after the Shkanes. I knew that no ship of Paz, not even the superb race-built galleons of Vallia, could catch a Shank ship.

Some of the very best galleons built in Valka might almost match a Shank vessel, and we were working all the time on improvements; but these Kataki vessels were mere small editions of argenters, broad and squat and with a pitiful sail plan. They were broad-beamed and capacious and designed to hold slaves.

We stood and jeered and fumed until the last Shank vessel vanished from sight, and then we turned back to the dolorous business of clearing up after the battle.

There was much talk, and much to talk about; but one single topic dominated every conversation.

Zena Iztar.

Dredd Pyvorr had been the first to drive into battle at her instigation. He, it was soon apparent, was the original martyr of the Order. His name would live enshrined.

Traditions were built in this fashion.

And, too, I detected a difference about these men. Some inner strength had been vouchsafed them. They were not the same men who had agreed to join the Order. They had been refined, refined in the crucible of agony and battle, and now they gleamed with a luster of spirit I found mightily reassuring—and also worrying in that nagging anxious way I have when events pour past without due design and thought spent upon them.

As with my membership of the Order of Krozairs of Zy upon the Eye of the World, I will not speak of much of our discipline. Much had been taken from the Krozairs, for their Orders are justly famed, and workmanlike, martial and mystic, devoted to Zair, and designed to sustain morale and spirit in the deepest of adversities. So I will content myself with a few remarks only. In the old days of Valka, when that island of which I am Strom was its own kingdom, they had their own knights, men of high-caliber, renowned, given the honor prefix of Ver to their names.

This, we chose to resurrect, and members of the Order of Iztar were called, among ourselves, Ver Seg and Ver Inch, and so on.

Ver Seg Segutorio was the High Archbold.

This I welcomed and refused to take on any particular position for myself, preferring to be a plain member, a simple Ver of the Order.

We called ourselves Kroveres.*

Kroveres.

The name rang and reverberated, as the name Krozair rings and reverberates.

We were the Kroveres of Iztar.

Also, and at the time much to my displeasure, another name was also used, and I asked questions and was told. Was told.

Seg said to me: "We are the Order of Kroveres of Iztar, Dray. Now we must build. This little Island has witnessed a miracle."

"Surely," I said as we rode lumpily for the Mound of Arial. "And you still haven't given me any idea why we came here in the first place—except to check up on progress."

He laughed.

"Why, you may as well know now. I think Elder Pyvorr will be mourning his son—" All the laughter fled. "It was a great deed, Dredd Pyvorr's. We shall remember him in the Kroveres."

"Yes, that is so. And?"

"And, my old dom, you were asked here to be given the new name of the island as a gifting. You are the Kov of Zamra. Zamra is just over the horizon to the north, and this little island is called Nikzm—"

"I know!" Nik as a prefix means half and as a suffix means small. In the names of lands and islands, however, the prefix often carries the meaning of small, for Zamra was by many times more than twice the size of Small Zamra, Nikzamra, Nikzm.

"The Elders and people of the island have decided and issued the necessary patents and the bokkertu has been concluded to call the island Drayzm. Drayzm. So, my old dom, we are also the Kroveres of Drayzm."

---

* Kroveres. Prescot spells this out. He pronounces it in the same way as Krozair, but does not spell it Krovair.   A.B.A.

So, as you can well imagine, I was not overly pleased.

I passed it off; but Seg gave me a hard look, and said a word or two about thick-headed, vosk-skulled ingrates, and how Delia was muchly pleased—

"Did Delia know about this, then?"

"Oh, aye. You don't think we'd go behind your back without consulting Delia, do you? You've told me how they made you Strom of Valka—well! This is no new title—and I know how you feel about them, as I do. They are useful in this world."

"That is sooth, by Vox!"

And Inch leaned forward to say, waspishly: "And if the Kov of Falinur lost that one, he'd not give a damn, hey?"

"Too right!" snapped back Seg. He had had great trouble in his kovnate of Falinur. "Except—except Thelda would—"

"Aye," I said. "Thelda likes mightily to be a kovneva. And so she should. She deserves it."

Inch laughed and chick-chicked his zorca and we rode on. But I began to think how best to relieve Seg of Falinur and find him a kovnate where he was not regarded with hatred, through no fault of his own but because of the ingrained animosity of the people to anyone who deprived them of slaves.

Then, of course, the problem would arise that the new kov would almost certainly approve of slavery, as did most ordinary men and women of Vallia. Slavery, Delia and I had sworn, was going to be rooted out of Vallia. I looked beyond that, as did Delia, I know now, until it was finally uprooted from all of Paz.

As we rode back this kind of talk naturally led on to the problems of Vallia, the huge island Empire. Delia's father, the emperor, had once more gained a breathing space with the destruction of the Chyyanists; but there were always fresh factions seeking to drag him down and install the puppet of their own choice as emperor.

"Mind you, Dray," said Seg, reflectively as we cantered gently into a defile ready to begin the last ascent to Arial's Mound in the last of the suns shine. "The nobles loyal to the emperor remain loyal, or most of them. He couldn't rule without them."

"But the opposition parties still continue, also," pointed out Inch. "They keep changing alliance and pattern; but they are still against the emperor, the whole family." Here he looked at me.

I nodded somberly. Vallia is an enormous patchwork of many different sized estates, run by nobles—by kovs and vads and trylons and stroms and all the others—and there are many parties and factions, not all of whom seek to destroy the emperor. At this time the main party was the Racter Party, and the second the Panval Party. The Fegters were growing in strength and there was always the North East of Vallia, an area traditionally troublesome. But when Inch mentioned the family of the emperor, he was thinking of Delia and me and our family.

"And, to cap it all," said Seg. "There's this Queen Lush. Thelda is still captivated by the woman. I fancy this queen has her eyeballs firmly set on the emperor. You'll have to have a say there, Dray."

"Sink me!" I burst out. "If the old devil wants to get married again I won't stop him." I added, nastily: "Give him something else to think about."

"Well, my old dom, you're still banished from Vondium."

I grumped in the saddle; and we rode on. By Zair! But I was anxious to see Delia again and find out about our erring daughter Dayra. And even Lela still had not put in an appearance. I'd not seen them for years and years. It was just not good enough. So I was not in the happiest of moods as the final rites were gone through, the Kroveres of Iztar dispersed to their homes, the island was renamed Drayzm, and, at last, at blessedly last, we could take off for Valka and home—and Delia.

# Chapter Three

## Of Processions and Mercenary Guards

The airboat swung in a wide graceful arc over the glittering sea and the dancing wavelets of the Bay of Valkanium threw back splintered shards of ruby and emerald, merging into a deepening golden-speckled radiance as the Suns of Scorpio sank beyond the bulk of the Heart Heights of Central Valka. The sight was gorgeous and nostalgic and always, invariably, awakes in me vast and moving memories. I slanted the boat down toward the high palace and fortress of Esser Rarioch, and joyed that I was coming home.

There was much work to be done. With a premonition I tried unsuccessfully to shake off, I faced a future in which the harsh clangor of strife, the wicked scrape of assassins' steel and the devious and vicious intrigues around an emperor's court held no lure for me whatsoever, and to the Ice Floes of Sicce with the headlong adventure of it all. But I would face danger and the most deadly peril, as I knew, as I knew, and as you shall hear.

The world of Kregen, four hundred light years from Earth, is indeed a beautiful world. It is also a horrific world. It is real. And yet I was more and more convinced that the beauty and horror cloaked far deeper truths. If the Star Lords, who had brought me here from Earth many and many a time, alone were responsible, as I had once thought, with the Savanti attempting to combat them, then how could I either resist or support so powerful a group of—a group of what? Were they men? Were they superhuman beings, divine in origin, godlike in power? I did not know. The Savanti, the superhuman but mortal men of the Swinging City of Aphrasöe seemed, at least to me, to have more easily understood aims. The Savanti wanted to make of Kregen a better and more civilized world, and they supported apims to do that work for them. Apims, that is, people like Homo sapiens, formed a goodly proportion of the various peoples I had so far met on Kregen. But whose word was it? Did it belong to diff or apim? Or neither? I did not know.

These wider problems of Kregen stayed with me as the flier landed on that high upflung landing platform and we stepped down to be greeted by my High Chamberlain, old Panshi. He looked grave. He bowed formally, his wand of office held just so in the prescribed position of welcome and warning.

"My prince! Messengers from Vondium came for the princess; they left sealed packets and have departed these three days."

"Well, Delia was off with her Sisters of the Rose, hunting up information on our wayward daughter Dayra. I trusted she was being assisted by our eldest daughter Lela.

"Thank you, Panshi." We walked swiftly in the last of the suns sets glow toward the outer chambers. "I will see the packets. First I will see the princesses—Velia and Didi."

As I stood by the cots and looked at the two tiny forms, cherubic, sleeping, tiny fists closed, puckered mouths breathing gently, I sighed. What future lay in store for them, on this harsh and hostile planet of Kregen? Delia and I had been blessed by our daughter Velia, when our first daughter Velia had been so cruelly slain. But she had given us little Didi, the daughter of Velia, my Lady of the Stars, and of Gafard, the king's Striker, Sea Zhantil, renegade and man. I sighed again and bent and kissed them and so left them to the capable hands of the nurses and of Aunt Katri, who shooed me away with a fine air of hustle. As the emperor's sister, she spent more of her time with the emperor's daughter and her children than she did in the capital of Vallia, Vondium the Proud.

Panshi handed me the packets as I sipped the first light wine of the evening.

Heavily sealed, they bore the stamps of Lord Farris of Vomansoir, Chuktar in the Vallian Air Service, a great man, utterly loyal to the emperor, who looked upon Delia as a daughter.

With a brutal tug I broke the fastenings and took out the letter.

It was circumlocutory, filled with respect and devotion; but its message was more brutal than the gesture I had used to unseal it.

Briefly; the emperor was gravely ill. No one could fathom out the nature of his illness. There were new doctors who promised much but could find no cure. The presence of the Princess Majestrix was requested.

Turko walked in and saw my face.

"Aye, Turko. Bad news. The emperor is like to die."

"Delia—" said Turko, on a breath. His magnificently muscled body and his handsome face reassured me. He understood.

"He may be an old devil. But he is Delia's father. He once ordered his guards to take off my head, instantly, but—"

Turko half laughed. "Aye! Seg has told us often enough. He has said your surprise when you saw him will last the rest of his life." Sharply, he added: "When do we leave? Now?"

"Aye."

"Remember, you are banished by the emperor's strict decree."

"To the Ice Floes of Sicce with the old devil's decrees. Delia will have other messages, so she will know. She will go. And there is danger in a capital city of an empire when the emperor dies. We will pack up and leave at once."

Panshi was summoned and ran instantly to do my bidding. I felt that grim chill of premonition again. There were many forces conspiring to drag down the emperor, Delia's father. I was an old sea-leem, a render, a paktun, a buccaneer prince, the king of a fabled far-off land—I admit it freely. I wanted to be in at the death—if there was to be a death. I must add, not for myself alone. Delia must be supported. The emperor's grandchildren must be apportioned their rights. I knew my Delia would think only of her father's health and life; and I being that same Dray Prescot who is more of a rogue than he appears, thought also of what might follow the death of the emperor.

One thing appeared to me certain at the time. I did not then want to be the Emperor of Vallia. I was sincere in that. But what was to happen would be in the hands of the various doctors, the wizards and the gods of Kregen, each acting his part, each with his own rapier to sharpen—or, in the case of the doctors, with his own needle to sharpen—and, as always, I took as my guiding light through the maze of conflicting loyalties and treacheries the single dominant fact of my life. The well-being of Delia alone mattered. For her I would throw over kingships, kovnates, princedoms. They mean little, anyway, apart from the obvious comforts and the powers to alleviate suffering. Even, I would cast aside all I worked for with the Kroveres of Iztar. Even—and I shudder to confess this, for it is a horrendous crime—even I would disavow the Krozairs of Zy for the sake of my Delia, my Delia of Delphond, my Delia of the Blue Mountains.

Banishment from Vondium still hung over me like a cloud. It seemed sensible to land first at my own Valkan villa at the crest of one of the reserved hills of the capital, and equip myself suitably for admission to the palace. So I donned decent Vallian buff, with tall black boots, and slung a rapier and main gauche at my sides. I clapped on one of those peculiar Vallian wide-brimmed hats, with the two oblong slots cut in the front brim. The raffish curling feather was red and white, the colors of Valka. Also, I wore a red and yellow favor on my left shoulder, to tell any inquisitive rast who wanted to know that my sympathies lay with the emperor. For Vallia's colors are red and yellow, as are mine, except that the Vallian cross of yellow on the red flag is a saltire. So dressed, and carrying a heavy pouch filled with tied leather bags of gold talens, I took a zorcaride up to the palace.

Turko, Balass, Oby and Naghan the Gnat refused any orders from me to remain in the villa. They said they'd go with me, even if they had to hang about outside the palace, and go they would and that was that.

"If Tilly was here, she'd go as well," said Oby, stoutly.

The little Fristle fifi, Tilly, was away with Delia.

I nodded. "Very well. But we don't want any swordplay."

"We do not want it," said Balass, evilly. "But we may get it, by the carbuncle on Beng Thrax's posterior."

At the time I knew little of Vondium. It is a great and wonderful city, split by many wide boulevards and by the canals that are the glory of Vallia. I knew more of Ruathytu, the capital of the Empire of Hamal, arch-enemy to Vallia. I knew the way to and from the palace from various points within the city—from the villas we possessed, from Young Bargom's inn, from some of the gates, from the prison of the angels. We rode out sedately, taking the broadest ways, determined not to get into trouble.

We came to an intersection, where a wide avenue passed over a canal—it was the Samphron Cut—by one of the myriad bridges of Vondium. This bridge, of ancient and weathered stone, had been decorated with sculpted heads of zhantil and mortil. The fierce old faces had worn away until now they looked merely pathetic, savage fangs blunted and broken, mighty jaws crumbling and lean. Across the intersection passed a long procession, chanting. Many and many a time have I seen these processions, garlanded, brilliant with colors, bright with banners, carrying the sacred images proudly aloft, sprinkling the holy dewdrops, winding in long sinuous trails through the streets and avenues of Vondium. They changed as they walked, the long rolling mesmeric singsong of "Oolie Opaz, Oolie Opaz, Oolie Opaz."

Usually the emphasis falls on the first syllable of each

word, so that the long chant goes on and on and on: "*OO*-lie *OH*-paz, *OO*-lie-*OH*-paz, *OO*-lie *OH*-paz." Up and down, up and down, a hypnotic singsong chant in time with the shuffle of many feet.

But now all the emphasis, although apparently the same, rolled into a melancholy dirge. Effigies of the emperor were being carried along, heavily draped in black. The yellow and red of Vallia was fringed with heavy black tassels. Many tall poles were entwined with symbolic leaves and flowers, and topped with gilded and silvered skulls. These people, devout, devoted to Opaz, mourned the emperor already. The signs of passionate intercession broke spontaneously from the long columns, men and women flinging themselves into ecstasies of supplication, impassioned bursts of oratory and prayer to preserve the life of the emperor. But the dominant impression remained of a funeral procession, of the pious regrets and observances for a departed monarch.

"By Vox!" I said. "The old devil isn't dead yet!"

We rode on toward the palace and the traffic flow thickened with many riders and palankeens and chairs, with the zorca-chariots flickering their tall spindly wheels, varnish and paint and gilding catching the light of the suns. At the time the palace in Vondium always caught at my throat by its sheer size, its grandeur—as always I reflected that this beauty and glory and power would have been flung aside as nothing by Delia when she would have fled by night with me, a penniless outcast.

Up to the various guard details we rode and, at first, a chingle of the golden talens and the swift transference of a bag procured our passage. These guards did not know me—as I did not know them. They were mainly apims; but a few diffs of the kinds most favored in Vondium stood their duty.

Further into the warren of courts the going became tougher.

Here were stationed the first details of the emperor's personal bodyguard, the Crimson Bowmen of Loh.

"No way through here, koter," observed a matoc, a non-commissioned rank, anxious to be promoted to Deldar and put his foot on the first rung of the long ladder of advancement.

The gold worked with him.

At the next court, where flower sellers waited in long lines, their flowers all blue—a color not favored in Vallia—the guard detail was commanded by a dwa-Deldar. He looked at me. The gold did not move him. We dismounted.

I said to my friends: "Wait here and do not cause mischief."

"But—"

"Wait!"

I took the Deldar aside confidentially. I showed him the gold. He started to shake his head in the shadow of the marble column and I put a dagger into the small of his back, twisted it so he could feel the point, and said gently: "It's the gold or the steel, dom. The alternatives are open to you, the choice yours alone."

He made the sensible man's choice.

When we went back I said to Turko and the others: "Do you go back to the main square. I shall not return this way." I spoke forcefully. "If you do not leave now you will be taken up."

Such was the evil nature of my face that they went, albeit grumbling.

Past the next courtyard I found myself in a portion of the palace I knew slightly, and so could duck through a small door and enter the more somber shadows of the inner precincts unobserved. There would be more guards yet. I did not think I would have skewered the Deldar; but it was no certainty.

Mind you, I did not recollect the Crimson Bowmen being stationed so far out of the main bulk of the palace before. They usually stood duty inside the palace.

Inside, as I strode along and mingled with the many people hurrying to and fro, a common occurrence in these huge households so that I was for the moment not noticed, I spotted a distinct change. The guards stationed at doors leading to the various inner areas were Chuliks. I felt surprise. Chuliks do have two arms and two legs, two eyes, one nose and one mouth; but they are diffs of so savage and ferocious a nature that many diffs, let alone apims, hesitate to call them men. They habitually shave their heads save for a long pigtail, their skins are oily yellow, they have two three-inch long tusks thrusting up from the corners of their mouths, which are cruel ratraps. They are trained from birth as mercenary fighters, and can use many weapons with great skill. They will remain loyal when paid, and sometimes afterwards, if the prospects seem good.

A few nasty ideas began to circulate around my thick old head. The emperor, despite one nasty experience and a recent scotching of another, still reposed trust in his Crimson Bowmen. Why, then, should he replace them with most expensive mercenaries who were generally disliked?

Perhaps I should have used more guile getting in to see my father-in-law, and instead of taking the direct, golden-paved route, have broken in through one of the many secret passageways.

Persevering, on I went, noticing the air of tension and gloom about the place, but ignoring that in my determination to get through. Long and overly-ornate corridors, mirror-faced, tiled with scenes of the chase and the hunt, led me on ways I knew. This was now the main corridor that led from the outer courts of the palace to the first of the succession of anterooms opening onto the emperor's private apartments. The thickness of the scurrying crowds thinned. Soon, as I approached a tall balass door guarded by two Chuliks, I stood almost alone.

They regarded me as though I had crawled from under a stone.

"You had best begone from here, calsany," said one. He wore a most fancy uniform of red and black, lavishly garlanded with golden cords, with black belts studded with bronze. At his sides he carried scabbarded a rapier and main gauche and in his right hand a three-grained staff. The tassels were red and black, the colors of the emperor's slave masters.

"Will gold unlock that door, dom?" I spoke up cheerily, most friendly. My hands hung limply at my sides. "I know it well, having passed through many times. The Chemzite Stairway lies beyond, and this door is seldom closed—"

The left-hand Chulik stopped my prattling.

"These are not normal times, rast. The emperor is dying. No one passes here save those with authority. *Schtump!*"

Schtump is a most abusive way of saying clear off, and in normal circumstances could never have been used by a Chulik mercenary to a koter of Vallia within the palace. But times they were a changing-oh.

"Since," I told these two yellow-skinned, pigtailed mercenaries, "you will not take gold—take this."

Oh, yes, it was foolish, vainglorious. Even as I twisted the left-hand one's three-grained staff free and clouted his companion over the ear with it, and brought it back to

46

drive the bronze butt hard into ridged gut muscle, I was ruefully thinking that I was becoming overly talkative in these latter days. But, by Zair, that would change!

I gave each one a thoughtful little tap alongside the helmet rim, just to make sure, and leaving them slumbering pushed the balass doors inward. I heard a gasp and twisted at once, fast, to see only the long golden furred legs and delightful tail of a Fristle fifi disappearing past a pilaster along the wall. Friezes of strigicaws and shonages ran along the cove here, and the door slammed sharply. I made no attempt to follow. Instead, I pushed on through and ran up the weirdly deserted Chemzite Stairway. In normal times the balass doors were thrown back and the Stairway thronged with courtiers and supplicants and advocates and nobles, all going about their business with the emperor's personal staff.

Now all those highly-placed nobles with access to the emperor were confined to a few of the great halls. I passed along through narrower stairways, walking the marble of a balcony, and looked down at them as I went. From all over the Empire of Vallia the lords and ladies had come to Vondium to be in at the death. Each one had personal reasons of avarice or ambition or fear. As I walked along quietly, looking down at the assemblage of waiting nobility, my lips wrinkled up. A fine crew they were! Not a one, I daresay, spared a thought in sympathy for Delia, their Princess Majestrix. Not a one thought for an instant that it was a girl's father who lay dying.

But, then, that was not entirely true, for nobles like Farris would care. Many of them I recognized. Some of them I have already introduced to you in these tapes, and many more there were of that crew waiting to step onto the stage and strut their little part, before shuffling off, and, by Vox, a lot of them horizontal, too . . .

But, adhering to my plan, I will tell you of these high and mighty nobles of Vallia as and when they came into contact with me. And, too, I did not forget that I had vowed to myself to be the new Dray Prescot, the quiet, conciliatory peace-loving man who would talk first. If the emperor died then the streets of the capital might flow with blood. Everyone knew that factions waited for the moment to strike. And, as is the way with desperate men banded together waiting for a single event to strike, each party believed itself to be the most powerful, or the most advantageously placed, or having the most moral force. A detached observer could see only tragedy ahead.

But, of course, there were few—if any—detached observers, for everyone had a zhantil to saddle. And I, Dray Prescot, I was not detached. Oh, I tried to be. I told myself I wanted none of it. But I knew if some hulking lout brandishing a sword and flaunting colors and feathers tried to steal what belonged to Delia, or what should rightfully belong to our children, then all my fine detachment would vanish and the old Dray Prescot, of the devil's face and intemperate manner and vicious determination, would jump in, sword swinging, as he had done long and long in the old days . . .

As was inevitable I was at last stopped by four Chulik guards before an ivory door banded in gold and emeralds. They wore the red and black and carried the three-grained staffs. They were less polite than the last. True to my desire to be the rational easy-going man I ought to be, I attempted to talk.

The polearm slashed toward me with deadly intent. They'd knock me senseless and hustle me down to the dungeons. The three-grained staff, very convoluted, very ornate, the black and red tassels swinging, the bright curved edges glittering with much honing against the solid olive of the metal head, struck for my skull.

I slid the blow, took the polearm, twisted it free and held it parallel with the ground. I pushed. The Chulik tumbled against the gold and emerald and ivory door. He went: "Whoof!" That was as much from surprise as from having the air knocked from his lungs.

His companions set on at once, so I had to twist the staffs free and, partially regretfully, tap their skulls. As the last slumped down I heard a hard, brittle voice say: "If you do not drop that staff this instant you are a dead man."

Without turning I knew what stood behind me. I dropped the staff. Without seeing the flight of an arrow it is damned difficult—nigh impossible—to judge which way to jump, which direction to use. Slowly, I turned around.

Yes—four Bowmen and an officer stood there, their bows fully drawn, and the lamplight glittered from the sharp steel heads. The odds were against me. I might have dodged, given the mystic disciplines of the Krozairs of Zy, had the occasion warranted. But I persevered in my peaceful overtures—here, in the palace of my father-in-law, for all that I was banished, here!

As it was, I said to the officer at the head of the four Crimson Bowmen: "I do not know you. It is clear you do not know me. I have pressing business—" I got no further.

"Take him to the cells," said this officer in his brittle voice. "Question him—Naghan the Pinch will know what to do. You know your orders."

The officer in his trim Crimson was a Hikdar, a waso-Hikdar, and the pallid hardness of his face and blankness of the stare in his blue eyes would give any nefarious culprit wandering the palace a severe case of the frights. I looked at him. I thought I knew this type—always a dangerous assumption—and I stared past him at the four Bowmen.

One, I recognized.

I said: "Lahal, Neg Negutorio. Why do you stand in the ranks? You were an ord-Deldar the last time we met. I would have thought you a shiv-Hikdar by now—"

That was as far as the officer was going to allow me to prattle on. My attempt at distraction would not fool him. Furiously, he bellowed out: "Seize him up! I'll have you all jikaidered, by Hlo-Hli! *Bratch!*"*

This was a threat no swod was fool enough to ignore.

Three of the Bowmen, taking their bows and arrows into their left hands, reached out with their right hands.

Neg Negutorio gaped at me.

"Dray Prescot!" he said. And: "The Prince Majister!"

The Hikdar took a step back. The hands of the three Bowmen fell away.

Neg shook his head. "Prince. Times have changed. There are many new faces in the Guard. Dag Dagutorio, our Chuktar, has been sent home, and replaced by Rog Rogutorio." He wet his lips. "As for me—I was degraded—it was a trumped-up charge—and now I must obey orders I care not overmuch for—"

"Silence, cramph!" shouted the Hikdar. He stared at me with venom in his face and a twitch about his jaws. "If

---

* Bratch: "Move!" "Jump!" Get about your duty or you know what will happen, and the punishment will be sore indeed. Not quite so vicious a word of command as the terrible "Grak!" shouted with killing intent at slaves; but still a hard word.     A.B.A.

this is truly Dray Prescot, the Prince Majister of Vallia, then is he forsworn! He is banished from Vondium! Seize him! Chain him! Send word to Kov Layco we have taken up a rare prize. Bratch!"

For a second a paralysis gripped the Crimson Bowmen. Then the four Chuliks groaned, more or less together, and opened their eyes. Like the fierce fighting men they were they came to their feet, grasping their ripped-free rapiers, and the points glittered, centered on my chest. These diffs would have no hesitation in killing me if that proved more convenient than attempting to restrain me.

"The Prince Majister is banished from Vondium and sets foot within the city at his own peril!" howled the Hikdar. "Seize him! If he resists—slay him!"

The Chuliks stepped forward. My hand gripped the rapier hilt. In the next second blood would splash luridly across the golden and emerald and ivory door—

"Hold!" rang a clear, perfect voice. A voice I knew. A voice that means everything in two worlds. "Hold! The Princess Majestrix commands! Touch the Prince Majister at your peril!"

# *Chapter Four*

## Ashti Melekhi, the Vadnicha of Venga

"The emperor my father has revoked the edict of banishment that should never have been passed on the Prince Majister! Get about your duties."

So, together, side by side, we walked along through the ivory and gold and emerald doorway. We left four Chuliks with blank, yellow faces, and three Crimson Bowmen disgruntled, and a waso-Hikdar raging with icy, baffled fury—and one Bowman with a single enormous grin plastered all over the inside of his martially stiff and unmoving features.

Delia!

She held my arm. I was dizzyingly conscious of the limber suppleness of her as she walked at my side. She wore a long dress of deep purple, unrelieved by any ornament save two brooches, one fashioned into the likeness of a rose and all of rubies and gold. The other was the hubless spoked wheel of precious gems I had given her, the emblem of the Krozairs of Zy.

"My heart—my father—he is ill, so very ill. He is dying, I am sure of it. The doctor—" Here she gripped the scrap of lace between her fingers.

"I will see the doctor. We should fetch Nath the Needle—"

"It is no use. Doctor Charboi is most highly respected, and his associates. But they will not let Nath the Needle see my father."

"I think they will," I said.

Nath the Needle had doctored me, and he had taken care of Delia. If the emperor's new doctors did not want Nath about them, that was a matter of concern to me. In the ante room beyond Seg and Thelda hurried toward us with Katrin Rashumin, the Kovneva of Rahartdrin. She was now wholeheartedly devoted to Delia. With them, Nath the Needle looked just the same, if a trifle absentminded rather than bewildered in this strange, claustrophobic atmosphere of the imperial palace where we waited for an emperor to die. And, too, here came Tilly, the gorgeous golden-furred Fristle fifi. Now I knew it was she I had seen running off to fetch Delia.

"And has the emperor really pardoned me?"

"Not yet. I said that, for it needed to be said. But he will."

I smiled at Tilly and she laughed, and sobered at once.

"You remind me once again of the Jikhorkdun in Huringa."

"And the silver chains are all melted down—master."

That little minx Tilly knows how to infuriate me, and how I detest being called master by her.

As for Thelda, Seg's wife, she could not do enough for Delia. She had been in Vondium, and Seg had called there after the meeting of the Brotherhood, arriving well before me. Thelda fussed and organized and sorted out all the tangles, she would have everybody running, and was properly reverential when she came within three doors' distance of the sick room. I do Thelda an injustice. She had made Seg a fine wife, and she was a good and loving mother to her children, and yet, and yet, still, I could not stop myself from remarking on the silver heart in blue flowers, from time to time, jocularly, and then feeling the biggest villain in two worlds. Poor Thelda!

"And Nath the Needle is most hurt, dear Dray," said Thelda. A magnificently-shaped woman, Thelda always looked incipiently plump, and yet was not. A disturbing trick to play on a man.

"Nath attempted to treat the emperor," said Seg. "He was rebuffed by this Doctor Charboi. He has an enormous reputation and is newly come from Loh. He is not," Seg added, "a Wizard of Loh. But he acts with all the high-handedness of one of those—those—"

"Yes," I said. Ordinary men perforce spoke carefully when they mentioned any Wizard of Loh.

"Aunt Katri was so upset," said Delia. "She frets in Esser Rarioch, I am sure. Everything seems so—so *odd*."

I could feel the unease within the palace as in all Vondium. Things had changed in Vallia, imperceptibly, and little attention had been paid when, for instance, the old Pallans died or retired and new Pallans—secretaries or ministers of state—had replaced them. Dag Dagutorio had left suddenly for Loh, and Rog Rogutorio had taken his place as Chuktar of the Crimson Bowmen. The emperor's chief adviser in these latter days was a kov I did not then know, one Layco Jhansi, the Kov of Vennar. His was a name I was to come to know passing well—to my sorrow, I may add—but at the time he was regarded as the savior of Vallia, the man who would hold the empire together, the emperor's Right Hand.

Automatically I thought of Gafard, the Sea-Zhantil, the King's Striker, who had died so far away from Vallia, loving still the memory of our daughter Velia, and I would sigh, and—then—wonder if this Kov Layco could give half the loyalty and allegiance past blindness that Gafard had given his mad genius King Genod.

We passed on and the presence of the Princess Majestrix opened all doors. Yet I gained the distinct and unsettling impression that our little group formed, as it were, a conspiracy, here in the palace. Once the difficulty of my banishment had been cleared up it should have been plain sailing. But it seemed to me, incredibly, as though we hatched a plot. And all we wanted to do was have a doctor we trusted give a second opinion on the condition of the emperor.

Slaves scuttled about their eternal tasks, always an affront. The Archer Guard of Valka which I had instituted had been sent, so I was told the moment I mentioned their absence, to Evir, the most northerly province of Vallia, to help quell a disturbance there. I felt as we walked on that I would welcome the presence of my Archers of Valka right there and then, above that of the mercenary Chuliks, for all their worth and valor as fighting men, and above the Crimson Bowmen, who were fresh strangers to me.

The mood of the palace baffled me. I sensed the heavy oppression, and yet I felt the heady intoxication of terror could not be adequately explained away merely by the emperor's inpending death. The factions would fight. There would be slaughter and murder. There would be burnings and looting. But, all the same, the intense, indrawn, coiled-spring of horror I sensed in the very air of the palace contained so much more of menace that, quite instinctively, my hand rested on my rapier hilt as we walked—rested not in an affected, courtly way of fashion, but in the hard professional grip of the bladesman ready to draw in a twinkling.

Doctor Nath the Needle looked exactly as when I had first met him, when I'd been recovering from the infection from the shorgortz and the intemperate orders of the man who was now my father-in-law, the man who was now dying and whom Nath had been forbidden to attend. Dried up, wispy, wearing his old dark-brown clothes, his tawny yellow hair roughly combed, he looked just the same, and he held the same old velvet-lined sturmwood case of acupuncture needles under his arm.

"I am happy to see you, prince," he said, most formally.

"And I you, doctor," I answered gravely. "I do not know what this nonsense is about your being refused an audience of the emperor; but we'll go in and see him now."

Nath nodded and then, because, as was proper, the Princess Majestrix walked first, and Thelda and Katrin walked a half-step to her rear, and Seg was trying to catch a bundle of wool about to fall from Thelda's bag, Nath and I walked at the rear.

Nath began to talk as these savants do, increasingly oblivious of his surroundings, absorbed by his own thoughts.

"The shorgortz poison—you remember that, I am sure, my prince—is proving of fascinating interest. The Blue Mountain Boys captured a specimen in a pit and, knowing my interest, for I sent messages and gold to Korf Aighos, they extracted the poison and forwarded me a sample. It is indeed remarkable. Incredible, if a doctor may ever use that word. I have conducted experiments, see—" Here he halted and began pulling papers from the pockets in the flaps of his old brown coat. I swear dust flew. He bashed the papers about—they were ordinary paper and not the superb paper made by the Savanti—and crumpled them up and dropped some. I helped him collect up these vital medical discoveries.

"I shall look at your work with great pleasure, doctor; but later. Now I want you to see the emperor and tell me just what is the matter with him and what must be done to cure him."

Nath the Needle favored me with a look, jolted back to the reason for his presence here. He made a singularly apt remark about Charboi; but he was perfectly willing to try again. He sneezed a couple of times, stuffing the papers away.

If I thought the obstacles to Nath the Needle seeing the emperor had all been overcome, then I was an onker indeed.

We debouched beneath overhanging arches lavishly decorated with exquisite mosaics depicting—oh, the pictures were filled with the fire and passion of Vallia's turbulent past. Across the wide marble-floored space where cool fountains sparkled in the perfumed air, where fruit trees bloomed and delicately colored birds flitted from branch to branch, the long white wall barring off the emperor's quarters as approached from this direction showed a solid crimson and black band along its foot.

The guards stood shoulder to shoulder, a Crimson Bowman and a Chulik, alternating. Pacing toward us came two Jiktars, high officers, one a Bowman of Loh, the other a Chulik.

Delia proved herself a princess in her handling of them.

Haughtily, yet with just the right amount of friendliness stopping this side of condescension, she avowed the Prince Majister was now free to walk in Vondium, that she intended to see her father, and her suite would go with her. The guards stood back. We walked through. Although I did not smile, my fist no longer rested on the rapier hilt. A little thing—but revealing. . . .

There was no mistaking the abrupt dispatch of a Bowman runner, a lithe young man fresh from Loh, learning his trade.

The light chilled. Heavy doors swung inwards. I knew just where we were, now, and had studied the plans of the palace drawn up many seasons ago when this wing had been built. At last, past a bevy of waiting nurses and minor doctors, we entered the sick room.

The place struck me with a chill repulsion. Delia visited her father constantly, had been drawn away by Tilly's startling news. He lay in the wide bed, on his back, the covers drawn to his chin and pettishly pulled half down one side. His wasted face spider-webbed with etched lines, the cheeks sunken in. I saw the hand he extended to his daughter and was shocked at its skeletal aspect. He had always been a firmly fleshed man.

His flesh was wasting away. His condition really was serious, and Delia's concern struck me, suddenly, with an anguish for her I detested and found biting and acid and altogether hateful. My Delia! Well, everyone must go through the agonies of seeing loved ones die. Because Delia and I had bathed in the Sacred Pool of the River Zelph in far Aphrasöe, the city of the Savanti, the Swinging City, we were assured of a thousand years of life and the rapid recovery from wounds and illness. The wounds I had taken in the jikai of the Brotherhood of Iztar against the Shanks were already healed. And yet, I had held my daughter Velia in my arms as she died. What agonies mortality tortures us with.

Nath the Needle moved carefully forward in his best professional manner and shooed us from the bed. He took immediate command of the four nurses, pale women, nervous, worried, and at his directions one of them turned back the coverlets and the others lifted the emperor's shrunken body and opened the fancy silk shirt over his sunken chest. I went with Seg to stand over in the bay window where a flick-flick plant looked as though it needed a heaping handful of fat flies. The six flunkeys, armed, who stood along the far walls, blankly regarding the proceedings, could be ignored. The emperor, apart from certain follies, lived a spartan life.

I said to Seg: "D'you know what's happened to Queen Lush? I thought for sure she'd be sobbing at the bedside."

"She had to return to Lome. Some pressing affair of state. The emperor saw her off—Thelda says he was in full health then."

"We haven't seen the last of her. She has designs on the emperor. This dire news will bring her scurrying back."

"Aye. It's bad, Dray."

"Yes. How stands Falinur?"

He knew what I meant. The old recklessness of his face sobered, for the men of Erthyrdrin, Seg's homeland, are fey and wild and also highly practical. "I have worked hard there, trying to make the kovnate into the kind of paradise you have in Valka. There are always cramphs against whatever I try to do. Their malignancy lingers on. They remember. I wouldn't take a sheaf of arrows on their loyalty."

I made no comment on this bleak if expected news. "And Inch? I fancy the Black Mountains will stand with us."

"The Blue Mountain Boys have resolved their ancient quarrels with the Black Mountain Men. That is more Inch's doing than Korf Aighos's—he is one man I wouldn't trust with my bow—but he is loyal to Delia. Between them they have made those mountains and the zorca plains into a stronghold."

"There are other nobles willing to stand up and be numbered. As for Delphond—" I sighed. I thought, then, that Delia's pretty little province of Delphond, a charming, lazy, contented place, now that the Chyyanists had gone, could never raise even a pastang of real fighting men. There had been changes in Delphond the last time I had been through, as you know; but the old carefree, easy-going ways persisted—and I would not change them.

"Lord Farris will bring in Vomansoir."

"Yes. And, if it comes to the fluttrell's vane, we can strike across quickly and so pinch out—" I stopped. Delia and Thelda with Katrin came over to us and the conversation became general, still concerned, low-voiced. I glanced at the doctor. Nath the Needle looked grave. He peered into the emperor's mouth, pulled down his lower eyelids, felt and prodded him, tut-tutting to himself. No acupuncture needles had been used by Doctor Charboi, and Nath had not opened his sturmwood case, so I gathered the sick man was in no pain.

Very carefully, using a piece of verss, that finest of snow-white linen, Nath wiped the emperor's mouth. He folded the cloth delicately and placed it into his lesten-hide satchel. Sight of the piece of pure verss reminded me vividly of the Kroveres—for verss represented the purity for which the old vers of Valka had been famed.

Nath glanced up and met my gaze. He nodded and indicated he was ready to leave, which surprised me, and the door burst open with a crash onto the somber sick room and a group of violently angry men and women entered.

As I stared at them, at their red faces and their gesticulating, ring-laden hands, the sumptuousness of their dress, their jewels and lace, all the habitual airs of wealth and command and authority, I felt repulsion. I felt revulsion. Their vicious unthinking demands on everyone about them they could master, these I had witnessed many times, on Earth as on Kregen, and despaired of, and resisted, and, I own the matching of violence with violence to be a sin, there, in that sick room of a palace where an emperor lay dying, I was particularly revolted by their violence. I am a peaceful sort of fellow, liking the quiet life, and yet I have, to my shame, been forced many and many a time to match violence with violence. The Kroveres of Iztar were one response. I own, I have never made a secret of it, I own the matching of violence with violence to be a sin, and yet I hoped for so much from the Kroveres in milder civilized ways.

But—these people. You will meet them all as my story trundles along. Of them at the moment it is fit you should see just three.

The first was Doctor Charboi. Here on Earth he would have been impeccably dressed, crowned with a distinguished mass of silver hair. He would have worn a neat Harley Street suit, and have commanded the highest prices for nostrums and soothing words from the highest in society. On Kregen, where a person's hair does not ordinarily turn white until past two hundred, Charboi had the red mop of Loh, and he presented the full-fleshed, country-club figure of a man in the prime of life, brisk, efficient, demanding. And violent.

"Out!" he shouted. He was violent. No doubt of it. "Out!"

The second man hulked in the room. Massive, bulky, he towered against the lamplight and it was clear from the set of his mouth and the clamping thrust of his jaws and chin that he spoke seldom. Apim, he was, but built like a Chulik. All the time his powerful figure remained planted at the shoulder of his mistress. He wore the heavy brown tunic called a khiganer, double-breasted, the wide flap caught up over his left side with a long flaring row of bronze buttons, from belt to shoulder, and from point of shoulder to collar. That collar stood stiff and hard and high, encircling his neck. Gold glittered there. He wore buff breeches and tall black Vallian boots, gleaming with polish, spurred. He wore no baldric; but the lockets for a rapier and empty main gauche swung from two jewelled belts. His sleeves were banded after the fashion of Vallia, indicating his allegiance. Brown and green bands, with three small diagonal slashes, marked him for Venga. The sheer ferocity of that lowering face impressed me, the lambent bestiality slumbering in the tiny dark eyes, the cragginess of the jaw. He was a notorious Bladesman.

This was Nath the Iarvin, ruffler, Bladesman, bought body and soul by his mistress.

The third person was a woman.

Thin, she was, hard-edged like a diamond, brittle and bright, with a flame about her that consumed all who were unfortunate enough not to know how to handle her. Her dark hair was caught in a diamond-encrusted net. She wore riding leathers of a sheening green, making her mannish figure even more angular, and long black boots, like a man. On her left shoulder was pinned a golden brooch fashioned into the form of a wersting seizing a korf, the vicious Kregan dog crunching down on the soaring bird. A rapier and dagger were scabbarded at her narrow waist. I fancied she could use them passing well. High, her face, white and scornful, with deep, grey-green eyes, and arched black eyebrows. Red, her mouth, thin and bitter and drawn in at the corners, red and like a wound above her sharp chin. She could have cut ice with her glance.

This, then, was Ashti Melekhi, the Vadnicha of Venga.*

She stared at us narrowly, reminding me of the way those carnivorous hunting risslacas stare unwinking at their prey.

"Get out," she said. And her voice, I swear it, hissed as

---

\* Vad is the title of Kregan nobility immediately below Kov. Nich is the suffix denoting the second twin. Nicha is feminine. Vadnicha therefore is the twin sister of the Vad, with certain responsibilities within the same Vadvarate. The Vad's wife is the Vadni.     A.B.A.

a risslaca hisses before he pounces. "Schtump! Layco Jhansi, the Kov of Vennar, the emperor's Chief Pallan, has placed me in charge of the sick room and of all the emperor's wants, answerable only to him. I do not care who you are. The Princess Majestrix may stay, because she is the emperor's daughter. The rest of you—out! Schtump!"

I did not speak.

She pointed her riding crop at me. It did not waver.

"You may be the Prince Majister. But you are nothing more than a trumpery clansman, a hairy barbarian. And you dare to bring in another doctor! Have a care lest you go too far."

The crop circled to include Seg and Thelda and Katrin, and then rested, accusingly, on Nath the Needle.

"Let the emperor die in dignity, as befits the end of a great man. You profane his greatness. This doddery buffoon pries and prods—beware lest your heads topple before the suns descend."

I opened my mouth—and then closed it. I speculated on the inner mysteries of philosophy, how the worlds roll through space, how a woman may change a man and the man change an empire, how violence breeds violence, how women are so often nonsensical creatures unfit for their own company, let alone a man's, how I was the new Dray Prescot.

She slashed the crop down. "Now get this rabble cleared out! Go, now. Or I call the palace guard."

Seg was staring at me with that old half-mocking smile on his face. I knew what he expected. Nath stood back from the bed, outraged; but keeping his composure remarkably well. Thelda was already boiling up and Katrin was standing by ready to lay in after. These two ladies were high born, coming from great families, kovnevas both. Delia—Delia looked at me and I managed the smile I can always find for her, and I shook my head, ever so slightly, and so she smiled back at me, uncertain, disturbed, but ready to follow my mood, trusting me. What a wonderful woman is my Delia among all women!

I did not speak. Conscious that I was acting a part, I felt a word would shatter that charade. I could have broken this headstrong woman, made her see the errors of her ways, given Doctor Charboi the fright of his life. And no damn guards would have stopped us, either. But I did not. Even now, had I done so, I am not sure it would have changed anything that followed. The details of the tragedy and the heartbreak might have been different; the end results would surely have been the same.

"Are you going?" demanded the bitter, icy voice. This Ashti Melekhi switched her crop around and on the instant would have shouted for the guards.

A weak, breathy voice spoke and for a disoriented moment, so wrapped up were we all in the tension of the situation, we could not understand who was speaking. Then Delia dropped to her knees by the bed, clasping her father's shrunken hand.

"Delia." The emperor gasped with the effort of speaking. "My daughter." He worked his thin lips around each word, as though forcing each one out against enormous forces pent within him. "Aph—" He stopped and swallowed, his Adam's Apple jumping erratically. "Hamal. Todalpheme—"

"No!" shouted Charboi, storming forward. "That is not to be thought of! Do as the vadnicha commands. Go!"

If the rast put his hand on Delia's shoulder to pull her away from the bed I would have forgotten my play-acting and being the new, considerate, understanding, nonviolent Dray Prescot. But he still had the sense not to commit such a flagrant act of lese-majesty. Perhaps, had he taken refuge in his doctor's status, and allowed his temper to lay a hand on Delia, and I had acted as I would surely have done, the world of Kregen would be a different place today. I do not know. I do not really think so. It does not matter. For what was to happen, happened, and that is all that matters, in the whirl of vaol-paol.

"You're not going to stand for this, Dray!" demanded Thelda. Her face betrayed shock and anger, and, also, another emotion. Seg put his arm around her waist and drew her away, and I looked at her, so she went, but not without a squib or two.

The Vadnicha Ashti Melekhi stared with those narrow grey-green eyes after Thelda, and I knew they had sparked before, like a diamond cutting butter—and, suddenly, I knew how much I cared for Thelda, my comrade's wife, despite all. That would not stop me from gently tormenting her, of course, or stop her from fussing and overpressuring and, in general, of being Thelda.

Seg looked back past me over Thelda's shoulder, and I put out a hand and so stopped Katrin from blowing up. Nath picked up his sturmwood case and walked with measured tread for the door, but he looked mightily offended. So, at last, Delia rose and kissed her father, the dread emperor of a mighty empire, and we walked out sedately, together, side by side.

Still I had said no word.

The brittle voice cut the air after us. "Good riddance to a rabble! Now, Charboi, see if you can undo the damage that doddering incompetent may have done. I am going to find Kov Layco and tell him to make sure these cramphs never have a chance to sneak in to pester the emperor again."

"Yes, my lady," said Charboi, very huffed with himself.

So I took myself off at the side of Delia, and I pondered.

# Chapter Five

## Of a Ruffianly Meeting at *The Rose of Valka*

"In the old days, my vovedeer, we'd have slipped six inches of good Zeniccean steel into the guts of the cramph! By the Black Chunkrah! I am astonished the fellow is walking about with a head on his shoulders!"

And Hap Loder tossed the rest of his wine down and roared for more. The inner private snug of *The Rose of Valka* resounded with heated talk and argument. I knew what must be done. But it must be done the right way.

"Yes, Hap, you fearsome rascal. That is the way of the clansmen who ride the plains of Segesthes. And I know that is what most of my comrades would have done. But unthinking violence will not solve the problems of Vallia now."

"That is right, by all the shattered targes in Mount Hlabro!" quoth Seg, who as a kov of Vallia much bethought himself of his adopted country's welfare. "I'll own I was surprised at first. But that she-leem would have called the guards. Then there would have been a right merry set-to."

Wine went the rounds. Palines and other luscious fruits lay heaped on bronze plates, ready to hand. The people gathered here and drifting in as the evening wore on were all my comrades, gathered from many areas of Kregen. After the adventures in the Eye of the World, when I had been saved in the nick of time by these same lusty fighters, we were enjoying one last carouse, although the dismal news of Delia's father laid a gloom across the meeting.

Inch had brought his lady newly arrived from Ng'groga, his home, a charming girl, all of six foot six in height, of a fiery nature and a bold eye, who, I felt with a twinge, would cut Inch down to size. Their taboos still operated, at least, to some extent, for they could not be married until—and then so much metaphysical profound casuistry erupted about our thick non-Ng'grogan heads that we could only rock back and hold our sides and laugh. Inch and his taboos....

I liked Inch's lady, Sasha, and she quickly became a part of our roistering group. Of Sasha there is much to speak, later....

My own Wizard of Loh—I say 'my own' but that is to pitch it too high, these famous wizards being their own men; but Khe-Hi-Bjanching owed not only his status but his life to me, and he proved trustworthy and loyal. Also, since those early days, he had matured. Now he was a wizard capable of extraordinary feats.

He listened gravely as I told him what the emperor had said and of Doctor Charboi's reaction, and what I felt I ought to do. He frowned. He looked—and I was startled—he looked most comfoundedly put out, frightened, even. This moved me to say, half-jesting: "What, Khe-Hi! A Wizard of Loh, scared of anything at all in the world! That is indeed a ponsho-bitten leem." Which is to say, something so extraordinary as to be almost unbelievable.

"By Father Mehzta-Makku!" said Gloag, his bristle hide most carefully groomed, his whole appearance sleek and elegant as befitted by crebent of the House of Strombor in Zenicce. "I would think three times before I accused a Wizard of Loh of being the cleverest man in all Segesthes—and then I'd hold my tongue."

Khe-Hi-Bjanching wet his lips. "I own I am grown different from other wizards." His voice held a falt deadness I did not like at all. "In the service of our prince I have grown into my powers. I am good. There is no sense in denying it. But I have access to some secrets I would not turn over, as I would not stick my head into a chavonth's jaws."

The racket around us in the snug subsided as they realized some serious talk was going on. They listened, soberly.

"Say on, Khe-Hi. You know, I think, what the emperor asked. You share Charboi's apprehensions?"

"Apprehensions!" Bjanching gripped a fist on the sturmwood table among the wine glasses. "It is more than that. We wizards, well, all men speak of our art. We are adepts. Sorcery is child's play to us. But if you seek out the Todalpheme of Hamal and they tell you—you will be as great a pack of fools as they!"

"But," protested Seg. "The Todalpheme are good, wise savants. They predict the tides. They are sacrosanct. No man dares raise a hand against them. How can the Todalpheme be evil?"

"They are not evil, kov. Of course not. But a secret has fallen into their possession and they do not understand it."

The samphron oil lamps gleamed on their faces. They sat and stood in a circle there in the private snug of *The Rose of Valka* in Vondium. I can see them now, so clearly. My comrades. Men and women who had gone through the fire with me, aye, and were to go through again—and damned soon, too. I am a lonely man, a true loner, as you know; yet I have been blessed with friends such as I believe no other mortal can ever have been blessed with. The charismatic power that clings about me, the yrium, so difficult to define and yet so starkly obvious when the truth is seen, that does not explain it all, not all . . .

Jaidur, my youngest son, sat very quietly for him, for the overturning of the misconceptions of his world were taking time to work through. My second son, Zeg, Pur Zeg, a noted Krozair of Zy of the Inner Sea, now the King of Zandikar, was away there in the Eye of the World, a great man, Bane of Grodno. My eldest son, Prince Drak, had been sent for. Vomanus of Vindelka, newly arrived from some far-off corner of Kregen, listened intently, and as the half-brother of Delia shared a lively concern over the fate of the emperor, who was not his father.

Yes, we were a ruffianly crew. The others of whom you know were there, and there were new faces, also—Dray,

Seg's son, and his twins, Valin and Silda. They listened avidly and spoke little, conduct very becoming. Seg had named his firstborn son Dray when he thought I was dead. This Dray's real name was Seg, of course, as the firstborn, so that he might carry on the Torio. Valin was a good Vallian name, and Silda was the name of Thelda's mother.

We argued on, with the wizard genuinely concerned to deflect us from what increasingly we saw as the only way to aid the emperor. But, you who listen to these tapes know far more than my comrades there in the comfortable snug of *The Rose of Valka*. Only I understood with Delia what the Wizard of Loh was hinting at. When the emperor's daughter had fallen from a zorca, he had raised heaven and hell to find a cure. He had been put into contact with the Todalpheme of Hamal through an airboat salesman, for at that time Vallia and Hamal were on more-or-less speaking terms. The information had cost a great deal. The Todalpheme of Hamal, it was rumored, knew also of a fabled land where miracle cures might be effected. Delia had been taken through the various secret channels in a flier and had at last reached Aphrasöe, where the Savanti had been too long in making up their minds whether or not to cure her. So I, that uncouth sailor, Dray Prescot, newly arrived from Earth and out of the thunder of the broadsides as the seventy-fours drifted down into the battlesmoke, had taken it upon myself to cure Delia.

That I had done so, and into the bargain assured her of a thousand years of life, was past history. But the whole business was wrapped about with mystery. During my journeys on Kregen I had asked always for news of Aphrasöe, the Swinging City, and no one had even heard of the place. To me, then, it had been paradise. And I had been thrown out of paradise. But real life had caught up with me and engulfed me, so that, for me, Paradise was Valka and Strombor and Djanduin and the Great Plains of Segesthes. I speak, you understand, of the time in Vondium when the emperor lay dying. Fragrant Azby, the other places, what has happened to me since—ah, well, all that must wait its due turn.

Even when I had at last discovered that the Todalpheme of Hamal had been the ones responsible—or, at least, could put me in touch with the ones responsible—I had been in no case to prosecute further inquiries or do any more about it. Real life has a habit of rolling along everything before its onward surge, ambitions, dreams, nightmares, the daily grind.

The gravity of the burden of our conversation was lost upon no one there. The light from the mellow samphron oil lamps gleamed upon our faces, and reflected without edged menace from scabbarded blades. The menace breathed all about us in the night of Vondium, under the seven moons of Kregen.

Even those two rogues sensed the atmosphere. One drinking happily, the other drinking seeming somewhat empty without a wench on his knee, my two favorite rascals, Nath and Zolta, understood what went forward here. And how they revelled in this whole new world outside the inner sea! Any fears I had had that they would be overawed, fail to fit in, become dejected and morose, had evaporated. Nath and Zolta! Fine, fearsome, rascally rogues, my two oar-comrades—and great-hearted Zorg dead and gone and food for chanks in the Eye of the World.

"I know, Dray," said Vomanus, carelessly, popping a paline into his mouth, chewing and swallowing—a barbarous habit, for the paline is a berry of superlative performance on a man's digestion: "I know what the emperor did and said when Delia crippled herself falling off that damned zorca. For a start he had the beast's throat slit. But this Opaz-forsaken airboat salesman was eager to sell, and we poor fools of Vallia eager to buy his rubbish." The old sore spot again. . . . "He gave names and addresses to the emperor, and Delia was sent, all neatly packaged. The fellow was some kind of defrocked Todalpheme acolyte, I believe. Came by his information evilly, I'll warrant. Still, it must have been successful." And Vomanus smiled broadly at my Delia as she regarded him gravely, thinking of those times.

We had told no one of our experiences in Aphrasöe.

"So we do the same," I said. "We take the emperor to this place known to the Todalpheme's contacts. We effect a miracle cure, also."

"Aye!" they shouted, ready to brave a world.

"But," said Seg. "How do we start? You saw how those rasts kept him mewed up."

"Aye. But we can find a key to open the cage."

"I would have thought, Dray Prescot, that the emperor's daughter and the Prince Majister, her husband, could take the emperor to a doctor without such a to-do!"

Thus spake Thelda.

Seg started to say something; but, quickly, Delia broke in gently to say: "We will, Thelda, my dear, we will. And you will aid us, I know."

"Well, of course!" Thelda turned to me, high of color, heaving of bosom, glowing with resolution. "Prince, am I not Delia's best friend?"

Very, very carefully, I said: "Yes, Thelda."

All the old subjection to the racters that had made of Thelda a tool for political designs had gone. Her family, well-born but poverty-stricken through foolish gambling of a rake-hell grandfather, had not been able to give her any assistance in life save that of offering her as a tool for the racters in return for gold. Her marriage to Seg and her friendship with the Prince and Princess, her own status as a kovneva, and the known wildness of her friends, had protected Thelda from the unwelcome attentions of those who might have sought to employ her again.

"It's high time we did something," growled Inch, very tall and grim in the lamplight.

"Aye!" roared those wolfish fighting men—and those vulpine ladyfriends and wives. "Aye! For Delia and for Dray!"

Well, it was all very pretty. But it shod no zorcas, as my clansmen would say.

The door swung open as Young Bargom, the proprietor hustled in. With him came Prince Varden Wanek and Natema who were staying at a merchant friend's house because one of the children's children had a slight fever. Nath the Needle had hurried round there, and now he came in with Varden and Natema, looking excited.

"What news, Nath?"

"It is as I suspected," he said, swirling his cloak off and sneezing and almost putting his satchel on the table. Someone caught it. He mumbled around and produced a small vial. It held a colorless liquid.

"I refined and clarified the emperor's spittle. There is no doubt. He has been fed solkien concentrate—"

A gasp broke from many gathered there.

Nath nodded, not pretending to lecture. "A most lethal and unpleasant poison. It is secret—and the secret of its discovery even more so. But," he said without false modesty, "I know it. A deadly mixture of the tree Memph, the cactus Trechinolc, a little of the bark Liverspot, one or two other spicy ingredients, all balanced to waste the flesh, to dilute the blood, to destroy most subtly."

Delia swayed. I put out a hand and she grasped it, staring into my face, trying to smile for me and failing.

"Oh—Dray!"

"Tonight," I said. Everyone hung on my words. "Tonight we will go in by certain secret passageways I know of, ways that were inspected with Largan the Rule, the palace architect—"

"Dead and gone these many seasons," said Vomanus.

"I'm sorry to know that. But we may make our way in and we may make our way out bearing the emperor. It is the way I should have taken today, but did not. Thelda! Can you see to the nursing facilities for Doctor Nath the Needle?"

"Of course!" She tossed her head, and then said: "And I do not wish to hear about vilmy flowers, and especially not about fallimy flowers! So there!"

Oby said: "I will see to the fliers."

Turko said: "I'll see to the provisions."

"Right. And, friends all, bring your weapons sharp."

"Aye," they growled. I own, trying to see them critically and not as the dear friends they were, they were a cutthroat bunch and no mistake.

Of course, it had to be Vomanus, careless, bright-eyed, casual, who said: "Mind you, Dray. My half-sister is heir. If the emperor dies you would have a good claim to the throne yourself."

I just looked. The rapscallion had the grace to look away and adopt a less negligent attitude, half-perched on a table. But the thought was there, hanging, ugly, in the air of the snug.

What each one thought I do not know. What I thought I am not sure. "I want nothing of the emperor save what I already have—his daughter. Unless—unless the evil days are too evil." My memories embraced Djanduin and what I had done there.

The door opened on the little silence and Bargom thrust his head in and bellowed: "Prince Drak!"

And here was my son, Drak, Prince of Vallia, most wroth, fuming with rage. He flung his cloak off in a great swirl and hurled it at a chair, snatched up a pot of wine from the table.

"By Vox!" he said. "By all the grey ones of Sicce! They wouldn't let me see grandfather. They threw me out up at the palace, that bitch Melekhi and her scum! And, on the way here, stikitches tried to do for me, assassins tried to skewer me. I tell you, Vondium is become a madhouse!"

## *Chapter Six*

### We Pay a Duty Call on the Emperor of Vallia

Two closed carriages took the raiding party to the portcullised gate below the Jasmine Tower. The bulk of the Tower wheeled against the stars, blazing in those familiar constellations over Kregen. She of the Veils shed a fuzzy pink and golden light, icing the gables and rooftops, contouring the domes with mysterious shadows, lending a deeper menace to the darkness beneath the craggy walls. The carriages, pulled by four krahniks apiece, rolled to a stop close to the edge of the dried-up moat. Here the old Canal of Contentment, very short, curved about the rear re-entrants of the palace walls. To either hand the long curtain walls vanished into the darkness, battlemented against the sky.

No one spoke a word. Seg and Inch and Turko, Balass, Vomanus, Hap and Oby.

We left the carriages concealed beneath the end arch of a colonnade where moonblooms opened their petals to the drenching moonlight. We crept upon the sentry like leems. We did not kill him, for he was a Rapa, and merely earning his hire. That he was a Rapa guarding the palace in Vondium itself clearly indicated that times had changed. His vulturine face with the fierce warrior eyes either side of his beak stared blankly up at the moon. Soon She of the Veils would be joined by the Twins, and then there would be too much light for nefarious purposes.

So, we respectable citizens of Vallia crept along in the shadows like assassins, spies, drikingers. Sharp left inside the narrow wicket I turned past the buttress and so found a narrow crack in the inner wall, a crack seeming merely the ruin of time, plastered over against the fall of the towers. But the plastering was a mere shell, covering stout wood, and the wood pivoted and revealed a square opening, a foot on a side. I gripped the iron handle, shaped like the handle of a spade, and pulled.

Almost soundlessly, so well wrought was the masonry, the section of stone pivoted about itself. The opening widened into a narrow doorway and onto stairs leading down.

Down we went and with the practiced knack of those accustomed to such things flint and steel lit the lanterns. The stairs leered below us, dark and sinister, running strips of water, darkly stained, brilliant in the lantern glitter.

Down we went.

Niter caked the walls lower down, and greenish slime hung in greasy tendrils. On we went along a jagged corridor where Inch appealed feelingly to Ngrangi, immediately hushing himself and rubbing that tall head of his.

These labyrinthine windings of corridor and tunnel and stair are virtually dictated by any palace architect on Kregen. A whole system of secondary channels exists alongside the proud and ornate halls and chambers. Many of these secret runnels I had had blocked up when first living here; but I had a map of those I knew of remaining in my head. To find the sick room was not difficult; merely tortuous.

I put my eye to the eyehole in the wooden screen and looked out into the room in which the emperor lay dying, in which Vadnicha Ashti Melekhi had screamed invective and had myself and my friends thrown out.

Doctor Charboi was in the act of rising from the bed. A glass shone in his hand. His smooth face looked well satisfied. He spoke to someone out of my angle of vision.

"He will sleep now. Quite safely."

The voice that answered, all cut glass and splinters, all vicious neemu-hiss, said: "Very good, doctor. See that he is not disturbed. Have the guards called at once. The young prince thinks he is very masterful. Kov Layco was most angry."

"I have done my work well, vadnicha."

We knew what devil's work that was.

"I do not deny it. You will be paid."

Charboi gathered up the implements of his trade and went toward the door. He knocked and the door opened. I saw the crimson-clad arm. So the Bowmen kept the door sealed, now, and opened only to those they knew. I did not smile. But I rather fancied Ashti Melekhi would have some hard explaining to do to Kov Layco Jhansi, the emperor's Chief Pallan.

If she chose to remain in the room she would have to take her chances with us. We would have to quiet her before she could cry out and warn the guards. Charboi had only just got away; I think I half regretted that at the time. But, there's no time like the present—I was about to bash open the secret door and spring leem-like upon her, when she appeared. She walked to the outer door, and paused, and looked back.

I waited.

I saw her face. All thin and white and scornful, that face, with its red mouth and arched eyebrows. And she smiled. That smile would have held a Manhound for a space. Bitter, cunning, devilish—and, yet, also, I guessed, a little regretful. I do not wish to paint Ashti Melekhi in colors that are all black. I believe she was an accomplished player on the lute. I know she kept an aviary of exotic birds. But, in the death of an emperor, it is hard to paint lighter tones when the emperor's daughter is your wife.

Then, with a small golden staff slung on a jewelled chain about her neck, she knocked upon the door. The Bowmen opened for her. She said: "Watch the door. Hold it."

"Quidang, my lady!"

No one was going to come into that room through that door this night, unless it was over the dead bodies of the Crimson Bowmen and their new Chulik mercenary partners.

So she went out, all feline grace and thin glitter, hard and brittle and oddly manlike and I wondered when I would see her again.

Gently the secret panel eased open and I stepped into the sick room. The nurse on duty sat looking at the emperor and, I swear, a tear glistered on her pale cheek. The flunkeys were gone. The nurse did not see me, she saw nothing more as the black scarf whipped about her eyes blindfolding her. Turko held her arms, very gently, and we tied her up and laid her comfortably on a thick rug of Zeniccean-made fleecy-ponsho, a gift from Strombor, with a golden cushion for her head. She did not struggle and, no doubt, poor soul, was scared witless.

We lifted up the emperor and placed him carefully in the litter we had brought, using his own bedclothes. He weighed pathetically little for a man who had once been so strong and robust. With a single quick look around the sick room we returned through the opening and I, going last, latched the secret panel shut.

Our return was uneventful. I began to think we had planned so well as to negate all problems. Onker!

We took turn and turn about to carry the litter, for each of my comrades knew my views on manual labor, the status of nobles, and the mumbo jumbo of aristocratic privileges.

We knew the routine of the palace guard. The Crimson Bowmen were professionals and would keep up their hired mercenaries to the same standards. The guard commanders changed the sentries every three burs—two hours by terrestrial reckoning—and we had taken almost the whole of that time. We anticipated leaving just before any trouble from the guard reliefs with their watchwords and their lanterns and their ready weapons.

With soundless speed we filed through the concealing opening, the emperor carried smartly if gently enough, and I reset the plaster-coated wood. At the opening of the gate we paused. Someone swore; but so low the words did not carry.

The two closed carriages were gone.

The pink and golden moonlight, strengthening slowly as the Twins eternally revolving one about the other gradually added their luster, threw odd shadows from the battlements. The damned carriages were not there. Someone had unmistakably purloined them, for they had been left firmly tethered under the colonnade, and the krahniks, useful draught animals, had shown no inclination to break free and trot off.

I caught Seg's arm.

"We walk," I said into his ear.

"The emperor—?"

"Once we clear the palace precincts we become a drunken party with a casualty. There are eight of us. We should not be molested—"

That, onker that I am, was as far as I got.

The devils were clever and they were quick and they very nearly had us.

The deadly glitter of steel in the moonlight. . . . The quick indrawn breath as killers pounced. . . . The scrape of sandals across time-worn stones. . . .

My own rapier jumped into my fist and I swear it was only a fraction of a second faster than my comrades', for we were a right tearaway bunch and, after the first quick shock of the ambush, a certain pitying sorrow for our would-be slayers afflicted me. In that, I suppose, the old haughty pride we all fight down reared more of its ugly head than is strictly desirable. Turko's brand-new parrying stick flashed with smooth-oiled steel and balass, and a lunging rapier skipped and twanged away. Turko put his hand on the fellow and the cramph went sailing up, spread-eagled marvelously against the moons.

"Hai!" said Turko, reflectively, unruffled, taking a sober enjoyment.

Hap's short clansman's axe whirled and bit, withdrew and bit again—fast, fast!

Inch licked out deftly with his great Saxon-pattern axe, and lopped, and reared up, stark against the stars, and so went with the swing, rhythmically, shearing blood and ribs and backbone in a dark welter of spraying offal.

Seg and Vomanus, who had been carrying the litter between them, placed the emperor down as fast as was decently possible. One of the attackers, mere ghost-like figures bundled in dark cloaks, shrieked and shrieked as he held, unbelievingly, onto his insides which were now outside. Silence was of no more consequence.

"Leave a few for me!" bellowed Seg, ripping out his blade, plunging on.

"And me, by Vox! Can't a fellow have any fun!" And Vomanus twinkled his rapier out, very smooth, in that typical careless way of his.

Balass and Oby, in the rear, struggled to get out.

I, Dray Prescot, just stood. I just stood there, my rapier glinting in my fist, and I wanted to laugh. Yes! I wanted to bust a gut laughing. What poor fools these fellows were, to attempt to slay a mean bunch like us. How comical!

So I took no part in that swift and deadly struggle beneath the Moons of Kregen. Balass got in a few whacks with his superb new sword we had built back in Valka. The others stood, weapons ready, crouched, looking about into the shadows.

Young Oby stalked out, mightily upset. His wicked long-knife gleamed sharp and clean.

"Not one," he said. "A right leem's nest. You might at least have saved me one."

The others laughed. Gravely, with broad smiles, they promised Oby first pick next time. They were not speaking altogether idly. So, I stepped out at last.

"Pick up all the gear. We are all reivers, mercenaries. We do not scatter good weapons about. Bundle the offal into the canal. And do not take all night about it. The guards will be here in less than no time."

"Aye, Dray," they said, but softly, already at work. We did not know what further hostile ears might be listening, affixed either side of eyes that had witnessed horror. I thought that no other stikitche who had witnessed what had happened to his comrades—there had been twelve of them—would want to come rushing out upon his death.

We all knew, deeply and with conviction, that this attack must herald some fresh horror, that what all Vondium feared must come to pass and the future lay drenched in blood. This was a prospect that appalled me, careless as I may be in these things. We had to take the emperor to Aphrasöe and there effect a cure and so bring him safely back to his capital and reseat him on his throne, defeat the dark plots of his many enemies, and bring a fresh period of peace and stability to all Vallia.

"Take up the emperor. Quick and sharp. Pull your scarves about your faces." I glared at Inch. "And, tall man, hunch yourself over. We have to win back to the inn."

Silently, feral as leems, we padded away moments before the guards arrived with much heralding of their coming, made our way back to *The Rose of Valka* where the supplies and the fliers were waiting for us.

Among the gear we had stripped from the corpses were twelve fine metal masks. I will have more to say on the subject of metal-work and masks—for the Masks of Kregen form a fascinating, beautiful and horrible story of their own—but for now I will say that these masks were built of fine-quality steel, crafted by a mastersmith. They were all alike; triangular nose, curved lip opening, cunningly slotted to slide above an apim's ears, with brow ridges over the eye orbits chiselled into the semblance of hair.

Mass production is, as you know from Hamal, practiced to some degree on Kregen; but of necessity hand-crafted objects like these must differ in detail, one from the next.

They were genuine stikitche masks, most costly; but they did not match the assassins themselves. Each one had worn ordinary clothes, buff, green, amber. I shook my head.

"Although it may seem a foolish thing to say, these do not appear to have been professional stikitches."

They all took my meaning. No assassin is going to parade around with a special badge that lights up and proclaims he is an assassin. But some marks of the trade do sometimes show.

"Look at these," said Oby, his nimble fingers turning over the badges in the lamplight of the snug.

The twelve badges were of a wersting with a korf in its jaws.

"The bitch!"

"Yet they must have followed us to the palace and waited—they cannot report back to her," I said. "This is serious. Ashti Melekhi considers herself powerful enough to assassinate the Prince Majister." No ridiculous thought of self-importance crossed my mind, only the facts as stated. "This must not deflect us from our purpose. The emperor comes first."

"I think," said Hap Loder, judiciously, "that I may return through Vondium. I may have a few words for the lady."

So we all laughed. Clansmen are regarded as the devils of barbarians they truly are in Vondium—was not I a Clansman?

Thelda was all tears and alarms as we bundled the masks and badges into a big black cloak; but Seg hushed her, and young Dray gently took her for a fortifying sip of strong wine. Sasha simply took Inch's fearsome axe and tut-tutted and taking up a cloth began to polish until the true steel shone. Inch caught my eye and smiled. "The lassies of Ng'groga are trained to support a man, in more ways than the merely amorous."

At this, Tilly bristled up, her fine slanted eyes catching the lights and gleaming, very cat-like.

"You apims think we Fristle girls are trained only for the arts of love, like your sylvies! Well, you are wrong—"

"But, Tilly," said my son Drak, very chivalrous. "All the world knows how the Fristle men care for their womenfolk."

"And we can show our claws, too, Prince Drak!"

I knew that to be true, by Zair!

Melow the Supple, recovered from the wound she had taken in defense of Delia, a story they would not tell me because it concerned the Sisters of the Rose, let rip one of her curdling, snarling chuckles. A ferocious Manhound, once of Faol and now of Valka, she said: "Women know how to look after their brats where I come from."

And her son, Kardo, who never voluntarily leaves the side of Drak, broke out with his own harsh laugh at this. I did not marvel. But I knew a whole lot of people on the Island of Faol who would never believe Manhounds, the fearsome jiklos, savage hunting beasts genetically manufactured from human beings, could ever laugh, let alone share poignant human emotions. As for Shara, Kardo's twin sister, well, she always went loping savagely at my daughter Lela's side, and where they were, Opaz knew.

Delia could tell me nothing of what was happening to our daughters, save they were safe.

The Wizard of Loh, Khe-Hi-Bjanching, pushed forward. We all waited respectfully for him to speak. The snug in *The Rose of Valka*, went suddenly quiet. "You are all going on this expedition. But, my prince, why not have the Melekhi woman arrested? The poisoning will stop then, and—"

Nath the Needle shook his head. "The process is too far gone. Only this miracle can save him." We all knew that Nath was a renowned needleman among his friends; he had no need to advertise. What he said we believed.

"But you are all mad, mad!" cried the Wizard.

"We are surely mad, Khe-Hi," I said. "Of a certainty. But I daresay we will muddle through. I shall go ahead to make the arrangements with the Todalpheme while the expedition is put together. We meet at the Risshamal keys— you can find at least one of the men who will know the rendezvous."

"So," said my Delia.

"One thing," I told them. "The assassins who attacked Drak must probably have been the same bunch. I think we will all be better off outside Vondium, anyway." My son's fate must be considered involved with mine by Melekhi— which it was not, in truth. He, as the Amak of Vellendur, had his own path to hew. I intended to find a stromnate for him as soon as may be; but he had run Valka for me with Tom Tomor and the Elders, and done well. As the son of the Princess Majestrix he must know that eventually, given the longevity of Kregans, he stood a better chance than most of becoming Emperor of Vallia himself. I finished somberly: "The emperor must be got to Aphrasöe, and nothing must stop that. Nothing. The fate of all Vallia hangs on that. Until the emperor is returned to the throne, fit and well, anarchy and blood will rule in Vallia."

These tough warriors of Kregen understood that. I could leave the final preparations in good hands. Weapons, food, drink, clothes, supplies, all would be taken care of. As for airboats, well, the gigantic skyships Seg and Inch had stolen from the emperor to rescue me in Zandikar had been returned, not without a sniff and a few cutting remarks from the old devil. So now we would fly in somewhat smaller vollers; but large, well-found craft, all the same, carrying spare silver boxes to uplift and power them in flight.

Of provisions we would take enough to withstand a siege. Of weapons we would take an arsenal, for that is the Kregan way. All in all, as we stood to say our Remberees, we were a most lively company.

Delia made sure I was, myself, accoutred and weaponed correctly. We said our private farewells in a small private room of Bargom's off the blackwood landing, where the samphron oil lamps burned low, and the smell of night-blooming flowers carried heady scents in the lustrous air.

Then the small voller I would use was hauled down from her tether. I kissed Delia and climbed aboard. The stars spread above, the lights glowed from the windows around the small courtyard, built onto the flat roof at the rear of Bargom's *The Rose of Valka*. I observed the fantamyrrh. I waved to the others.

"Remberee," I shouted down. The voller rose. "Remberee."

"Remberee," they called up, dwindling into the shadows below. "Remberee, Dray Prescot, Prince Majister of Vallia . . ."

If they finished my interminable ridiculous rigmarole of titles I lofted up and far out of earshot long before they finished.

# Chapter Seven

## Hamun ham Farthytu Asks Questions

Speed was vital. There was no time to scout my approaches to the hostile and malignant Empire of Hamal. I had been there before and knew my way around. The voller flashed through the sky of Kregen, heading south, over the sea, on course for Denrette on the east coast of the southern continent of Havilfar.

Hamal's capital city, Ruathytu, lies some sixty dwaburs to the west up the River Havilthytus. This great river empties into the Ocean of Clouds opposite the southern end of the Island of Arnor. The city of Denrette stands at the mouth of the river, and I found it a strange and yet compelling place, filled with the bustle and clamor of fisherfolk, tainted with that dourness so characteristic of Hamalians, yet not without a certain energy that, three hundred miles from the capital, gave it a semblance of the shadow of the real, a reflection of the dark glories of Ruathytu.

Down by the shore, of course, the place stank of fish. But set atop small hills the houses and villas of the wealthier folk bespoke the nature of their affected reflection of the splendors of the capital. The city was large enough to boast an arena; but I steered well clear of the jikhorkdun. I had had my fill, for the time being, of fighting in the arena away down south in Huringa, the capital of Hyrklana. There happened to be a sennight of games in progress as I arrived. For a single mur I was tugged by nostalgic memories. For a heartbeat I considered going in to join the multitudes to discover how went the fortunes of the Ruby Drang. But I did not. Anyway, quite often here in Hamal the colors and the orders were different from those I had known in Huringa.

Instead, knowing a sick emperor waited, I took myself straight to the Akhram.

The Todalpheme, the wise men of Kregen who measure the tides and keep track of the suns and the moons in their courses, who predict eclipses and who are sacrosanct, would welcome me as any ordinary traveller, anxious to improve his knowledge, of the world and of their lore. Their secrets are open, freely given to those will join them, and difficult of access to people without that astronomically oriented frame of mind. I carried fine gifts we had put together in Vondium.

The information could be bought, for the emperor had bought the knowledge once before, and where once gold has eased the way gold will find the opening easier of attainment.

Set boldly atop a promontory right out at the eastern escarpment, with a sheer drop to the ocean below, the Akhram presented a massive picture of authority and power and ancient wisdom, its craggy walls one with the rock on which it stood. The dominating pharos would beam out at night, warning the imperial skyships of Hamal and the constant mercantile flying traffic, directing them on their inward courses toward Ruathytu. The Hamalese are not great sailors of the sea. They do not have to be, seeing as they manufacture the vollers which can fly through the empty wastes of the sky.

I walked quickly up the winding path. The river flowed in its deep gorge below, cut through the living rock. Away to the north various channels of the river emptied out and the marshes stretched remote under the suns, filled with immense flocks of wildfowl. There, also, prowled the aerial predators, saddle birds gone wild, and, among them, the untamed chyyans.

The air smelled sweet with the sea tang. The blaze of the suns fell about me, the twin intermingled rays of red and green from the Suns of Scorpio. Antares, the double star, poured down floods of light. I breathed deeply of the wine-rich air, swinging the lesten-hide bag containing so much wealth. The thraxter belted at my waist seemed in that limpid air and in that sybaritic setting to be an anachronism, unnecessary.

Yet—I could never forget I trod the stones of Kregen.

Carts were toiling up the hill, carts loaded with the produce of an empire, drawn by massive old quoffas with their patient faces and hearth-rug hides, bringing a pang of remembrance. I gave a shoulder to help heave a cart from a rut and the Xaffers, diffs so strange and remote they were always a mystery to apims, thanked me in their fashion, and I strode on, filling my lungs, my eyes fixed on the grey dominating pile of the Akhram above with the gilded domes flashing brilliantly.

The carts and the workpeople toiling up served the Todalpheme. For a single instant I had the horrified thought they were on the same errand as myself, seeking the whereabouts of the Swinging City. This was a nonsense. The secret was known to very few. The voller salesman who had sold it to the emperor for Delia's sake must have been an adept in a secret society of one kind or another if he had been ejected by the Todalpheme. Secret societies always seem to flourish when men and women think about their world and their place in the scheme of things. I walked on, trying to appear inconspicuous.

The knee-length white robe did not materially help in that, for it was a rustic dress, telling these folk I was a country bumpkin. They wore the working clothes of Ruathytu, blue or grey or green, where they were not slaves, and they knew my dress as provincial. Even the thraxter marked me, for the rapier and main gauche had grown apace as a fashion in Hamal.

The guards carried thraxters and shields, in the fashion of Hamal, and stuxes, also, the spears of varying kinds for varying work. The Shanks who raided from over the curve of the world generally steered clear of the coasts of Havilfar, the southern continent that contains Hamal and Kyrklana—and Djanduin to the south west. These guards were here to protect the Akhram not from Hamalese, although they would do that quickly enough if necessary.

With a polite greeting I was passed through. The Akhram! Well, these observatories of the Todalpheme are marvellous places, to be sure. When a world possesses two suns and seven moons the mysterious workings of heavenly bodies and the conflicting surgings of the tides demand a man's application to mathematics and accurate observation and a thorough-going knowledge of his world. These attributes the Todalpheme possess to a high degree. Once, I had been offered the opportunity of joining the Todalpheme, and had gracefully declined.

Akhram—for usually the chief Todalpheme calls himself just Akhram—lifted up the golden necklace. The gold and rubies glistered back at him in the rays of the suns through the arched windows overlooking the sea. Wide-winged birds pirouetted out there and the noise of the waves reached us, although the beach was not visible. The chamber was airy, light, with a flick-flick plant, and many scented flowers. That superb Kregen tea had been served, and, gratefully, I sipped watching Akhram as he stared at the treasure heaped over the lenken table.

"Fine, fine, Amak," he said. "Princely gifts."

"I respect the Todalpheme too much to weigh the price of gifts." I spoke bluffly, stoutly, cunningly. "It is not the value that matters."

He smiled that remote little smile with which the ascetic will acknowledge the gluttonous follies of the world. A tall, grave, distinguished man, Akhram, almost a hundred and eighty years of age, in the prime of life, with much work still to be accomplished. I will not go into overmuch detail of the transactions in the Akhram of Denrette. They kept me waiting for a space, to cool my heels, then suggested if I sought a cure it would be better to consult doctors, or seek spiritual assistance from any one of the many Bengs and Bengas whose saintly miracles could cure. Akhram himself seemed to size me up, and we talked, and I convinced him that my desire to discover the whereabouts of Aphrasöe was not mercenary. He nodded, and put the necklace back among the piles of treasure.

"We, Amak," he said, "are not the scarlet-roped Todalpheme. You will find them. They know the secret. We can but point you in the right direction."

He called me Amak because I had, naturally, assumed my sceret identity of Hamun ham Farthytu, the Amak of Paline Valley. I use the overly dramatic word secret. As Hamun ham Farthytu I was a real person, with a real identity, able to move freely about Hamal, the mighty empire in deadly opposition to my own country of Vallia. But that is what comes of being a spy.

He understood my intense desire for speed, for the person dearly beloved by me—and others, I added significantly—was a most highly placed personage and it would not be too much to say that a deal of Hamal's future depended on the recovery. Thus he said, with a small, deprecating smile: "We have given this information before, for a price. There is a tortuous route to follow; but we have learned ourselves shortcuts. I think—"

"For Hamal, Akhram," I said, most seriously.

"Yes." When he told me I understood why no one I had

spoken to hitherto had heard of Todalpheme wearing scarlet ropes about their waists. The old color had come back again to haunt me. I did not smile; but I took up the map Akhram showed me, and with my old sailor skill committed it to memory. Right over to the west, west of the Tamish Channel of Havilfar, out below the forbidden island of Tambu, the island of Bet-Aqsa. Bet-Aqsa.

There we must go, and at once, to inquire of the scarlet-roped Todalpheme the whereabout of Aphrasöe.

Listening as Akhram spoke in his quiet voice in the high-vaulted library of the observatory where we had gone to find the map, I had the suspicion he did not truly know how the secret had come into the hands of the Todalpheme of Hamal. As a puissant empire, the strongest power in Havilfar—if, in my arrogance, you excepted Djanduin—it seemed logical for Hamal to come by strange shreds of knowledge, secrets gathered from the four corners of the continent. Maybe some of the Todalpheme down in the Dawn Lands might also know that the Todalpheme of Bet-Aqsa knew of a place where miracle cures might be effected. All that concerned me now was to take my flier as fast as she would fly to the rendezvous up among the Risshamal Keys.

More and more I was determined to avert the consequences of the emperor's death. For the streets of Vallia would run red with blood, the alleys pile with stinking corpses, the crops would burn, the livestock starve, thousands of hapless wights would be branded and herded off to slavery—all these atrocities would happen—might happen, would probably happen—if the Emperor of Vallia died.

Making all due observances as I took my leave, giving them Remberee, I took myself off and walked smartly back down the stony path to the waiting flier.

The Risshamal Keys are merely a number of long, fingerlike extensions of small islands, rocks, cays, shoals and reefs running out in a northeasterly direction from the northeastern corner of Havilfar. I had been shipwrecked there in the old *Ovvend Barynth*. In setting up the rendezvous we knew the certain men who could aid us. As I took off and flew up into the streaming radiance of Antares I wondered who it would be who would guide my friends to the island of the Yuccamots along the Risshamal Keys.

Flying eastward out over the sparkling sea I cleared the coast and then headed north. The Island of Arnor passed away astern. The suns poured their floods of opaz light upon the sea, and I saw a few ships sailing there—not many. A number of vollers passed; but none offered to stop and search me. The simple precaution had been taken of painting out the Vallian recognition signs, and the voller might have come direct from Ruathytu or Paline Valley for all anyone might know. I flew northwards and Bet-Aqsa lay to the southwest. I had always harbored an inkling that Aphrasöe might lie upon some island in the Outer Oceans, and had favored the easterly direction. Maybe—and I hoped most fervently that I was wrong—maybe the Swinging City was situated on the other grouping of islands and continents on the other side of Kregen, around the curve of the world. Kregen runs a longer mileage in the equator than does Earth, for all the fractionally lesser gravity, and there is a damned lot of ground to cover.

The continental grouping in which, so far, all my adventuring had taken place, is called Paz. From the other continents and islands around the curve of the world sailed the fearsome Fish-Heads—call them shanks, shants, shtarkins, shkanes, it makes no difference to their viciousness—to plague and harry us. Every so often their marvelous fleet ships would sail upon an unsuspecting shore and there would follow horror and desolation. I had fought the shanks before the jikai with the Kroveres on Drayzm, and would fight them again. Always, like any sailor of Paz, one eye was always roving the far horizons to catch the first glimpse of those tall wing-like sails of the shank ships.

And then, as I plunged on through the thin air toward that brave company of friends awaiting me at the Risshamal Keys, I looked up and saw a giant scarlet and golden bird, flying high, circling, watching me with bright black beady eyes.

I swore.

I shook my fist.

By Zair! Not now, not now!

The great hunting bird circled. The raptor was a familiar sight, a hateful sight. This was the Gdoinye, the spy and messenger of the Everoinye, the Star Lords.

Through their malign agency I had been flung about space between worlds like a yo-yo. When I had so intemperately refused to obey their orders I had been chucked back to Earth to rot for twenty-one infernal years. If the

Gdoinye was spying on me, all well and good, for I knew the Star Lords kept an eye on me from time to time. But if the Opaz-forsaken bird was warning me that I would be required to perform again for the Star Lords. . . .

I sweated. I clenched my teeth and stopped myself from shouting up insults, as I usually did when the golden and scarlet raptor hove into sight.

If the bird did swoop down and speak to me I would try to be conciliatory, be the new Dray Prescot, refrain from hurling abuse and calling the thing a cramph, a rast, a kleesh. But it swung about up there, glinting magnificently in the opaz radiance, and then calmly flew away.

I let out a great gusty breath of relief.

What a time to be dragged away from Kregen!

# Chapter Eight

## A Brush with Flutsmen

Thinking that, with the appearance of the Gdoinye, the Savanti might have sent their white dove to spy on me, I cast a good look around. I could see no sign of the dove. Well, that meant little, although, to be sure, it made more sense for the Savanti to spy on me now, seeing that my intended destination was their secret island.

The long low straggle of islands of the southern fingering of the Risshamal Keys showed as an extended yellowish grey stain upon the water ahead. The Yuccamots inhabited many of the little islands and gained a precarious living fishing and trading, in communication with the local sailing craft. I had no fear of them, for they were a simple folk and had shown us kindness before. They are, I am glad to say, enormously proud of their broad thick tails, and of their webbed feet.

The Hamalian Air Service was another matter. They maintained a string of stations along the Keys, and it behooved me to avoid those.

What did happen, with the blinding speed of precipitate action upon Kregen, whipped up a nice little froth to send the blood thumping through the veins and open the pores a trifle.

Out of the roseate glow of the red sun Zim shot the dark forms of riders urging on their saddle flyers.

With my fingers up against my eyes I peered into the dazzlement even as I thrust the control levers hard over and up.

They were flutsmen up there.

Flutsmen!

By this time I knew a little of their nefarious ways. Later, I was to learn more. But now, these mercenaries of the skies, flying their fluttrells with sure confident skill, out for plunder and lopped heads, bore down screeching on me. To them, I represented loot, easy pickings, a lone flier in a voller.

If they could take me before I rose and speeded enough to elude them, why, then they'd toss me over the side into the sea, and pilot the voller back to their base. They'd sell her and her contents and get drunk on the proceeds. Then they'd go reiving off for more easy plunder.

Usually, the flutsmen work for hire, bands of professional mercenaries, paktuns of a sort. I'd hardly demean them to the low quality of masichieri, those scoundrels who are more employable bandits than honest mercenaries, but often enough they came close, by Zair. I fancied this band were freelancing, tazll, harrying for themselves. There were about thirty of them, too long odds for me to want to tangle with them, in view of the urgency of the task before me, unless I had to.

The emperor must come first. A fight could wait. There is always opportunity for a fight on Kregen....

The voller lifted. Slowly. Too slowly.

The fluttrells turned their big heads with those large ridiculous vanes into the wind and opened their jaws and lanced down.

I glared up savagely. By Krun! I wanted no fight. But if these haughty, vicious flutsmen wanted to come to handstrokes, then I'd accommodate them. With a juicy Makki-Grodno oath, having to do with the putrescent diseased innards of Makki-Grodno's disgusting liver, I snatched up the great Lohvian longbow. If I couldn't shaft a few of the yetches before they reached me I hadn't been trained by Seg Segutorio, the master bowman of Erthyrdrin!

Down they swooped, their green-feathered harness tight about them, their closely-fitting green-feathered caps with the flaring knotted clumps of ribbon streaming out in the wind of their passage. Flutsmen on the rampage present a brave spectacle. Completely confident of themselves they swooped down, each man ready with crossbow, volstux or long whippy sword.

Before they could start shooting I cast the first shaft.

Clean through the feather-adorned armored body of the leading flutsman the clothyard shaft punched. The brilliant blue feathers of the shaft's fletching came from the crested korf of the Blue Mountains of Vallia. Always, Seg would say that the king korf's blue feathers were just that fraction superior to those of a crested korf; but he would affirm that the beautiful bird, the korf of Kregen, provided the best feathers for the shafts cast from a Lohvian longbow. I thought about this as I loosed again.

Before the leading flutsman had time to slide from his high saddle and dangle from the leather straps of his clerketer, the second shaft took his wingmate. The third shaft took the third man in the vee.

Shouts of rage battered down . . .

"Cramph! You should know better! To slay a flutsman is to die!"

I didn't bother to reply in words but sped another shaft that parted the teeth of a yelling flutsman and did nasty things to the back of his skull. His saddle flyer spun past, spraying bits of the flutsman's bone and gobbets of brain.

Yes, the korf provides the best fletchings. We'd been experimenting in Valka with the rose-colored feathers of the zim-korf. I'd had a few shafts made up and the warmly-glowing red feathers dyed a brilliant blue. Seg, when I'd tried him, had expressed himself as perfectly satisfied with the shafts, and why was I making such a thing out of it. When we washed the dye away, letting the blue color leach out to reveal the brave old red, Seg's face was a picture.

But, as the other flutsmen closed in, I had time to loose twice more—loose the blazing blue feathered shafts in deadly true arcs. Each time the arrow punched cleanly; then I took to my sword.

The Krozair longsword felt good in my fists.

Ah, me! How often I have thought that. But now, with

an emperor sick and near to dying, was no time to consider my new image, the quiet, conciliatory, peace-loving Dray Prescot. With the Krozair longsword in my fists, my hands spread in that cunning Krozair grip, I went to work.

Mind you, the first and chief use of the sword at the moment was to ward off the shafts that sliced toward me with the artful two-handed flicking taught in the Krozair disciplines. I battered the bolts away joyfully. I own it. The blood thumped around my veins. The voller shot up now as the speed increased vertically and we went slap bang through the middle of the fluttrell formation. In a clashing smother of flapping wings and raking talons the voller shot up and broke through. For an instant I was slashing and hacking away to my heart's content. Thrusting is a chancy business in these circumstances, for obvious reasons.

The voller clanged as the wooden hull gonged to repeated blows. But she won free. We sprung through the giant saddle birds and up into the suns shine—save for one. One fluttrell rose abruptly directly before me.

There was no chance to swerve the flier. Bird and boat crashed together with an almighty smash.

Staggering, I kept my feet, braced, wrathful, the wicked Krozair brand slanted up and forward. The bird was entangled with the stem of the boat, where the fancy gilding was all scraped away. The stout leather harness did not break. Its wings thrashed. The rider, freeing himself from his clerketer, leaped right nimbly down onto the tiny deck, superbly balanced on supple legs, came for me directly. His green feathers flaunted in the light.

"Die, onker!" he shouted, and cast his stux.

The spear flew. The Krozair longsword flicked and the spear, ringing like a gong, caromed away into the blue.

Nothing daunted, the flutsman came on, drawing his thraxter. He presented the sword, point first, the Havilfarese cut-and-thruster held in skilled firm grip, leaped down with a wild panache. Powerful, he was, limber in his strength, supremely at home in the air. The longsword flicked left, halted, surged back, twisting. The thraxter spun up in the air, end over end, sparkling. The sharp steel point of the Krozair brand held without a tremble on the throat of the flutsman, just above the green collar of his lorica.

He glared at me, panting, disbelieving. He was a strong well-built Brokelsh. His bristle body hair bristled even more. A strong, virile race, the Brokelsh, and many people consider them coarse and uncouth. Not apims, of course, the Brokelsh. Had this fellow been wearing a silver or gold trim to the collar of his lorica I might have had a little more exercise in twitching his sword away.

He gaped down at the sword. His expression was one of enormous surprise, as though he awoke from a dream of midnight houris and wine to find himself in this predicament.

His goggle-eyed amazement amused me.

"Why should I not slay you now, dom?"

He shook his massive head and licked his lips. His mannerisms were those of a man, diff or apim, both. "I am a flutsman, apim."

"Aye! A reiving mercenary of the skies who owes no allegiance to any save his own band, despite the hire fees you take. Well, many of your band have gone down to the Ice Floes this day. What say you, Flutsman?"

His blunt chin went up. Uncouth they may be, the Brokelsh, exceedingly hairy with a coarse black body hair; but they are men.

"I am Hakko Bolg ti Bregal, known as Hakko Volrokjid. Perhaps I deserve to die. I do not think so. I have a great hatred for all you Hamalese—and mayhap that will serve."

"In that case, by the disgusting tripes of Makki-Grodno! I shall not slay you. I do not want your blood on my blade."

I said this, you will perceive, to conceal the truth.

He squinted his eyes down, this Hakko Volrokjid. I, too had had trouble with volroks, those winged flying men of Havilfar. "And this blade," he said. "I have not seen its like before."

"And I've not heard of Bregal."

"A small town, in Ystilbur of the Dawn Lands."

"I have heard of Ystilbur. An ancient land."

"And razed with fire and swords by you rasts. By Barflut the Razor Feathered! I would dearly love to slay you all!"

"Seize your fluttrell, before the onkerish thing strangles himself on his own harness. Get you gone. I am not a Hamalese. And, dom, if you meet me again, remember, and tread small."

He glared for a heartbeat at me, his bristly face working, then he scrambled back and grappled his bird, who would have bit at him had he not clouted it over the head. I spoke big, like that, to conceal deeps I did not want this Brokelsh flutsman, Hakko Volrokjid, to see revealed in me.

He freed the bird and vaulted up into the saddle, doing all this with the practiced ease of your true flutsman. He buckled up the clerketer. His bristly face lowered down on me.

"I shall not forget you, apim. Be very sure of that, by the Golden Feathered Aegis!" He drew up the reins, handled most cunningly in one fist. Then he shouted down words that surprised me, although they should not have. Many a paktun—although he was far too callow to have earned the coveted mortilhead—would not thank a man for giving life. They might feel shame, depression, humiliation, the outrage of their professional ethics, depending on their beliefs. But this young flutsman bellowed down: "I thank you for my life. May the Resplendent Bridzikelsh have you in his keeping. Remberee!"

And with a great beating of wings the fluttrell swooped away and this singular flutsman was gone.

I poked my head over the side of the voller.

The flutsmen toiled along after me, all in formation, the wings of their flyers going up and down, up and down. Hakko Volrokjid spun away through the level wastes to join them. Then, all in formation, they swung away and strung out in a beeline for the coast to the west. Hakko flew strongly after them. So, guessing what was afoot—or, rather, in the air—I looked ahead and there were the fliers lifting from the scattering of cays and bearing up for me.

A single look reassured me.

They were not vollers of the Hamalian Air Service.

My friends, waiting at the rendezvous, had witnessed the little aerial affray and were no doubt thirsting to get into the fight.

This was true—deplorably so.

The moment my voller touched gunwales with Seg's impressive craft he yelled across; "One missed, Dray—the blue flash of feathers was not to be mistaken."

"My finger slipped on the string."

"Aye!" he roared, joyously. "You always had slippery fingers."

Inch bellowed across from his flier. "A good long axe, Dray—that's what you need up here in the sky."

Other greetings rose from the other fliers. We formed a

little fleet, a tiny armada, there off the coast of a hostile empire. But we wanted nothing of Hamal on this trip.

I landed the little voller across the deck of the large flier Delia had provided for us. She waited for me, alight with joy at my safe return. All my comrades and their families were here, in good spirits, although chafing to have missed that little spat of a fight. So I knew the emperor was not yet dead.

Delia smiled at me, her face pale.

"He still lives. But he is weak, so very weak. We must hurry."

I shouted out the course to Vangar.

"Southwest! Southwest at top speed."

We were on our way to Bet-Aqsa and the men who might tell us where away lay Aphrasöe, the Swinging City of the Savanti.

# Chapter Nine

## In the Akhram of Bet-Aqsa

The encounter between the ranked Pachak swods and the Rapa Deldars had been sanguinary in the extreme. Two Chulik Jiktars, powerful, had been swept away in the bloody rout, and an apim Paktun and a Brokelsh Hikdar were thrown with the others regretfully back into the velvet-lined box.

"Do you yield?" demanded Delia, most fierce.

"Aye," I said. I did not tip my king over in the terrestrial way of chess but I pushed back in the chair and, looking on the ruin of my forces, said: "Aye, I bare the throat."

Jikaida is a game where women can be so damned deceitful it amazes mere mortal men. But I could not help adding: "I notice you are using as your Pallan a female figure. I still do not recognize the representation."

"You are not meant to."

I glanced out through a port. The airboat fled on through the level wastes of air, speeding towards Bet-Aqsa. We had slept and eaten and I had thought to occupy the mind of Delia by Jikaida, that absorbing game that dominates so much of Kregan intellectual thinking, giving opportunities for rigorous mental disciplines. I did not pick up her Pallan, the most powerful piece on the board. But I cast the gorgeous little figure a most baleful glance.

Delia smiled. "She carries the yellow cross on the scarlet field. What more could you ask?"

I grunted. "Only that she play for me, woman!"

At this, Delia laughed, and so I knew much of her fear for her father had been damped by the amazing success we had so far enjoyed in our mission to save his life, and with it the life and well-being of all Vallia.

Most people have a game of Jikaida stuffed away somewhere in a dusty cupboard; most people play from time to time. It demands much more than the game Jikalla. Some folk play so often that the game becomes their life. Gafard, the King's Striker, who was our son-in-law and who was now dead, had once earned a living as a Jikaidast, a man—or woman—who sets up in a suitable place and challenges all comers for wagers. Such Jikaidasts are regarded differently in various countries; usually they are given honor and I, for one, gave them due honor within the craft.

Most people who are halfway serious about Jikaida also own at least one personal set of playing pieces. Although the opposing colors are usually blue and yellow, sometimes black and white—almost never red and green—the individual figures are embellished in wondrous ways. I happened to have been using a mixed set in which diffs and apims filled the functions of representing the various pieces. I admired the fine martial appearance of the little warriors, of whatever race they happened to be. Delia had produced a marvelous set, all of delicately carved ivory and balass and gold, including Pachaks and Djangs. With, of course, her confounded mysterious female figure as her Pallan.

Now, lifting up my own Pallan, a neat little apim with a finely wrought Lohvian longbow and a sword too long for comfort, I laid him away in the balass box.

"Having bared the throat, will you wet it with some wine?"

Our son, Prince Drak, came into the stateroom just then and did the honors, pouring Gremivoh, the vintage favored in the Vallian Air Service.

"It is all going amazingly well," he said. He still experienced difficulty in calling me father, and Jaidur always avoided the embarrassment." The island will be in sight within a bur or so."

We spoke for a few moments of the trip and the prospects, ground we had covered time after time. Drak expressed himself as most pleased that when we had stopped off in Djanguraj for fresh provisions, nothing would stop Kytun Kholinn Dorn and Ortyg Fellin Coper and their families from joining us. Then, speaking to Delia although looking at Drak, I said: "Can you tell me why this well set-up, handsome son of ours has not married so far?"

Drak's powerful features lowered on me at this, and Delia shook her head in a quick admonitory way.

"That is my business," said Drak.

"Oh, aye," I said. "But the emperor is your grandfather. We are going to save his life. Rest easy on that. But, one day, it is likely you will be emperor."

His head went up at this. Powerful, Drak, hard and strong, filled with a dark purpose I could only admire at a distance.

"Yes. Consider that well. With a family to sustain you, you will seem an even better choice to the people and the Presidio."

"And you?"

"Me? I want only your well being—as for the emperor—throne, crown, title, wealth—they are all gewgaws. I have enough of that kind of thing already." Here, again thinking of Djanduin of which land I am king, I paused. "At least, if it comes to it, and if your mother agrees, why, then...."

Drak set his glass down carefully. He was worked up, his handsome face, dark and powerful, set in harsh lines of determination that, I suspected, were very like those lines I see in the mirror when I shave.

"I do not anticipate becoming emperor while you or mother live."

He went out then, quickly, and the sturmwood door slammed somewhat too hard.

"I really do not know what to make of that boy," I said.

Delia laughed: "You do realize, my heart, that because

of our dip in the Sacred Pool of Baptism, we are younger than he is?"

"Deuced odd that, by Zair!"

She became grave, on a sudden. "They—the Savanti—they would not let me go—you remember—and you—it was a dreadful journey to the pool—" She bit her lip, and said, on a rush: "Suppose they will not let father be cured?"

"I have thought of that. We fly directly to the Pool of Baptism. Once we are there and your father is cured, it will be too late for the Savanti to interfere."

So we agreed on the plan between us. I felt some confidence that with the tearaway bunch of ruffians with us, and with the fine navigation of Vangar—I would help, of course—we ought both to find the River Zelph and the Pool and take care of any opposition along the way. What the Savanti might say I did not much care. I own I felt some concern over what they might do. But they were, as I knew, a civilized people who wanted to make of Kregen a world fit for people to grow into fulfilled lives without the dark fears that plagued them now. The stakes were too high to draw back now out of phantasmal fears of what might be.

We went up on deck into the clean swift rush of wind.

Our friends were peering ahead from every flier. Wersting Rogahan, who could shoot a varter and hit the center of the Chunkrah's eye every time, had been the man they had found to guide them to the Yuccamot island in the Risshamal Keys. He had been shipwrecked with me in the old *Ovvend Barynth*, a rough-tongued rapscallion, an old sea-dog; but he was a man I fancied I understood and could rub along with. He had advanced just one step in rank since I had had him made up to so-Deldar, and was now a ley-Deldar. He still wore that dark strip of chin beard under his jaws, his lean knowing face was just the same with the broken nose and the mahogany tan of a life spent at sea. Up here in a flying craft he had donned a buff shirt where normally he went bare-chested, and the old buff trousers cut off at the knees might have been the same pair he'd worn when we'd shot our varters in competition against the pursuing shanks.

"Land ho!"

The shrill yell skyrocketed up from Oby, perched high. He pointed ahead.

Soon we all saw the low dark outline of coast, with hills

beyond, and the cream of surf and the wink of rivers. Bet-Aqsa was a sizeable island, triangular in shape and some one hundred eighty or so dwaburs across at the widest part, smaller than the forbidden island of Tambu to the north.

Kytun Kholin Dorn, my fearsome four-armed Djang comrade, bellowed across the wind-rushing gap between fliers; "So that's where those Drig-loving reivers live, is it? Now we know, by Zodjuin of the Silver Stux! we will pay them a visit and return their gifts to us in fire and the sword!"

Well, knowing my Djangs as I do, and knowing of the raids they suffered from the sea people—not the Shanks—I could not be surprised.

If the inhabitants of Bet-Aqsa as distinct from the Todalpheme of that place made a habit of raiding the western coasts of Havilfar, secure that their home was far enough west to deter anyone reckless enough even to think of sailing that far into the Ocean of Doubt, then they would be in for a nasty shock. The place was secretive enough, Zair knew. Events were changing fast on Kregen, and the world would never be the same again.

Over the horizon to the north and east the forbidden island of Tambu presented no lure. I had met men who claimed to have been there and the stories about the place, not all apocryphal, I feel sure, were calculated to curdle the blood. Gruesome, distasteful, the stories, most of them, as I was to discover. The thought did cross my mind that perhaps the forbidden character of Tambu could be explained away by the unsuspected presence there of the Savanti.

That, we would soon discover.

Over the island we flew, seeing towns and villages of peculiar aspect, and long rolling downlands, forests, marks of cultivation. A few fluttrell patrols winged up after us; but we flew vollers high and fast and left the laboring saddle birds far below. Also, there arose other flyers riding beasts new to us, flying steeds of remarkable appearance, all speckled with ruby and amber feathers, with gappy jaws and long whiplike tails. Still and all, despite their efficient wingspan, long and wide like an albatross's and despite the gesticulating figures upon their backs, they were outdistanced also.

"Straight to the Western Akhram, Vangar," I told the captain of my Valkan Fleet, admiral, chuktar, flag-captain and skipper of whatever voller I happened to be flying in all rolled into one efficient, loyal, great-hearted man. He nodded and bent to his map, the self-same map I had drawn out for him from my memory of the one shown me by Akhram of the Todalpheme of Denrette.

Soon at the best speed of our vollers the western coast came in sight, a green-blue glittering expanse of water stretching out beyond the last fingerings of land, a vast mass of empty water stretching out no man knew whither. This was the Ocean of Doubt.

"There!" screeched Oby, pointing, the wind in his hair.

A collection of yellow-green onion domes rose from the edge of an inlet. Ships lay moored and signs of activity from what were clearly dockyards showed that these people kept themselves busy, an impression heightened by the size of the town strung along the water's edge. The low yellow fortress guarding the mouth of the inlet was not lost upon us. These folk trafficked upon the sea, and yet they built defenses. We all thought we knew for whom those stout walls had been built.

The Akhram stood aloof from these mundane pursuits, the cluster of onion domes glistening in the limpid air.

How far we had come! Right to the edge of the known world—over it, for all we had previously known of these foreign parts. Where one might have expected to discover an uncouth half-savage people, it was clear there was wealth down there, industry and commerce—and, for sure, a deal of loot from the coasts of Havilfar, including Djanduin.

I had argued with my friends and overborne them.

Delia said: "But I should go with you! I have been to Aphrasöe before. Therefore—"

"Therefore you will stay here, with the fleet."

She pouted at me, making a mockery of my heavy-handedness. But I would not be swayed. I had brought a fleet and a large body of fighting men, for that is the best way to travel on Kregen when you are in a hurry and will meet foes—and carry a bedridden, dying emperor. The very best way, of course, is alone, like a savage clansman in hunting leathers—and, truly, better even than that, is just the two of you, just the two, alone in the whole wide world of Kregen. . . .

So I would not be swayed now. Nath the Needle said he dare not leave the emperor. The poison wasting away the once stalwart frame was insidious, and any cure that might once have been possible was long since too late, by far. All he could do was administer what antidote he could. Every bur the emperor had to take a teaspoonful of the nauseating mixture Nath prepared, swallowing it down past clenched teeth we had gently to prise open with silver levers. Also, acupuncture needles had to be used, carefully inserted in the right nodes and along the correct lines to ease the increasing pain. I had studied assiduously with Nath the Needle as well as other eminent doctors to discover all I could of the arcane myseries of the needleman's art. I could insert a needle now and know with sure certainty that it would do the work intended.

Making preparations as the fleet hovered over the Akhram, I gave my last instructions. "I go alone and hope to win through with gold and peaceful talk. If I am not back within three burs then, Seg and Inch, you'd better fly down and see what is keeping me. I trust you will bring a few sturdy fellows with you, and, as well, leave another pack of sky-leems up here to guard our return."

They nodded. They were not joking, even if I tended to treat this whole escapade as just that. They didn't like me jaunting off by myself. Even I had to admit that that was because they cared for my leathery old hide, and not, as I dearly loved to believe, because they fancied I was hogging all the action.

All my experiences on Kregen so far indicated that the Todalpheme were quiet, studious, peace-loving men who wished only to get on with their tasks of tracking the course of the moons and the suns and of predicting the tides. They kept up a force of brown-clad workpeople who were not slave, superintended by the Oblifanters, answerable directly to the Todalpheme. The Oblifanters and their work force were not cloaked by the universal acceptance of the sanctity of the Todalpheme. They might be entrapped, made slave, killed. So they were a rougher bunch. Their methods of work I had seen at the Dam of Days.

The voller spun away and I was lunging for the cluster of greenish-yellow onion domes within the long walls.

While it is not true to say that one Akhram is very much like another, they must all share a deal in common as to the purpose of their architecture. They each possess an observatory and a library and a refectory. As I expected, after a wait, I was shown into a small room where Akhram would see me. Gold, even among the Todalpheme, sometimes eases the way. But the Todalpheme welcome students visiting them, and within the framework of their vital occupations will delight in conversation with visitors, seeing that they are usually cut off from normal human intercourse. As a rule they lead solitary lives, at one with the waves and the winds and the tides. I anticipated only the problem of convincing the Todalpheme of Bet-Aqsa that I was genuinely in need of secret information.

Some thought had been taken as to my dress.

To go with the orange favors of the Djangs would be to excite instant suspicion if not hostility. To go as a Vallian would mean little, except to create wariness almost as much as a Hamalian. Finally I donned a simple short russet-colored tunic, edged with a deep yellow, belted with lesten hide and a great golden buckle—petty ostentation, this last, but designed with a purpose. A rapier and dagger swung at my sides and the old longsword jutted up over my shoulder. I hung a long white cloak around my shoulders, clear of the hilt of the longsword, and fastened off the bronzen zhantil-head clips. The unworldly combination should provoke interest, at the least.

"And are you a prince, dom?" said Akhram, coming into the chamber and sitting down. He was a fat and fleshy man, with pursed lips despite the fat jowliness of his cheeks, and pouchy eyes. I did not like the sound of that "dom" which is common among ordinary folk as a greeting name, and among friends as a mark of affection. For the first time I felt unease, that I had blundered.

"That is not of importance." I put to him the reason for my visit. I opened the lesten-hide bag and showed him the contents. As I did this I watched his eyes. My hackles rose. He was a Todalpheme; I do not deny him that. And, also, I knew there was much and much I did not know about Kregen. But he was like no other Todalpheme, least of all an Akhram, that I had met before.

"Pretty baubles," he said, lifting the golden chains. But his face betrayed far different emotions from his words.

"All yours, excellency." I used the word deliberately. "The man is very sick. Only the Savanti can cure him."

He looked up quickly, the golden chain swinging from his soft plump fingers. "So you know their name? The brothers grow careless. And you have come far?"

"A goodly way." I pushed the heavy bag nearer. "Tell me where lies Aphrasöe and these are yours and I will leave at once."

No strangeness afflicted me as I considered what I said,

what I demanded. The search for information had upheld me for long periods of my life upon Kregen. It was a secret I had hungered for, suffered for, something I had thought meant more to me than anything else in two worlds. Paradise! I had been thrown out of the paradise that was Aphrasöe, the Swinging City. I had asked and asked and always to no avail, and then real life had taken me in and the Swinging City had dimmed. And now, here I was, calmly offering gold to buy the secret. Weird!

So the strangeness of it all did affect me, after all.

"I think, dom," said this Akhram, touching his lips, which shone, moist in the lights through the open windows. "I think the bag of treasure is mine, whether I give you the secret or not."

"How so?"

"We do not impart this to everyone who asks. It is a high trust placed in our hands."

Again, I blundered.

"I do not believe that. You came by the information by chance—"

"Do not presume!" He flared at me, shaking already with an anger he did little to control. This Todalpheme showed a petty emotion. "We have sent our men before. Good men. In vollers that cost a great deal of money in far Havilfar."

By saying "far" Havilfar, he sought to entrap me into some kind of reaction by which he might judge my place of origin.

Stony-faced, I said: "I need the information and I need it in a hurry. I do not quarrel with anything you say of your acquisition or trust of the secret. The man is like to die. You will tell me."

"And if I will not?"

I put my hand on the bag.

He sneered. "We have sent brothers to Aphrasöe and often they do not return. Gold will not buy their lives."

"I do not ask any escort."

Then he said the revealing thing I had sensed and which had caused my blundering, my stiff-necked talk.

"No," he said. "No, we are not as other Todalpheme."

He wore a fine sensil robe of yellow. His thick waist was girded by a scarlet rope. He was, in truth, one of the Scarlet-Roped Todalpheme, men I had sought over the face of Kregen. And now I had found one of that brotherhood and he was proving two-faced, obstinate, greedy, attempting to cheat and defraud me, attempting, also, to browbeat me.

He reached out a hand and touched the bag of treasure.

"I think this is mine, already. I think you had best be gone before worse befalls you."

I said: "Do you consider yourself sacrosanct?"

His astonishment was genuine.

His eyes glittered through abruptly down-drawn lids. Yet he answered obliquely. "You wear swords, dom." He paused. His use of the word dom continued to offend me. I saw quite clearly in it a patronizing sneer; dom is the word between friends for friend, or the kindly word indicating no hostility. Except, of course, when it is used in irony, and then the circumstances are perfectly plain. There are subtleties in the use of words. Here, this Akhram was baiting me. Why? He thought he could take the treasure and kick me out. He had guards, powerful armed men at call.

He put his hands together and continued, heavily. "You wear swords. Only a madman would offer violence to a Todalpheme."

Yes, on occasion I am mad. But I was not as yet mad enough to risk everything on a cheap retort, something like: "I am mad, dom, mad enough to do your business for you if you do not speak up—quick!"

Instead, I said: "What impediment is there to telling me? Surely the gold is not all there is to it?"

He hesitated again at this. I can judge time passably well. The three burs were drifting away through the glass.

"We have been warned by the Savanti. They do not relish strangers visiting them."

This sounded likely. I remembered the vexation with which Maspero, my tutor, had greeted the arrival of the flier carrying Delia. With her had been three yellow-robed, scarlet-roped men—and they had all three been dead.

He leaned forward. "Perhaps, if you told me the name and identity of the sick man. . . ?"

Now it was my turn to pause. Information. The Todalpheme were avaricious for news of all kinds. A mistake now—in all sober truth the fate of Vallia trembled on what I said, hung there, stark and brutal before me.

I said: "It is the Emperor of Vallia."

"Ah." He pushed back in his carved chair and smiled. He glanced at the bag of treasure. "One bag of gold is an insult."

"So that is it. You are greedy."

He flushed. "Take care, rast, lest you regret hasty words."

All I had learned as a good Kregan warred within me with myself. I have a nature. My nature has to be quashed. The Todalpheme are sacrosanct; no sane man will raise a hand against them. But what of tradition, what of the truth of the question when a great empire may run red with blood? Where lay my duty now?

He watched me slyly. He saw the twitch of my hand toward the rapier hilt. He smiled wetly. "The fate of a man who rasies a hand against a Todalpheme is awful— awful."

Was my just punishment if I violated the basic tenet of this solemn Kregan belief worthy payment for saving the life of an emperor, of preventing the torrents of blood that would follow? Would my Delia thank me for destroying myself in saving her father?

The decision was mine.

## Chapter Ten

### "In Aphrasöe You Will Find Only Death!"

Everything so far had gone with such amazing ease I should have been warned. Khokkak the Meddler should have been heeded. Trip the Thwarter should have been propitiated. We had spirited the emperor away from his would-be murderers. We had arrested the insidious work of the poison so that he still lived. We had tracked down the clues and found our way here to where the secret would be told. And now we were thwarted by this cunning, greedy, deceitful onker of a man.

He was after the gold, surely, and information, and he did not intend to let me leave alive, I fancied.

What could I say to move him in a spirit of conciliation?

If it was a mere matter of gold. . . .

"If you require gold, then you must know it is yours for the asking. Vallia will pour out her treasures for the life of her emperor."

"Yet you bring one miserable bag."

The answer to that was easy.

"It is but an earnest."

"Ah!" The avariciousness in him was plain now, plain and ugly and degrading. "How soon can you bring more? Much more?"

"As soon as the emperor is well—"

"Not good enough."

"There is no time to be lost. You have my word."

"Words are cheap among the canaille." He used another word; but that is what he meant. I kept my seat. For the moment I had postponed the decision that would destroy me.

"What more do you want of me—treasure—?"

"You could start by showing proper respect and by calling me master, or san, or Akhram."

I nodded. I'd have to force the words out as a constipated man forces himself; but for the sake of Vallia I'd eat humble pie. And, not really for Vallia. For my Delia. . . .

"Listen to me, Akhram. Tell me plain. I can have as much gold as you can imagine brought to you. But it must be clear to you that it is not with me now. Yet the emperor must be treated at once." Then I put a little snap into my words. "If you do not tell me and the emperor dies, you will get nothing."

He put a hand to his mouth at this, pondering the truth.

I gave him no chance to bluster on. I blustered a trifle myself. "Take the gold we have. Save the emperor. Then you will have the reward of a good deed well done, besides the treasure." I leaned a little closer and my hand dropped to the rapier hilt. "You say you are not as other Todalpheme, and I see that to be true. You have threatened to kill me. But I am not as other men of Kregen. A Todalpheme has little respect from me if he does not act as a Todalpheme is expected to act. If the emperor dies, I think you may die, also."

He started up, pushing away from the table, his heavy face red, from shock or indignation or fear, I did not know and didn't damned well care. I had made no conscious decision; I still sought to sway him with words, even if the words were brutal and barbed and vicious.

"I am sacrosanct!"

I ignored him and he sat down, shaking his hands falling from my sight beneath the table edge. "You know of Vallia. I am aware of that. You know that Vallia has beaten the Empire of Hamal. I do not think you would relish a great armada from Vallia wreaking just vengeance on you."

He had regained his composure. "You would not find the swods or the officers who would lay a hand on a Todalpheme!" He sneered the words, getting his courage back, vicious.

So I saw the answer.

I stood up and glared down on him and all the old intemperate evil power must have flooded into my face, for he started back in his chair, unable to rise, all his new-found bravado fled.

"Listen to me, Akhram! If you do not instantly tell me where we may find the Savanti and so save our emperor, then a great armada will come from Vallia. They will not attack the Akhram. They will leave the Todalpheme alone. But they will utterly destroy your island of Bet-Aqsa. All your people will be slain or enslaved—save a few. Save a few who will know why this calamity has fallen on them. They will bear hatred in their hearts for those who caused their destruction. Who do you think will receive that enmity? Whom will they blame for the calamity that will have fallen on them? Who by refusing to help a sick and dying man wrought such terrible retribution upon the heads of an innocent people?"

I glowered down, hard, horrible, hateful. "Think on, Akhram. Your people will refuse to work for you, to support you. They may not kill you; but they will not lift a finger to help you. What will your life be like then? Think on, old man, and be quick about it."

He pointed a trembling finger at me. "You—you devil!"

"Aye! Believe it. And tell me."

"There will be a reckoning. . . . But I will instruct my people. Your emperor must be blindfolded and we will take him—"

About to bellow a vicious: "No! We will take him!" I paused. I had pushed. There would be another way, now, than that of violence, which I abhor.

"The doctor cannot leave his side."

"Our doctors can attend him."

"Then ready your flier and hurry."

The commotion that broke outside the door made my lips rick back. The cunning leem probably had a bell-push hidden beneath his chair. Various combinations of rings gave his instructions. Even an onker could guess what he had rung his minions and his guards for.

"You have boasted and threatened, cramph." His heavy flushed face ran sweat. He descended to insults, also, which is not the way of your true Todalpheme of Kregen. He had waited his time, and now: "Now it is my turn! My people will deal with you utterly. You are alone and although you wear swords I do not think you will stand against my Oblifanters and their swods. Whatever the truth of your story, no one in the whole world will ever see you or hear of you again."

"You make a mistake."

"My mistake was in listening to you. Yetch!" He was suddenly shaking in a paroxysm of fresh rage, bloated, purple, rising to confront me. "You dare to threaten me! Calling yourself a devil! Should the Empire of Vallia lay waste to the whole of Bet-Aqsa and the stupid canaille left refuse to bring their offerings to the Akhram and to work for us, why do you think that would concern me? Do you think there are no other places I might go? An Akhram? Sacrosanct?"

"The Ice Floes of Sicce for one."

"Now my people are here—listen to them and the clink of their steel. You are doomed, rast, and I shall spit; but not on your grave, for no mortal man will know where that is."

The door opened. It did not burst in. It opened, all the same, with a pretty smash. The Oblifanters and the guards would tramp in, now, and we'd have a right merry set-to. All my plans had gone wrong—

"Where d'you want these, my king!" bellowed an enormous voice.

Kytun bounced through. In his lower left and right arms he carried two squirming soldiers, almost crushed against his massive ribs. His upper left arm was lifted and his broad hand gripped a writhing Hikdar, his fancy uniform flying, kicking and yelling aloft in the air. In Kytun's right hand a djangir gleamed. The very short very broad sword of Djanduin shone brilliantly, clean steel, without a trace of blood.

Over Kytun's head an Oblifanter sailed up, to land with an almighty crash on the floor between us, so I knew Turko was busy out there. Seg and Inch pushed through, their faces grim.

"Todalpheme!" said Seg. He looked disgusted. "We kept out of sight and sailed in on time. By the Veiled Froyvil, my old dom, this place stinks!"

"If these are Todalpheme, judging by what I saw," put in Inch, "stink is too mild a description."

"Aye," I said. "This man here, this Akhram, will show us where away lies Aphrasöe. He has been told what will happen if he does not."

At the ruination of his plans Akhram shrank. He shook.

"You would not lay a hand on me!" He shrieked, in mortal fear, for the first time in his life, no doubt. "Defilers!"

"Not on you," I said. "Remember. Ponder what I have said."

I was not proud in a loose sense of what I had done. I remembered other Akhrams I had known, and their worth did not excuse my treatment of this worthless example. But he, like the scorpion, only followed his own nature. But, being a man and not a scorpion, and being bound by vows, and being in a high position of trust and privilege, he should have made better attempts to curb his own villainy, and acted his part as an Akhram.

So I leaned, as I used to lean, a little, to my shame.

"And do not think there is a single place in the whole wide world of Kregen where you could scuttle that the arm of Dray Prescot, Prince Majister of Vallia, could not reach out and find you—and, finding, punish!"

Well, it was petty, I'll allow. But the fellow had mizzled me. Delia's father lay dying, and this kleesh had done what he had done, despite my earnest endeavors at concilition. Ends and means, means and ends, they are all the same according to the wise divines of Opaz, for one creed alone, and so I stand branded as an evil-doer. But, would I not take upon myself all the evil of two worlds for the sake of Delia?

So, after naked, brutal force had been used, and not against the Todalpheme, to overwhelm them in the person of this Akhram, by the threat of violence only, he gave us the directions we coveted. I did not think he lied. Lying would bring upon his head his total destruction. He knew this. If the emperor died because of his treachery in giving us the wrong directions, he knew we would return and great would be our fury.

All the same, as we soared up, the malicious cramph had the last word.

He tilted that heavy face back, and the redness staining his forehead and cheeks glistened in the waning lights of Antares. He shouted up, gloating, crowing, cocksure we were doomed.

"The Savanti will not welcome you! You will never return! If you go you are dead men!"

Then, with a triumphant cackling screech, he shrilled:

"In Aphrasöe you will find only death!"

# *Chapter Eleven*

## Of Weapons and Colors—
## and the Scorpion

"In Aphrasöe you will find only death!"

Threats of that kind had little effect on our company—By Krun! they had no effect whatsoever. We were a roughneck, reckless, hairbrained bunch, and with the end of our long journey in sight, any tension that might have been expected did not show itself as these tough warriors—old and young—skylarked and joked, treating the whole expedition as a giant escapade put on for their especial benefit. Concern over the life of the emperor had sensibly diminished now we were so close to the Pool of Baptism where he would be cured.

No doubts or thoughts of failure entered anyone's head.

The laggard burs flew past. The large island on which Aphrasöe was situated rose out of the sea before us as the Suns of Scorpio rose, blinding in their opaz radiance, streaming their mingled lights of jade and ruby across the sea and the black mass ahead. What perils awaited us there, in that mysterious island? No sense in anticipating problems; they would find us quickly enough. So, thoughtfully, competently, like the old professional fighting hands we were, we prepared for what the future might bring.

Over the coast we soared. The sea and the land looked like any sea and land ought to look—and yet, and yet this was the island of the Savanti!

Somewhere on this island I had for the very first time been dumped down on Kregen. Floating along the Sacred River Aph in a leaf boat, with only an enormous scorpion for crew. That was long and long ago, by Zair—before I even knew of Zair, or the Krozairs—or Delia.

The powers of the superhuman Savanti were immense, unknown, frightening. I made up my mind for the umpteenth time that we must fly straight for the Pool, following the course of the River Zelph rather than the Aph, cure the emperor, and then high tail it out of Aphrasöe, if we could. There would be no hanging about, no stopping for Lahals with the Savanti. I would not go swinging in the Swinging City. There was too much at stake—and, anyway, I had found my paradise elsewhere.

Well, men grow corn for Zair to reap, as they say.

Again and again I went over the plan. Delia knew what it was necessary to do at the Pool itself. All my magnificent fighting men—aye! and their ladies also—knew what must be done.

So we flew through the brightening morning air and the red and the green mingled and fused into that glorious opaline radiance, streaming golden and clean from Antares through the sweet air of Kregen.

The coastline itself trended away and showed no sign that we could see of life or habitation, and we saw not one sail. But, as we flew inland, the ground swarmed with life. I own I felt amazement.

Down there, as we flew over, huge herds of animals in myriad forms of animal life grazed and ran and heaved in a long rolling sea of heaving rumps and wicked upflung horns. We hung over the rails and watched the hunters, leem and graint, chavonth and strigicaw, a whole mad medly of the savage animals of Kregen, all roaming the plains and valleys and jungly defiles below. Just about every kind of animal I had encountered on Kregen passed below, and many more that I saw there for the first time. Kregen is so marvelous a world and so populated with wonders that it is sometimes difficult to remember that this incredible Earth of ours has probably almost as vast a range of different forms. But on Kregen the varieties have been wildly intermingled, and the artful hand of artificial genetic breeding has been at work, and the combinations of animals—and humans—appear much more startling.

Wild animals would from time to time cross the high passes of the craggy mountain ring that surrounds and protects the Swinging City. I had hunted graint with the Savanti, carefully packing them up and sending them back over the mountains unharmed. Now I saw the reality of the enormous profusion of life. It seemed that examples of every kind of animal sported below.

Oby licked his lips. "What a sight!" he stared down, hungrily.

"We shall not starve, that is sure," said Turko. "Seg with his great bow could feed us single handed."

Vegetarianism is known and practiced on Kregen; but if a man is starving and a fat deer passes by—well, a man must live unless he wishes to surrender to the fate high ideals may bring. It is an argument that continues.

"Look!" yelled Oby. And then, as I had taught him, amplifying any sighting report: "Rapas! A whole village of 'em!"

We soared over the Rapa village, and the vulture-headed diffs barely bothered to glance up at our vollers. We passed over other communities of diffs: Chuliks, and Ochs, Brokelsh, Khibils, Fristles, of Blegs and Numims, of Pachaks and Underkers. As we sailed on over the vastly extensive expanses below we passed many and many a village and town inhabited by one or another of the races of Kregen.

Now this, as you will surmise, puzzled me mightily. I also noticed, and thought I was not mistaken, that the people down there would not look up at us, were frightened to look up, as though the sight of a flying craft in the sky would damn and doom them.

But nothing must stand in our way. Nothing. We flew on.

Mountains rose in a white dazzlement ahead.

I shook my head as Delia glanced at me.

"I think not. They do not wear the same appearance as the mountains ringing the Swinging City."

Vangar spread out the maps. He sucked in his cheeks.

"I would suggest, my prince, that in those mountains yonder rises this fabulous River Zelph."

I felt very conscious that we were a band exploring unknown territory. But I agreed with Vangar. "And we follow that river down. We do not deviate."

Then it was time for those closest, who would be in command, as it were, to come across from their own fliers and to sit with us to a sumptuous meal in Delia's voller. We looked after ourselves, for we had brought the minimum number of servants, and of slaves, of course, there was no sign.

When the palines in their silver dishes were being passed around Nath the Needle came in. He looked grave. We quieted our quick talk at once.

"My prince!" he began. "My princess!" My heart sank. "The emperor is sinking. All my art—" He spread his hands in self-disgust at his own lack of skill.

At once, bravely, Delia said: "You have done all you can, Nath. How soon—is it—can you tell?"

Before Nath could answer, I, foolish and loving, burst in with: "Sink me! We'll reach the Pool before your father is any worse. He will be well again and then we'll fly back to Vondium. I'm waiting to see the faces of those rasts who tried to poison him."

"Aye!" said Seg, forcefully. "That Ashti Melekhi will get one almighty shock, as Erthyr the Bow is my witness."

I took comfort from Seg's words. He does not often swear on the name of the Supreme Being of Erthyrdrin.

The others broke in, also, roundly declaring we'd reach the Pool well in time. I warmed to them. Comrades, all! If any power of mortal man or woman could get the Emperor of Vallia to the Pool of Baptism, then, surely, that power flew here with me!

Nath nodded, saying: "I think there will be time. . . ."

I stood up, crushing down a last paline and I looked around the table on my comrades. I felt the silly, choked up feeling that betrays me for a weakling. But I spoke up harshly enough, grating the words out.

Believe me, I did not overlook the fact that the emperor could easily die before we could save him. Then I would have to return to Vallia and take charge. I fancied I would have to do that, although detesting the work. Some men I knew would be amazed that I did not throw the emperor overboard at once and sail back to claim the throne. And, there was no guarantee in this bitter life that any rescue could succeed. I had not raced to save my daughter Velia? Had I not failed?

So I spoke pungently to the assembled company, knowing they would pass my words onto everyone in the expedition.

"Remember. Nothing must stop us from winning through to the Pool. Once the emperor is cured, we may return. No casualty must deter us. Let no man, beast, god or wizard stand in our way. *Nothing*!"

They roared at this, determined, dedicated, and Nath the Needle, looking at me, nodded as if to say that, well, perhaps his hopes were strong enough, the Emperor would live.

And, as for me—brave bluff words from an inspired leader? Onkerish words from an onker of onkers, a get onker? Reaction to my own dark thoughts? But, all in the fullness of time, I suppose, every man gets his comeuppance. I am not too sure about women, though. . . .

Of only one thing I remained sure. These my comrades would get through to the Pool of Baptism if it was humanly possible. No matter what happened, they'd go on. After the emperor was cured the Savanti might rail—the deed would be done.

With a few final words that reinforced my orders—for, make no mistake, what I told this roaring reckless rout of ruffians to do was an order, hard and incisive—we parted to kit up for the final run in to the Pool.

We must go well-armed and accoutred, for I did not forget the ravening monsters Delia and I had met on the struggle to reach the sacred grove and the rocky overhang and the Pool.

In our stateroom Delia pulled out the long length of brilliant scarlet cloth. Well, now. . . . I made myself smile, and smiling always comes easily for me with my Delia, and I said, lightly: "The scarlet of Strombor and the yellow cross of my Clansmen—yes, my heart, I think it appropriate, for they are the colors of Vallia, also."

"And the orange and grey of your fearsome Djangs."

"Our fearsome Djangs. Of course. And the red and white of Valka. And, for the place grows dearer to me, the yellow and blue of Zamra. I think," I said, twisting up the scarlet around my waist and drawing it through my legs and tucking the end securely in, and then picking up the broad lesten-hide belt with the dull silver buckle. "I rather think we look like popinjays, these latter times."

She laughed; but she, too, understood the importance of colors and badges and signs. In the midst of the dust and hurly burly of a battle, a man needs a flag to rally to. Colors and badges tell you whom to kill and whom not to kill. That is a matter of importance for anyone, and particularly to anyone who wishes to live for very long on Kregen. So my Delia laughed at my words; but her thoughts were with the sick man, her father. I chided her.

"Once he is well again we will fly back to Vallia. There all those who sought to profit by his death will receive the nasty shock Seg and the others promise. There are loyal people in Vallia, still—"

"Oh, yes. But few, I think, very few."

"Once the emperor is seen to be fit and well the waverers will suddenly realize what side they are on. Anyway," I went on with a rush of confidence. "This new Chief Pallan your father has brought forward to such power, this Kov Layco. He will keep things running while we are away. He has shown a misjudgment of character in appointing Ashti Melekhi—but that will be forgiven him, I daresay, if he is as skilled and clever as is said."

"He is clever, no doubt of that. I try to like him."

"Oh?"

"You are so often away, Dray. It is difficult. Once it is all settled you will tell me this dread secret that you feel will—will—I tremble to say it—will come to—"

"Do not say it, my heart. Nothing can destroy our love." I believed it, passionately. "But I do fear to tell you. I feel—I feel the burden I shall impose on you is—" My thoughts were muddled. I had kept putting off and putting off telling Delia of my origins. To her, I was a savage clansman, with a strange underspirit that did not come from the plains of Segesthes. But—Earth! How could I tell her I came from a star in the sky she could barely make out? How could she possibly believe in a world which possessed only one sun? What sense was there in a world with only one moon! And, how could any sensible person of Kregen believe in a world that contained only apims as men and women, where diffs were unknown? My story would be taken as the ravings of a madman. I ploughed on somehow: "You will find it hard to believe me. But I shall tell the truth. I swear it. I swear it by Zair."

"I shall believe—"

Turning for the arms rack I groped around and took up the scabbarded Krozair longsword with the plain strappings that would secure it to my back, the hilt comfortably jutting over my shoulder by the blue-fletched arrowshafts.

I remember, through the maze of impending agony through which I would have to go trying to convince Delia and my family that I was not a raving lunatic, I sought a little tawdry comfort in thinking of ordinary things. I thought I would have to see about a proper supply of the rose-red feathers of the zim-korf for my Archers of Valka, and I also remember thinking I was growing far too accustomed to wearing the longsword sticking up over my back instead of jutting almost parallel with the ground at my left side. I was thinking I would like to see my new aerial cavalry of Valka mounted on flutduins performing against those rascally flutsmen. A torrent of vague thoughts poured through my mind.

So I turned again to pick up the superb shortsword Hap Loder had brought me, a present from the Clansmen of Viktrik, the new clan who had given me obi, a blade built in Zenicce to the very highest standards, a blade to shame any Genodder of the Eye of the World, and I took the chunkrah-hide and gold scabbard up into my hand and a red and brown scorpion, glinting, ran from under the arms rack.

I felt sick.

A scorpion!

Symbol of the forces of the Savanti or the Star Lords, symbol of those powers that could hurl me about Kregen or banish me back to Earth, contemptuously tossing me about like a puppet, that scorpion stood on its eight hairy legs, waving its vicious stinging tail at me in admonishing authority.

Not now! Please Zair! Not now!

But the blue haze dropped upon me, and I felt the coldness, striking through like the clammy hand of Death himself, and the scorpion grew and bloated, radiant with the blue fire, and everything spun away in two worlds, and engulfed in agony I fell into nothingness.

# Chapter Twelve

## Strife Among the Star Lords

This nothingness differed from those other nauseating nothingnesses in which I had suffered so often before.

Always, so it seemed to me, I had been snatched away by the blue-limned radiance of the scorpion, caught up, whirled through nothingness, spun through an achingly cold void, smashed down with a hint of the red fire of Antares, slapped head over heels, all naked like a newborn infant, sent toppling helplessly into a new world.

But, this time . . .

A difference.

I was stark naked, and that I expected.

I was no longer in the voller and that, too, I expected.

I tried to open my eyes and realized they were open. I could see and yet, seeing, see nothing.

The hint of echoes, as of the rushing of a distant torrent far below ground, pent between eon-old walls never opened to sunlight. . . . The whisper of insane voices cackling over the edge of a world, pringling clammily against my skin. . . . I felt the coldness touch me, and ebb, and return. I saw—I saw blue whorls of light gyrating, and, across them and irradiating them with wheels of crimson, red streaks of fire pulsating. The blue was a pale, luminescent blue, and the sharp blue and the crimson struggled for supremacy. And—green! An ominous tinge of green washed across the lower corner of the firmament, clashing with the struggling blue and crimson.

Where had I see blue and crimson before, recently? My head rang with soundless echoes. I struggled, and did not move.

The sky colors fought and writhed, waxed and waned.

Yellow! Where was the yellow of Zena Iztar?

I bellowed out: "Zena Iztar!" and only a dolorous croak passed my lips, my corded throat bursting with effort, a croak like a frog with hernia.

Blue of that brilliant beckoning luminosity was the color used by both the Savanti and the Star Lords when they sent the Scorpion after me. Yellow had been used triumphantly by Zena Iztar, as I believed, to save me. As for that mysterious woman, who on Earth called herself Madam Ivanovna, I knew nothing—or practically nothing. She came and went at her own whim. Glorious she was, aye, that is true. She showed no fear of the Star Lords or the Savanti; but if she worked for them or against them, or for one or the other, I did not know.

I fell.

As I fell I remembered—remembered Zena Iztar and the Kroveres of Iztar, and the crimson flag and the blue device.

I fell. All naked and bruised, I fell into a thorn-ivy bush and I cursed by the foul anatomy of Makki-Grodno. What was happening I had no idea; all I wanted to do was get back to the voller and Delia and go cure her father.

By an effort of will I had succeeded in erecting a kind of structure of deceits so as partially to mollify the anger of the Star Lords. I had managed to convince them I should stay on Kregen and not be dispatched to Earth. I had also, after some success along the way, like an onker resisted them, wilfully, and so been banished to Earth for twenty-one horrendous years.

Resistance might once again cause another banishment.

What Maspero, my tutor in the Swinging City, had told me did make a kind of sense. He had said: "Only by the free exercise of your will can you contrive the journey." That journey had taken me for the first time from Earth—I was literally up a tree at the time, being chased by savages—to sail my leaf boat down the sacred River Aph and after the welcome departure of the scorpion crew to discover a little of what life on Kregen was like and how I would measure up to it—and at last so reach Aphrasöe. Could the Savanti not draw me at will, then? Their monstrous creature in the sacred Pool of Baptism had flung me back to Earth, and it had been the Everoinye, the Star Lords, who had picked me to labor for them about their mysterious purposes on Kregen.

So I exerted my will.

I roared it out, and produced only a croaking sighing

like a pair of bellows shot through by musketry. "I will stay on Kregen! I will rejoin my wife in the voller! You have no powers over me, Star Lords! Savanti—I would have worked joyously for you; but you disdained me! Why torture me now? Why?"

And, all the time, I looked for the welcome yellow to gush up among the gyrating colors staining the firmament, and no yellow came.

From the susurrating wash of background noises, from the color-dripping sky, from the mingling scents and perfumes, past the thorn-ivybush, from everywhere and from nowhere, a voice spoke to me. A voice spoke to me.

"Insolent onker! You are a mere mortal man—do not presume."

I tried to bellow back, and merely wheezed.

I thought. I tried to hurl my thoughts; and the voice crashed down, masterful, dominating.

"I command you now, Dray Prescot. And I demand from you more than you have hitherto given—more than you appear willing to give. But that more I will have." The voice whined suddenly, and became incoherent. Then: "Hearken unto me!"

And, another voice, harsher, deeper: "The man is ours!"

"You do not use him to the full!"

"We use him as we see fit. He is, after all, but a mere mortal man."

"And fit therefore to be driven—"

"He is often stubborn. He is not an easy man—"

"I would drive him! I would—" Again that acrid voice became incoherent. I listened my mouth dry, my eyes fairly starting from my head, and my backside jabbed thick with the thorn-ivy needles.

This could not be the Savanti, arguing with the Star Lords!

Could it?

The thorn-ivy needles jabbed me cruelly and I rolled away, cursing, feeling harsh rock and stones beneath me, broken twigs, the detritus of a wild animal's lair.

Brittle bones crunched under my hands as I struggled to rise.

"We wish him—" continued the second voice.

The acid voice, the voice that had spoken first and so allowed me a listening post, illuminating with sound the black silent recesses, that voice that kept wavering as though the speaker strove to pierce through the tumult of a tempest, lashed back. "I shall run him now!"

"Not so! He works well—when he does work—"

"Does he know—?"

"Of course not! How could he? He is apim. Apim."

"Then perhaps I shall let him know a little—" The bitter voice trailed. Suddenly I found myself urging the voice to return. He'd tell me what, the rast?

These were not Savanti. I held that conviction with sudden deep resolution. Star Lords. They were the Everoinye.

"He is still too soft. The knowledge might destroy him—"

"I am prepared to take that chance."

I stood up at last and shook my fist at the gory viridian dance of colors against the sky. "You'd take the chance, you kleesh! With my hide! With my sanity!"

Well, that was a mistake.

Like a blind lashing up on a runaway roller, I opened my eyes anew, and stood up, and, lo!, I stood on a wide and dusty plain, the thorn-ivy bush at my side, and before me men and women fought among themselves.

I took a breath of sweet Kregan air.

This was more like old times!

A quick glance aloft showed me blue sky—and a whorling diminishing struggle between the blue and the red. And—and! A long beautiful streak of yellow coiled and drifted away into laypom and lemon and so vanished into the clear blue vault of the sky. I let rip a great sob of thankfulness. The yellow, so fragile, creeping in, told me Zena Iztar was at last aware.

I knew I had been brought here—wherever here was—to rescue some wight among that struggling throng, to preserve him or her for the pleasure of the Everoinye. I had served the Star Lords in this fashion before.

Or, so I believed.

I took one step forward.

And blue radiance dropped about me, and I tumbled head over heels, gasping, falling upwards, and so stood with a thump upon a high rampart atop a lofty tower, with a great city spread beneath me. Boulevards and kyros, avenues and temples, spread out beneath the glitter of the suns. And the city burned. Dull wafts of brown smoke rose from the bright buildings. Hordes of crazed people fled in every direction, wildly, not caring where they fled. The smell of blood and fire cloaked the doomed city.

From the air echelons of warriors, all steel and bronze and leather, flying their winged saddle-beasts of war, swooped mercilessly down, casting death before them. The beat of the wings sounded the death knell of the city. Fire, destruction, desolation—from that high tower I looked on the casting down of a city.

Where, in all this violence, was I to find the wight I was to rescue? Or, failing to rescue, to find myself packed headlong back to Earth?

Again, I took one foolish step forward, and the light changed.

The crimson beat in, drowning the blue. In crimson flakes of fire I was borne up, whirled headlong about, sent crashing down. I felt the heaving deck of a swordship beneath me and saw the banks of sweating rowers pulling, saw the tangled heat of striped sails about the mainmast, the severed rigging, the varter bolts embedded in the wood of deck and bulwarks, the smashed and splintered scantlings where varter-flung rocks had wreaked their destruction. Up in the bows both below and above the fore-platform where the varter lay scattered in useless shattered timbers and sinews the frenzied struggle battered on between men who cut and hacked and slipped in blood and shrieked and died, their weapons fouled and glistening in the opaz radiance of Antares. A varter bolt flew past my ear. Fierce bearded men with golden rings in their ears and tall golden-feathered helmets, their eyes alight with the joy of killing, their scale armor glittering, bore down howling on me.

Whom to rescue on the command of the Star Lords? I bent to snatch up a fallen sword—and the crimson light trembled, and faded, and gushed deeply, and was gone and the yellow light limned me, drenching me in golden glory, and I tumbled full length into that damned thorn-ivy bush.

Bellowing aloud that Makki-Grodno's diseased intestines would provide a capital sleeping bag for Star Lord, for Savanti, for whomever sought to drag me away from the voller and Delia, I pulled out of the thorn-ivy bush, stung to blazes.

The struggling mass of people had vanished from the dusty plain. The doomed city no longer existed. The swordship had gone.

I stood alone upon that dusty arid plain, stark naked, prickled by sharp thorn-ivy spines, and I looked about on nothing save dust.

"By Zair!" I roared, shaking my fist at the sky. And then I could not think of anything relevant to say. There was too much pent up within me. I had no real idea of what had been going on. I turned three hundred and sixty degrees and saw nothing save that dusty plain and the thorn-ivy bush.

So I stood, fuming, filled with an enormous baffled rage—and, also fully aware of my ridiculous position.

A voice ghosted in from nowhere, from everywhere, riding the radiance, ringing sweetly from the distant sky, fading.

"Go north, Dray Prescot! North. This is all I could contrive, all I can do...."

The voice of Zena Iztar! Yes, I knew that voice. That mysterious woman who could charm men and animals to a magic sleep, that woman of whom I hoped for much, that woman who seemed to offer sanity in a universe of madness; well, she was trying to help. I felt sure of that. But....

"By Vox, Krun, Djan and Kaidun!" I bellowed. I stamped my foot. "What an infernal waste of time!"

"Fight, Dray Prescot. Go North. Jikai, Ver Dray! There is nothing else...."

The sweet voice faded and was gone and I stood alone under the opaline radiance of the Suns of Scorpio.

Useless to pretend I had not been profoundly shaken by that unearthly experience. Unearthly—Unkregan! I had been a witness to a titanic struggle among superhumans, seeing a tiny corner of the veil of mystery lifted. All was not sweetness and light among the Star Lords, then....

Maybe an old paktun rogue like Dray Prescot could use that information. Yes, I thought, where werstings squabble the gyp gets the bone.

I stuck my old beak of a nose into the north, pulled a last spine from my rump, and set off on my bare feet.

The more I thought about these recent occurrences the more I fancied the Savanti were not involved. They were mere mortal men, superhuman, admitted; but men. They were the tiny remnant of the Sunset People who had once dominated Kregen. Their buildings lay in ruination in many lands. They it was who had constructed the Dam of Days and built the Grand Canal. Now they lived in the Swinging City and sought to train savapims to work for the betterment of Kregen. No, I did not think the Savanti had been involved in that cosmic struggle.

I plodded on.

The air remained warm, the suns shone, a few birds wheeled about above and you may be sure I favored them with a close scrutiny although their presence comforted me. They would not fly about here if there were no game to hunt. Mind you, I might be the Sunday dinner they had in mind; but I was used to that, and by certain signs near the thorn-ivy bushes I knew small animals lived in this waste that appeared a wilderness but was not to those who knew how to survive. So I trundled on northward, trying to be philosophical.

By Vox! But it was hard. What were my people doing now? How was Delia reacting to my disappearance from the voller? She would shake her head and sigh, and say, no doubt, more or less: "So he's off again." I thought of the gaudy array of weaponry I had been in the act of belting on. By Krun! I could do with some of those edged and pointed weapons now. Particularly, I needed a bow.

The bow I had intended to take had been a good greenwood bow of Erthyrdrin, its manufacture superintended by Seg. Although a kov he would indulge his passion for creating better and better bowstaves, working with his hands. The stave, like any bowstave, looked lumpy and sullen, following the grain of the wood, cunningly built to avoid any weakness. But it looked marvelous in the eyes of a bowman. Bows that look flashy and wonderful do not always work as well as those that follow the grain; they never do. With that bow, six feet six inches, a yard in the pull, I could cast an arrow and fetch up my supper with no trouble.

So, perforce, I stomped along in a foul humor and picked up a sharp stone and carried the thing in my fist and looked about with a fine predatory eye.

The ravening monsters of the air and land that ringed and protected the central mass of mountains would scarcely allow a naked unarmed man to pass. Thought had to be taken.

A black dot on the horizon almost directly on the back track attracted my immediate suspicious attention. I stopped moving at once and crouched beside a thorn-ivy bush. I watched. The black lump came on, growing in size, pirouetting with the heat devils, lumping and parting, coalescing, gradually drawing nearer.

Soon I made out a riding animal carrying two persons.

The beast looked to be some kind of member of the trix

family in that it had a blunt wicked head, six legs and a coat of coarse greyish hair. The riders—I whistled. The man was a numim lad, a lion-man, well built, glorious in the numim way with his great golden mane, hardy. The girl was a Fristle fifi, delicate, beautifully formed, charming, her slanted eyes and frolicsome tail eloquent of all that is best about the cat-people. They sat close together on the uncomfortable back of the six-legged animal and they were totally engrossed in each other.

Now numims and Fristles may sometimes get on well together, seeing that they are both of feline stock; and sometimes they spit and snarl and rick back their lips and tear great chunks out of each other. I had an inkling of what was going on here and although I did not smile—I did not forget the indignity and the sheer awful frustration of my predicament—I felt a little lift of my flinty old heart.

It has been my experience on Kregen that a man must make what he can of the situation in which he finds himself. Until I could rejoin Delia and my comrades I must work and fight to stay alive, and take an interest in all that occurred, trying to use events to my own advantage.

So, feeling an intruder, I stood up from the thorn-ivy bush and shouted: "Llahal, dom, domni. Llahal."

The stux whipped up in the lad's hand.

"Lalhal, dom. You are apim. I bear you no grudge."

"Nor I, you."

"Shall we make pappattu?"

"Assuredly."

"I am Naghan—" Then, his manners catching up with him, he stuttered and started over. "You have the honor to be in the presence of Fimi Shemillifey. I am Naghan Mennelo ti Sakersmot."

"I am Dray Prescot."

"Now that we have made pappattu—" and here he put up his stux, so that he could finish the pappattu, which means, as you know, more than a mere formal introduction. "I would ask you why you wander alone and naked in these perilous parts."

The answer was glib. "My caravan was set upon by drinkingers. And you?"

"We elope—" And then he stopped himself, and Fimi, his little Fristle fifi, giggled, and so I attempted to scrape up a smile. So wrapped up were they in their brave and foolhardy solution to their problem they barely heeded my own thin story.

"If you wish, we may continue our journey together." My eyes regarded his water bottle.

He shook his head. "As to the companionship, right gladly I welcome it, even though you have no weapons, for you look a fighting man and the Khirrs prowl hereabouts. But, as to the water. . . ." He shook the bottle. The confounded thing was nearly as dry as my throat.

"As Oxkalin the Blind Spirit chances," I said, resigned.

"Oh, for a long cool drink of parclear!" sighed Fimi.

Naghan chided her. "When we reach Great Aunt Melimni she will welcome us and you may drink all the parclear in Ba-Domek."

Incautiously, always a garrulous onker, I said: "Ba-Domek?"

"Why," says this Naghan ti Sakersmot. "Do not tell me you do not know where you are?"

If the twin suns had fallen from the sky upon my foolish head I do not think I could have been more shattered. Of course I had assumed without thinking that I was still on the island of Aphrasöe. And, instead, I was somewhere else on the surface of Kregen! I felt my face going red and my eyes must have betrayed all the killing passion in me. This Naghan ti Sakersmot reined up, smartly, flinching, staring down at me, starting back.

"This is not," I got out in a strangled voice. "This is not the island of Aphrasöe?"

At this both young people shrieked and clapped their hands over their ears. Their young faces expressed extreme horror.

"Do not say that!" screeched Naghan. "Never! We have not heard! As I love Fimi—I shall cut you down!"

"Brace up, lad!" I bellowed. "If you do not tell me where I am or what is going on—for I admit I am lost— how can I know? Tell me of Ba-Domek."

Relief at their reaction to my use of the name Aphrasöe made me weak. I had thought—what a horror that would have been!

"Why," Naghan said, cautiously taking his hands from his ears and the imp had heard me clearly, right enough. "Why, this is Ba-Domek. The city of which you speak is a place forbidden."

Of course. Trust the Savanti to spread a little ghoulish rumor about the Swinging City. I would not press this

119

young couple; but I felt sure they could retail grisly stories about the goings-on in Aphrasöe. So I was still on the island. Zena Iztar had managed to keep me here, at the least. I swallowed down, dry as a bone, for I could not spit.

"So you ride together. In that direction." My arm sliced down toward the north.

"Only for a ways. Then we turn off down the Valley of the Twin Spires. I feel confident of the way," he said, eagerly. "Even though I have ridden it but once before. Always, the way was through the River Feron's lowlands. This is a dangerous route."

"This city of which we do not speak. Where away lies that?"

"Down the other River," he said. That made sense.

Now I had to find where the river began—or where I could join it. I didn't care if it was the Aph or the Zelph.

In answer to my query he looked around the featureless horizon, undecided. He squinted up at the suns. He frowned.

Then: "I think, dom, I think—that away."

He pointed due north.

# Chapter Thirteen

## How Fimi Obtained Her Wedding Portion

For a space then, our ways would lie together.

The six-legged saddle animal, a gnutrix, walked along with that awkward swaying gait of the six-legged, and I tramped on alongside. The two young people made nothing of my nakedness and, partly, I suppose, that was because I was apim and they diff.

Their story was soon told. Miscegenation is not the true word for this kind of marriage across diff-boundaries, where the people in question are closely related. All the same, their own people were not happy; a chance meeting at a fair, the growing realization that a genuine love existed between them, the hostility of their families and, finally, elopement, all added up to this flight across the barren land to the sanctuary of Great Aunt Melimni's house—a fine villa with fountains and arbors, Naghan confided with pride—situated in the best district of Lowerinsmot. This town, he said with just the hint of doubt, was situated perhaps a little too close to—and here he paused, and ran a hand around his collar. I asked more questions in a general way, and gathered that Naghan knew a fair amount of the geography of this part of Ba-Domek, being a travelling salesman of a sort. I gathered as much from what he did not say as the information he parted with that Aphrasöe did indeed lie at the center of the island surrounded by the ring of sheltering mountains. He confirmed that the island swarmed with animals and birds and diffs. There were few apims. No city of Homo sapiens like me was known. And, of course, of those within the Swinging City itself, nothing would induce Naghan to venture there. He knew what apims were, of course, and regarded me with a lively interest as the representative of a strange and exotic breed.

Always before when I had been summoned by the scorpion and been flung head over heels pell-mell to Kregen I had awakened stark naked, faced with the immediate problem of rescuing someone or other from pressing peril. So, this time, I kept an eye on these two elopers. I did not think I had been dragged from the voller for nothing; equally, I was aware that the circumstances this time were greatly different from anything that had gone before.

"As soon as you reach Lowerinsmot all our troubles will be over." Fimi clung to Naghan, speaking with perfect confidence.

They wore simple tunics of a flaxen color, and Fimi's was trimmed and hemmed with bright embroidery. They had a satchel with dried meats and fruits. Their only weapon, apart from a bronze knife, was the stux, and he handled the spear smartly enough but not, I judged, as a warrior. Traveling salesmen, he said his family were, going from village and town around the countryside. Sometimes there were fights; but few people like to pick a quarrel with a numim.

But for the two suns in the sky—and a fellow gets used to those pretty quickly—and the cat-girl and lion-man riding a shambling six-legged mount at my side, this dusty plain with its willy-willies and its scraps of thorny bushes might have existed on Earth. I might be trudging along on the planet of my birth. But that was dangerous nonsense. I was on Kregen. At any moment deadly danger could spring at us, seeking to rend us into bloody shreds. The wild animals of Kregen would make an Earthly tiger, or elephant, or crocodile turn tail and flee. Those savage beasts of Kregen would look on us all as tasty morsels for dinner. Three appetizers and a couple of mouthfuls, with blood running and white bones splintering. So, as we walked, we kept a sharp lookout.

"I do not fear the strigicaws," said Naghan stoutly. "And we can outrun the graints. As for leems—" He pursed up his lion-mouth, and gripped his stux.

Fimi shivered. "Leems are terrible," she whispered. "But if we meet the Khirrs—"

Looking back as I surveyed our rear and observed the track of our march, I said: "Whatever these Khirrs may be—there are riders following—"

Both Naghan and Fimi let out cries of consternation. The riders behind spurred on fiercely. I could make out the ungainly forms of gnutrixes like the one ambling beside me. The wink of weapons told plainly what was in store.

"Your family, Fimi!" shouted Naghan. "They have tracked us—they will not let you go."

"Ride on." I spoke calmly. So this was the reason I had been dumped down here. Useless to rage. Useless to question the value of these two young people against the value of the emperor of Vallia. The Star Lords kept to their own purposes and to them an emperor might weigh no more than a Fristle fifi. But, was not that a part of my philosophy, also?

Already I had seen the result of similar handiwork. Had not my rescue of two young people at the commands of the Star Lords produced a great genius king, a mad king, who sought to rule all the world he knew?

I gave the gnutrix a slap on its hairy hide and it bounded away. What future lay in store for the child of these two, this Naghan ti Sakersmot and his Fimi, what veiled destiny?

Scattered about on the brown plain at my feet lay stones. Rough, sharp-edged stones. There were four riders. Stooping, I took up four stones of suitable size and shape.

Always a show-off, I suppose, the old onker Dray Prescot.

The riders slackened speed a trifle as they came within range. That fancy showing off was like to cost me dear, for the fourth stone missed its mark. The last rider, seeing his three companions slipping senseless from their saddles, let out a great roar and lowered his head—whereat my rock missed him—and charged, his sword whirling.

Now, the racial weapon of the Fristles is the scimitar. I hopped and skipped and ducked the sweep of the blade. His booted foot slipped at first through my clutching fingers and I had to roll under his beast, taking an infernal banging from the middle pair of hooves, before I could rise wrathfully up on the far side and so grab his leg and hurl him from the saddle.

"You great onker!" I bellowed. "I don't want to hurt you."

He came up on a knee. Quick and vicious, Fristles, particularly in anything touching the honor and well-being of their women folk. Their family would be shamed by Fimi's elopement. He retained his scimitar. The long curved blade glistered finely in the streaming radiance.

"Nulsh!" he screamed. He jumped in, recovered from his fall, scything his blade wildly.

I was not deceived.

At the last second that savage swashing would abruptly turn into a smooth thrusting drive as the scimitar revolved around the center of its artful curve—and the blade would carve me neatly through.

Turko the Khamorro would have relished the situation.

Armed with the Disciplines of unarmed combat instilled by the Krozairs of Zy I was able to feint one way, go the other, and then—very nastily—rake back and so tweak the scimitar from his grip and, instead of running him through or bashing him over the head with his own blade, present the point smartly at his throat.

He lay on his back, hands gripped into the dust, glaring up in murderous fury.

The little exercise was not worth a "Hai Hikai," the unarmed man's equivalent to the swordsman's "Hai Jikai." I had given Duhrra, who had then been called Duhrra the Mighty Mangler, the Hai Hikai after our first encounter, for I recognized in the gigantic wrestler a true man. I had given Duhrra the "Hai Hikai!" not the swordsman's "Hai Jikai."

This is important upon Kregen.

If this Fristle flat on his back wished to make of this little spat a jikai, he was welcome to try. I told him so. I finished: "But although I do not wish to slay you, and will not do so unless provoked beyond reason, I must warn you that Naghan and Fimi will depart in peace."

Three heavily armed Fristles slumbered in the dust and a fourth glowered up at me, flat on his back. I own it must have made a pretty sight. But I was in a hurry.

"Choose, dom. Let them go—or your life answers for it!"

He believed me. I suppose, looking back, I must have appeared to him a dark malignant demon, broad-shouldered, naked, sweat and dust molding those muscles of mine, ridged, iron-hard, turning me into the semblance of a man of iron. I felt only the need for speed.

In the end, believing me, he took himself off with his three companions. The four rode off on two gnutrixes, and one of them had fewer clothes than when he'd started and all had damned fewer weapons.

So, mounted up, rejoined with the two elopers, accoutred with scimitars, stuxes, we rode on.

Also, we had a filled water bottle and that, you may be sure, I kept under my hand.

"I shall return all these things, the gnutrixes, the weapons, the clothes, to you, Fimi, when we part. After all, they can be regarded as a wedding portion from your family."

Naghan laughed at this. "You are a strange man, Dray Prescot."

"Aye."

When the wind got up and blew devilish stinging sand into our faces we were glad to pull up the sand-scarves, although when I referred to my sand-scarf, calling it a hlamek as we do in South Zairia, my companions tittered and said it was a flamil. The Fristle from whom I had taken this flamil had been violently upset when I removed it from him. But I did not argue. From all I had heard and seen I was beginning to believe I might have stumbled upon another example of the work of the Savanti. All these jumbled animals and people, all living cheek-by-jowl around the outer portions of this large island—surely they must all have been brought here by the Savanti? Brought here to serve the purposes of the superhumans of the Swinging City?

Another explanation did not occur to me. Had it done so I would have seen it only as a further example of the cynicism of the Star Lords.

This island was in a mirrorlike way a representation of the rest of Kregen—or at least of the continental and island grouping of Paz. Diffs lived and worked and raised families here, Katakis prowled on their evil slaving raids, Chuliks maintained their strict Spartan training as mercenaries, along with all the other races who carried out the tasks for which they were best suited. Kings there were, too, so I heard, and wars and harryings and all the old evil ugly patchwork of human ambition and greed, along with the finer things of humanity, like art and love and religion and good works and music.

"Songs?" I said as we jogged along, the sand-storm blown away, the suns shining refulgently from a copper sky and the green of watered land showing on the horizon. "Aye, let us sing."

We took a good swig of the water bottle, for the greenery ahead promised, and started in. We sang *The Pachak with the Four Arms*, which is highly scurrilous, abusing a fine people I greatly admire. Fimi possessed a sweet singing voice, and Naghan roared out lustily and I joined my own bullfrog bellowings. A pang rose up to torture me— aye! The hostile territories . . . I remembered. . . .

So I launched into *The Bowmen of Loh*, leaving out certain of the stanzas, and found they were not too familiar with that famous and notorious old song. Then we had *King Naghan His Fall and Rise* in honor of the Naghan who rode with us. We were just about halfway through *Golden Fur*, a famous and beautiful song of both Fristles and numims, when the chavonth leaped.

This chavonth was a fine large specimen of his family, a six-legged hunting cat of formidable destructive powers. His hide was all patterned in hexagons of blue, black and grey, and his whiskers bristled and his fangs glinted as he leaped.

Treacherous are chavonths. He had my poor gnutrix. The animal went down squealing, his hide ripped by razor claws.

I rolled and the scimitar came out and I took a wild swipe at the cat as it sprang. At the last minute I managed to get out of the way and the chavonth hit the grass beyond my head. Faster than the cat, so fast I almost overran it, I leaped in and brought the scimitar down in an angled slashing blow. The blade grated into the bones of the chavonth's neck as the bright blood welled. It let out a tremendous screech and wrenched around and the blade snapped clean across.

For a moment we hung together, the six paws with those slashing claws clashing beyond my back as I strained to keep its head away. Fimi had screamed and Naghan's gnutrix had bolted. But all the world was concentrated into that struggle as, locked together, muscle against muscle, the chavonth and I sought to wrest the mastery. The fangs dripped. The red tongue lolled. I thrust back, feeling my muscles strain, feeling the blood thump in my head, feeling all the savagery that had been contained and repressed within me over the past days surging up, bright red, bestial, deadly.

Clamped together, we thrashed across the trampled grass beneath the small bluff where the chavonth had lurked. With every sinew straining, holding him back, my fists gripped around his throat, I pushed his head back and with my leg hooked about his body, hauled him in to me so that his claws could not disembowel. As it was he took a long raking chunk of skin and flesh away, and my blood dripped.

Then, with a last final, bestial effort, a great surging thrusting of bursting muscles, I smashed his head back and the chavonth's neck snapped across where the stupid broken scimitar blade jagged out.

Flinging the corpse from me I stood back. I drew in huge draughts of Kregen's sweet air. I dashed the sweat from my ugly old face. I know I was wearing that frightful devil's mask plastered in blood and sweat across my features.

"By Vox!" I said. "That was close."

"Give thanks to Farilafristle," said Fimi, shaking, her eyes large and horrified. She had stopped screaming and yet, for all her brave words, she turned with a sob of thankfulness from me and the chavonth corpse as Naghan came racing back, flogging his mount unmercifully.

"I give you the Jikai, Dray Prescot." He spoke gravely, dismounting and helping Fimi down.

"As to that," I said. "I must walk again, by Krun."

Gods and goddesses and spirits come in all shapes and sizes on Kregen. Few people bother over much which deity is sworn by or appealed to, so long as their own beliefs are not crudely touched. So, collecting the gear I thought necessary and leaving the two corpses, the gnutrix and the chavonth, we set off again through this new tangled wooded country.

The rips in my hide would heal; but they smarted sharply.

"Sooner a chavonth than a Khirr," said Naghan. He held his stux at the ready. His flamil rested under his chin. He looked down at me. "Also, apim, it is best to have your flamil handy. Be ready to draw it up over your face instantly if you see a Khirr."

"What? Do they freeze with a look?"

"No—they are no Gengulas of legend. They are real. They spit."

The way became easy after that and we spent five or six nights in comfort, with ample fresh meats and fruit. We were beset on a number of occasions; but fought through. In the process I acquired a knife, a miserable thing; but better than nothing. Gradually Naghan became more nervy. Fimi rubbed the fingers of her left hand over the atra she wore in the form of a bracelet on her right wrist. We were camping in a cave, and she looked about, wondering about a fire. "It is all—so dark and mysterious when the suns sleep and the moons are tardy."

About to make some hard common-sense reply, I hesitated, for Naghan, too, was rubbing his atra. He wore his amulet slung around his neck. I have spoken little of the atras, the amulets and lucky charms, the mystic spell-holders, worn by many people of Kregen. Superstition is as rife there as on Earth, mingled with sorceries and religions, demonic possession and necromancy. The bazaars and souks of cities and towns contained stalls where the magic talismans might be bought, and more money spent brought more protection. Blessings from as many sources of psychic power as possible also helped, and people would go from temple to sorcerer, brazen, bare-faced, to pay for a protective spell and a blessing.

"We are well-protected." Naghan pushed his atra back down inside his tunic. No doubt he believed that had saved him when the chavonth leaped on me, a man without an atra. And then, heartening me, he hefted his stux and added: "Let us rely on ourselves this night, my love. A fire. . . ?"

Naghan, knowing fire would drive away wild animals, would not have asked the question if there were not more behind a mere fire than that.

"What enemy is there," I said. "Apart from men, who does not fear fire?"

And, as he opened his mouth, I knew. So, together, we said: "Khirrs!"

This explained Naghan's increasing nervousness. We had a way to go yet before our directions parted. "Humm," I said, just like a frigate captain making time to think before giving his orders, a weak habit, it is true. "Fimi must have food and she will not eat raw meat—?"

Fimi shuddered eloquently, so that was that.

We set the fire as close to the overhang of the cave as we could, and letting the smoke take care of itself in the darkness of the groined stone arch, shielded the little flames by boulders. Soon the Twins would be up and there would be light.

The Twins sailed up as I sucked on the last bone. The space of woodland before us showed indistinctly at first, bathed in the fuzzy pink light, and the glade glimmered ghostly in the moons' light.

A dark round object appeared at the edge of the trees. Another and then three or four more moved among the pink-tinged leaves. I watched, motionless.

Near man-height, rotund, dark, hairy—I could make out little more. They looked to have two thin twinkling legs apiece. They stood for some time, and then they melted back into the forest. I let out my breath.

Naghan crouched at my side. He trembled.

"Khirrs," he said. *"Khirrs!"* His voice quivered. "May Numi-Hyrjiv the Golden Splendor strike them all with their own spit!"

# *Chapter Fourteen*

## The Fight with the Leem

That night we took turn and turn about to keep watch; but we saw or heard no more sign of the monsters.

In the morning we ate the rest of our last night's meal and drank cold water and prepared to set off.

The land presented a fair prospect of rolling tree-clad hills and tumbling streams and open glades. No distant views were easily obtainable but far ahead I thought I could make out the distant glint of snow-capped peaks. We did not follow any of the tracks and occasional roads that crisscrossed the land, and we avoided the easier paths running beside rivers. In this I took Naghan's advice. We would eventually reach the point at which he would turn off down the Valley of the Twin Spires. He had traversed this way only once before, and then in company with a strong band of well-mounted and well-armed numims, a good guarantee of safe passage most anywhere.

To sustain me during this time I had the comforting knowledge that my Delia was safe. She was surrounded by a group of the toughest warriors in Kregen. She was protected by a wall of steel and bronze, by a band of men and women devoted to her. They would get through to the pool despite my disappearance. No, thank Zair, I had no fears for the safety of Delia.

Ever and anon I cast a glance upwards.

"You look for something, Dray, apart from aerial foes?"

"Aye. Aerial friends."

They smiled a little uncomprehendingly at my words. The Savanti would keep command of the air in their own hands, and that adequately explained the general absence of vollers in Ba-Domek. Truth to tell, there were aerial foes aplenty. We hid from massive coal-black impiters out for a square meal. We bypassed likely looking places where chyyans might nest. Also, we avoided towns and villages, for Naghan advised that they would be unfriendly to us. I did not argue.

Life on Kregen has taught me to be wary of armed strangers, while always being ready to extend the hand of friendship with a cheerful Llahal. We pressed on by lonely ways. The Khirrs, too, infested the outskirts of towns. Scurvy, unkempt, hairy, the Khirrs scavenged around the outskirts of civilization.

Emerging out of a stand of trees and skirting along the edge of the wood so as not to climb over the brow of a hill, we saw below us a road, which with dusk, which we would cross.

A quoffa, huge, shambling, patient, ambled along the road drawing a high four-wheeled cart loaded with local produce. The cart also contained four Rapas, taking it easy, their weapons cocked up lazily and their hats tilted over their eyes so that only the wicked vulturine beaks showed beneath the brims. Two other Rapas, big bold fellows, strode alongside the quoffa, arguing away over some topic dear to them.

There are many kinds of Rapas on Kregen, as I have said, and it would be wearisome to detail all the different kinds, by name and color variation and shape of beak and crest, as by nation or belief. These fellows wore bright yellow markings about their black beaks, and their eyes were of a virulent purple. I noticed their pieces of renovated armor, mostly leather but with a piece of bronze and steel here and there. They carried stuxes and swords.

"Hold still," whispered Naghan. Not many races get on with Rapas, so we held within the shadow of the trees to wait until the Rapas and their quoffa cart had passed.

The attack swept in with startling suddenness. The white dust of the road abruptly churned under spindly twinkling feet. The coarse black hair of the Khirrs concealed powerful muscles under that rotund frame. They sprang. They pounced. Instantly the Rapas flung their scarves about their faces, shrieking to their comrades in the cart. I saw—quite distinctly—the quoffa shut his huge luminous eyes.

Naghan gulped and Fimi squealed, instantly silencing herself.

One Rapa was slow. He leaped from the cart, screaming, tearing at his face. The round bulbous bodies of the Khirrs darted in an uncanny grotesque fashion across the road. And now I saw they did have arms, and claws, scarlet talons that raked in razors of destruction. But the Rapas fought. Rapas stink in the nostrils of most peoples, diff and apim, but one becomes accustomed to their smell after a time. I had once had a good Rapa comrade, Rapechak, whom I could not believe dead and drowned in the River Magan in distant Migladrin, and my opinion of them was still slowly changing.

Two Rapas were down. The ones from the cart were slashing and cutting blindly. Two had a kind of transparent eye-mask; but raking claws ripped them away. I half-rose.

Naghan seized my arm.

"Suicide," he said. He was a numim, and he shook with the fear consuming him. "It will not be long."

I hesitated—fatally. It was all over.

I saw—quite clearly—the amber glint of liquid globules spurt from a tube in the center of a hairy face of a Khirr. A fleshy spout protruded, ridged, flexible, jutting forward like an obscene brown concertina and shooting its noxious liquid and then withdrawing. The spit struck a Rapa in the face. His scarf flapped. He was down, shrieking, tearing at his eyes.

"Spitballs," said Naghan. He shuddered. "They eat out a man's eyes—ghastly, ghastly."

The streaming mingled lights of Antares shone down refulgently upon that scene of horror. The Khirrs spat their drops of poison with uncanny accuracy. Now they hunkered around the bodies of their victims. Claws opened cavities. Below their round staring eyes, half-concealed by lank hair, the tubes pierced warm flesh and the Khirrs settled down, sucking, to their ghastly meal.

Fimi was sobbing. Naghan held her close. Quietly, we crept away from that diabolical scene.

"Spitballs, they are," said Naghan. He looked fierce and yet cowed. "They spit their poison and no man is safe."

Once again I had witnessed another of the myriad forms of life upon Kregen. Among all the menagerie men I had stumbled across these Khirrs, these Spitballs of Antares, and I knew if the cramphs spat their foul poison at me I'd have to skip and duck and swat as, perhaps, never before on Kregen.

Well away, we mounted up and, this time, Naghan and

Fimi shared a gnutrix and I rode the other. We cantered off in that awkward swaying gait of the six-legged riding animal, and I pondered. Spitballs of Antares—well, a more perceptive critical mind attuned to euphony—and alliteration—would call them Spitballs of Scorpio. But they were real, vitally alive, scavenging on the outskirts of civilization, vermin in that sense; but, as ever, I saw they but acted out the commands of their natures. They were made to act as they did, and so they acted thus. To condemn them for being themselves was the height of foolishness. They did not appear to have the intelligence that brings thought of consideration and consequences and thus a juster condemnation of evil acts; for to themselves, clearly, they were not evil. It merely behooved any sensible man to give them a wide berth—unless they offended too greatly and insisted on continuing the attack.

So as I rode on with a lion-lad and a cat-girl over the savage surface of Kregen I gave thanks that I was still alive.

We found a grassy hollow later on suitable for a small camp and dismounted and decided to light a fire and cook a meal. Once more, with those shifts of fortune, I was back battling against the perils and heart-stopping dangers of Savage Scorpio.

The two gnutrixes cropped the grass. Naghan and Fimi tended the fire, carefully, and I was just turning back from the edge of the trees with my arms full of branches. I had found a superb paline bush and was feeling pleased. Beyond the two young people and to the side, the long, lean, feline shape of a leem advanced to the grassy lip of the hollow. My mouth went dry.

A leem! The leem is deadly, a feral beast found in one form or another over most of Kregen. Eight-legged, it is furred, feline, vicious, with a wedge-shaped head armed with fangs that can strike through oak. Its paws can smash a man's head in like a pumpkin. Its claws can open rips in chunkrah hide. This was a well-grown specimen, sizeably larger than a leopard, low to the ground, weasel-like, filled with the animate energy of primordial savagery. I could see the beast's dusty ochre hide pulsating along his flanks. His eyes regarded the two elopers with all the bright interest of a gourmet reading a menu.

Among the branches I carried the palines glimmered yellow. I did not break off a handful of the superb berries and pop them into my mouth, as I longed to do.

The leem's tail moved lazily. He was well aware of his power. That tail carried no tuft; and for that, at the least, I gave thanks to Zair, for I carried no great Krozair longsword, no Savanti sword, only a curved silly little knife called a kutcherer. The kutcherer can best be imagined by thinking of a butcher knife, with a hook jagged a third of the way back from the tip, a wicked tooth of metal jagging up from the thick back. The kutcherer can be deadly against the right opponent. But, with this, I would have to go up against a leem.

Slowly, noiselessly, I placed the branches on the ground. And then, because, I suppose, I am Dray Prescot, my brown hand twitched a fingering of palines free and I did pop them quietly into my mouth. The dryness vanished.

Carefully, quietly, I drew the kutcherer. Always a tricky operation that by reason of the curved metal tooth, it was done this time soundlessly and quickly. I took a step forward and, even as my foot came soundlessly down, a thought so horrible, so blasphemous, entered my mind that I stopped stick-still, frozen.

Idiot! Always before I had been hurled to some new part of Kregen stark-naked at the behest of the Star Lords to become instantly embroiled in headlong action saving some wight from destruction. The injunction on me was to ensure the safety of the chosen ones until they were safe and I might go about my own pursuits. But, this time? Onker! This time—and I remembered Zena Iztar's words—this time there had been strife among the Star Lords. I had been kept here on the island of Aphrasöe only because Zena Iztar had contrived to thwart the others' plans. But that could only mean the Star Lords had not dispatched me here. I recalled the burning city, the boarded swordship. Surely, then, if this was Zena Iztar's doing I was not brought here to rescue anyone? She had kept me as close as she could contrive to my friends. These two young elopers, they had just happened by, as is the way of Kregen.

I owed them nothing.

The leem flicked his tail and prepared to charge, choosing his time. The two young people busied themselves at the fire, all unknowing. They, themselves, would say of the situation that they were all unknowing of the ghastly fate that leered upon them. But Kregen is full of ghastly fates, and one must do what one can. Was this ghastly fate any different from a thousand others? Yes—for a leem is a leem.

But—why need I embroil myself?

I was Dray Prescot, a stubborn onker; yet I could clearly see the foolishness of rushing down there armed only with an overgrown knife with a hook and trying to slay a damned great leem. Why, a leem could chomp me in half, could knock me over the head and rip that stupid head clean off those broad shoulders. And then where would all my plans for Vallia and Valka, for Djanduin and Stromber be? What would my Delia say? How could I be a helpmeet to her if I was being digested in the guts of a leem?

Yet—at the behest of Delia I had clambered down into a pit, somehow, brought out people I would have left trapped. Delia had explained it to me then. If she could see me now, would she act any differently? I wondered—for my Delia is the most perfect woman in two worlds, and a perfect woman does not ask her man to imperil his life needlessly.

The thoughts rushed through my brain whirling arrow fast, arrow sharp.

Onker! Idiot! Dray Prescot—stupid hulu!

This was no business of mine.

And there was this prickly question of honor. . . .

A fighting man, a warrior, let alone a Krozair Brother—how could such a one leave two helpless youngsters to the claws and fangs of a leem? Was the situation one in which, with honor, I could turn tail? Of course it was! My duty, my life, my honor lay with Delia and the children and all the bright promise of the future for our friends and our countries.

What of the evil plans of all those who would bring down the emperor and bathe Vallia in blood? What of the evil devil, that foresworn Wizard of Loh, Phu-Si-Yantong? He had sworn he would dominate the world of Kregen. With all humility I fancied I might stand in his path and hinder him. Dare I jump down to almost certain death for the sake of an honor that demanded a sacrifice beyond the worth of the prize?

I sweated. I, Dray Prescot, Krozair of Zy, the Lord of Stromber, stood there like a petrified calsany, glaring hideously on the horror that stalked Naghan and Fimi.

No. No! I had fought leems before, and regretted it.

Had I a deadly Krozair brand—but I did not.

Had I a Lohivian longbow—but I did not.

Had I a Savanti sword—but I did not.

Had I any suitable weapon I think I would have gone charging down, roaring out "Hai!" in the old reckless way of Dray Prescot.

But I gripped only a little kutcherer and I did not want to leave this marvelous world of Kregen and all I loved—even for the sakes of a young numim lad and a pretty Fristle fifi.

My motives appeared as murky to me as the muddy depths of the crocodile pool of debased Forglinda the Forsaken.

Busy about the camp fire, Fimi began to hum and then sing a few snatches from *The Bowmen of Loh*, variations on that rollicking old song I had taught her. My lips ricked back. By Zair! I am a fool, an onker, a great hulking hairy idiot of a fellow! Even to this day I cannot adequately explain to myself why. I knew I did wrong. Had I not, painfully but with devastating speed, reasoned it all out? Come to the right conclusions? I knew the codes of honor and chivalry were phantasms against reality. Yet reality demanded these phantasm become real. I knew so much, and I knew damn all. . . .

I was wrong, I knew I was wrong, dreadfully wrong, making a hideous mistake as I whipped up the barbed knife and went roaring down into the glade. Bawling, bellowing, kicking up an infernal racket so the leem would turn his attentions to me and away from these two tender morsels by the fire, like a lunatic, I, Dray Prescot, get onker, went charging down. . . .

Barely two heartbeats had elapsed since I had begun this fruitless reasoning.

"Hai!" I screeched. I leaped and cavorted and ran, ran fleetly, waving the knife. "Hai, leem! Hai!"

Oh, yes, a fool, an onker, an idiot—but, then, that is me, Dray Prescot, for you.

If I came out of this little lot alive, I remember the single scorching thought, I would not, most certainly would never, tell all of it to Delia.

By Vox, no!

The leem switched his wicked wedge-shaped head around. He sized up what tasty dish made this noise. He halted his first incipient charge, his tail flicking. I had been in time. Just in the nick of time—but only just.

His tail lashed.

His head went down and his eyes gleamed like coals. Belly low to the ground he advanced on me, putting down those eight claw-armed engines of destruction one after the other, with precision, like a cat. He slunk along, stalking me. The enormous wedge-shaped jaws gaped abruptly and his fangs caught the lights and gleamed, brilliant swords of death.

I ran full at him.

No chance to do any of the clever weaving and shearing I had done with the Krozair longsword in the Jikhorkdun of Huringa. Now only speed, and vital energy, and more speed, could save me. Even then as I charged I was aware of the horror around the fire. Naghan and Fimi sprang apart, shrieking, and for a moment as I ran like a madman they came together again, and clung. Then the gnutrixes at last caught the scent of the leem, for the cunning hunter had crept on them from downwind, and they screamed, rearing at their tethers. For the last blazing instant I saw Naghan hoist Fimi onto a mount, leap up with her and slash the gnutrix across the flanks. In a clashing bounding of six legs and flying tassels, the gnutrix raced away.

Then it was only the leem and me.

I remember little.

By rights I should have been dead. I have had my memory fortified by the dips in the Sacred Pool; but the memories here jog scarlet and ragged, fading and mocking, tormenting and frightful. The first feral leap could be slid, although one dagger-claw gouged a bloody chunk from my left shoulder. I got on his back. Somehow I held on and the kutcherer went in as far as the tooth of metal would allow. And that was not far enough to reach the leem's lesser heart, let alone his main heart. I tried to cut his throat and he whirled his interlocked shoulder blades and I spun catapulting off. I caught an ear in my left fist and held on, burning pain dripping down my arm, and was dragged, and felt claws rake all down my side.

The ground smashed at me and the claws drank my blood. But I was clinging to him like a burr, trying to serve him as I had the chavonth. The strength of a leem overtops lesser wildcats; a leem is no chavonth or strigicaw—a leem is a leem!

Sliding and dangling I was aware I slid in blood dabbling his fur. My blood. My blood, hot and red, mingled with some of his.

Again I tried to slit his throat and felt the blade kiss across fur and windpipe. He bucked and I held on, held on, and the world crashed and whirled about me. With the kutcherer reversed and leaning over that fanged wedge-head I brought the tooth of metal down and dragged back, reeling, gasping, and so pierced into one of his eyes. His roars shattered into the hot air. He swerved. He arched his back bucking, contorting, trying to fling me off. All the time he hissed and screeched and foam flew. The stink of him broke with fetid strength into my nostrils. Fur and sweat and blood all mixed together. Somehow there was strength enough to hold on. Muscles bursting, lungs afire, pain scorching, body hammered and beaten, somehow, somehow I held on.

I sawed the blade across his throat. We rolled. His weight near crushed me. Half suffocated I wrenched violently aside. A claw came from nowhere and razored half an ear away.

His claws scraped again; but I held myself in, clinging, limpet-like, shaking, gripping his fur, grabbing him anywhere, hauling our rolling bodies together, fast locked in a grip of death.

Over and over we rolled. His hisses and spittings shocked frightfully into my ears, through my head, drumming and howling like condemned spirits. But I held on and sawed and slashed and stabbed—stabbing was useless, useless with that tooth of metal halting the clean inward drive of the blade.

His struggles grew ever more vigorous, gaining in power and viciousness despite the loss of an eye as I felt my own strength waning. My left hand, daubed with blood, slipped. I grasped desperately at his stinking fur. The blood oozed through my fingers and I felt the fur slide away as a man slides his fingers down the neck of a chicken. I gasped and heaved back. I was rolling over and over and the leem was high in the air before me, pouncing, leaping, soaring through the air in that long superb leap of the leem.

He landed on his four front paws and that cruel wedge head split wide and the gaping maw opened and closed and the bright fangs crunched around my left arm.

I hardly noticed the pain for the fury that filled me.

If I was to die then I'd be dying a fool!

The kutcherer stabbed forward and up. The point shattered through his remaining eye. His screeches racketed in maniacal howlings. The stink of blood and sweat bathed me in a stench that mingled with his pungent leem smell. I could not feel my left arm. He opened his jaws to screech and I jerked free, and fell, and tried to stand up. The world was going up and down in hideous waves. He swiped at me—one swipe of those paws and my head would burst asunder like a rotten fruit—I ducked and the knife stabbed and hacked. I backed away. Crouched over, panting, drenched in blood, half-crazed, half-ruined, I backed away. He could not see. But he could smell. I could barely stand. I backed, seeking an opening. He followed, blindly. I slashed again, leaping in. I opened his throat. The dark blood pumped out, gushing, shining and viscous, welling in a red stream over his bedabbled ochre fur.

I staggered and fell. I could not move. He lifted his paws, blindly, slashing out. He advanced. Somehow strength fountained from somewhere, with the blood leaching from me, and I slashed again with the hooked knife and his screech sounded as though it echoed up from Cottmer's Caverns.

The ground struck hard under my knees. I tried to stand and could not. My head hung down. I caught a single horrific glimpse of my own left arm—of what had been my left arm. The skin and flesh had been stripped off in his fangs. The pink and white of bone gleamed through, with the blood bubbling; it was a skeletal arm, and the hand hung askew and mangled, broken into an obscene lump. I could feel nothing.

I fell forward from my knees onto my face. The dust stung into my face, smeared and slicked with sweat and blood. The kutcherer, a mere mass of shining blood, dropped into the stained grass. I tried to lift my head. If this was the end then I'd husk out a last Hai Jikai and so take my last voyage down to the Ice Floes of Sicce.

The will forced me up. There was no physical strength in this thing. The will, the driving force of spirit—I was on my knees, my head dangling, feeling blindly about for the knife.

The leem crouched before me. He was not yet dead. It is extraordinarily hard to slay a leem. His hearts pumped blood out through the ragged gaping rents in his hide, from the slashes in his throat. His punctured eyes streamed ichor. His ochre fur sheened with spilled blood. And his cruel mouth dribbled blood that belonged to me.

With that dark effort at which I have long ceased to marvel I forced myself to stand. My legs shook. My knees quivered. Wavering, reeling, gasping with wide-open mouth for air, laboring, I stood up. I grasped the knife again. I did not recall finding it in the grass and picking it up. The handle was as fouled with blood as the blade. And the metal tooth was gone, snapped off, wrenched away.

And so, more falling than leaping, more toppling helplessly forward than thrusting, I fell onto the leem and drove the knife home into his main heart.

He thrashed. He quivered in the last frenzy before death. His hind legs caught me and knocked me head over heels. I smashed into the dirt and rolled and a bony skeletal object, loosely articulated with a few threads of gristle, wrapped about by a few shreds of flesh and skin, flapped about me as I rolled and I realized that ghastly blood-spraying flailing skeletal thing was my left arm.

The bones of my arm clashed with the bones of my ribs, exposed, showing through the cut and lacerated flesh of my body.

The darkness that was beyond the darkness of Notor Zan flowed over me. I felt—I felt nothing.

I saw the leem. He lay awash in his own blood.

Stupidly, I collapsed onto the dirt.

So I lay there, and my head sank down to the dusty blood-caked grass, and I slept.

# *Chapter Fifteen*

## Shadow

That I speak to you in these tapes is proof I did not die.

How close to death I drew I do not know. By my immersion in the Sacred Pool of Baptism my body had been endowed with remarkable powers of recuperation and recovery from injury. But my left arm had been stripped away, mangled, practically wrenched from the socket, destroyed. That would not be repaired. It might not kill me; it would never be a sound left arm again.

Someone was shouting at me. The leem fight brought back ghosts.

"By Kaidun! D'you want the glass eye and brass sword of Beng Thrax to do it all for you! Go in, you coys, you hulus. Go in and fight for the Ruby Drang!"

For the Ruby Drang! Aye! I would fight for the Ruby Drang.

And, another voice, leading on the war hosts: "For Vallia! Valka! Valka!"

And, again, yet another voice, shrilling over the war trumpets and the heart-pulsing pounding of ten thousand voves: "Felschraung! Felschraung and Longuelm! Zorcander! Zorcander!"

And, too, the voices bellowing joyfully: "For Djan! For Notor Prescot and for Djanduin!"

The surf-roar of a hundred ghostly voices beat about me, roaring in my head. Visions passed before my eyes. Flames shot up, smoke billowed, the horrendous sounds of combat flowered in my head. Demands were being made upon me. Urgent decisions were called for. There was no time for rest. Rest was a sin.

"For the Kroveres of Iztar!"

I groaned. The weight was too much. I was a mere mortal man and could not support the load. The voices, the demands, the urgency, beat and battered at me, and I moaned and rolled over and so, stupidly, sat up.

The last phantasmal voice roared, proud, defiant, ready to challenge a world: "For Zair! Krozair! Krozair!"

I opened my eyes and winced, shuddering, and so looked about blearily, and remembered.

I had not bled to death.

My left arm pained. The amazement that that was all it did must be pushed aside. A mere string or two of sinew, broken splintered bones, a few scraps of red meat—that was all there was hanging from my shattered shoulder.

What the hell Delia would say I shuddered to think.

My thoughts were not even as clear as that. It is a surmise from later. The disgusting remnants of my arm must be bound up and the gaping cavity in my side staunched, and I ripped away at the tatters of the flaxen tunic to make a sling and pads.

I was, I think, still reasonably coherent at this time.

Later the delirium would seize me. If a fever shook me I'd have to fight that, too. I can recall hauling at the gnutrix and clumsily mounting. I had a filled water bottle. What else there was besides a remnant of an arm in a sling and a mangled side I did not know, do not remember. I started off, kicking the animal along, jolting cruelly in that damned six-legged gait.

The corpse of the leem lay there bathed in shining blood, black and green with flies. I left him without a word, without a parting jikai, left him to rot.

Although the long-term calendar of Kregen is based to a large extent on the precedence of the red or the green sun through the sky, and the forty-year cycle, plus the orbital movement of the planet itself, these give only the broadest outline to calendar measurements. Most immediate date measurements are made by months of one moon or another. For the journey I must now undertake I fancied I'd need a whole sheaf of months, culled from all the seven moons.

What passed along the way remains hazy. Blurred snatches of memory jag through the mists. I think I met a group of little Ochs, who tut-tutted over my arm and gave me potions. Ochs are funny little puff-chopped folk, with six limbs, the center pair used either as hands or feet. I have been helped before by Ochs, as well as being savagely beaten by them when a slave.

They gave me a piece of clear crystal hung on chains from a circlet they cautioned me to wear on my head. Drunkenly I put the thing on and the crystal hung down before my eyes turning the world into a phantasmagoria as though I peered through the bottom of a bottle. I thanked them—I think I did—giving them a proper Remberee, riding on, lolling in the saddle like a man sodden with dopa and too far gone to fight.

The way proved long and tiresome. Go north, Zena Iztar had said, and I had obeyed. Now I crawled along with an altogether more dreadful reason. Now, despite all, I must win through. Forests, tracks, trees, streams, boulders, defiles. I staggered along, reeling in the saddle. Yes, snatches of it come back to haunt me in nightmares, now. I was growing steadily weaker as the dreadful injuries that surely must have killed any normal man fought against the healing properties my body had acquired from the Savanti.

Of all that painful journey only a few incidents stand out at all clearly. Of them, the most vivid, if not the most evil, wrenching in its violence, occurred as the gnutrix lolloped down a slope toward a stream bowered in trees where I could quench the torturing thirst and soothe my burning lips. My thirst tormented and drove me insatiably.

By this time I must have been pretty far gone. Only the memory of the incident remains, like a child's picture torn from a book and mounted in a frame, isolate, individual, related to nothing else.

Katakis moved about the stream, making a camp, busy in the familiar tasks of creating a base for the night. To one side the bound slaves, hallmark of the Katakis' trade, moaned in their winnowed lines of suffering. I stared, sick, almost falling off the gnutrix, glaring madly upon these devils who debarred me from the water. My whole body wracked with cramps, I burned, yet coldness brushed me with ice crystals. Shuddering, reeling in the saddle, I had to face the terrible fact that there was no water for me at this stream, not with the Katakis and their slaving habits in the way. One look at me, the instant summation I was useless as merchandise, and they'd whip up a tail-blade and finish me.

Even now, I believe no single thought occurred to me that this might be a blissful end to all suffering.

Low-browed and with a gap-jawed mouth filled with snaggly teeth is a Kataki. His thick black hair is oiled and curled in a fashion far different from that of the Eye of the World. His eyes are wide-spaced, narrow and cold. Evil, vicious and rapacious, Katakis, slavemasters, manmanagers, batteners on human misery. Perhaps the thing that gives a Kataki his greatest pride is his tail, a long sinuous powerful tail to which is strapped a sharp steel blade. So, sickly, I stared down on these vile diffs and I could not summon a single curse.

Jerking the gnutrix away was bewilderingly useless. He scented the water, parched as was I, obstinately thrusting his blunt head toward the inviting stream in the darkling light.

He started off and I sawed the reins and he resisted, disregarding the pain in his mouth for the lure of the water. We picked up speed jolting down toward the stream.

Had I had the use of two arms; had I been even a little stronger, I would have held him. But he ran away with me. So I did the only thing I could do, plunging down to certain death, trying to husk up the last of my voice, to make a good shouting show of it.

"Khirrs!" I shrilled, and my voice wheezed and cracked. "Khirrs all about you!"

Croaking though my voice was, the Katakis heard. Instantly, like the black-hearted reivers they were, they gave thought only to themselves.

The camp boiled with frenzied activity. Pounding down I went, catching a guyline in a gnutrix hoof and pulling the whole lot down, knocking a cooking fire blazing, scattering pots and pans, bounding along like a scarecrow. Katakis were forming and each swung a crystal oblong before his face, so they knew about Khirrs. On lumbered the gnutrix for the stream. Katakis were running to the edge of the camp, their weapons bright, shouting in confusion, ferocious and malignant. The animal reached the stream and plunged in and I sailed over his head into the water. The sweet coolness helped. I lay for a moment, winded, and then tried to crawl, all lopsided like a beetle. The water sloshed about me and I sucked in thirstily. The far bank appeared dwaburs off.

The stream deepened. The current knocked me over and I rolled along banging against the bottom. I am not sure what I felt as what remained of my left arm scraped the gravel; but I expect some more pieces of me fell off.

Somehow the gravel oriented itself under me and I was staggering up out of the stream. But I was still on the same side as the Katakis and their shouts told me that no Khirrs had arrived and the Katakis wanted to know what was going on and to get their hands on the lunatic who had caused the furor. A zorca stood by the bank. He stood impossibly tall on those four spindly powerful legs, close-coupled. His magnificent twisted spiral horn stuck up arrogantly from his forehead. To his saddle were belted sword, bow, saddlebags. I grasped his reins in my one hand and tried to vault onto his back and landed on my belly, dangling across, and he snorted and bucked, so I kneed him, anyhow, and we went galloping off, bashing through the low bushes into the trees.

The next thing I recall, not so luridly, is trotting out into another glade with a rockface and a trickle of water and of falling off and still grasping the reins of crawling until I could lash the reins around a broken stump and then plunge my head under the water.

I must have slept, for the shrilling of the zorca awoke me and I sat up, sluggishly, that awful dead feeling in my left arm and side reminding me my time was running out. I peered foolishly out into early morning suns shine.

They flitted out from the trees, their spindly legs twinkling, their harsh hairy bodies rotund and hateful in the mingled radiance. I blinked. Spitballs of Antares. Vermin. They crept upon me as I slept, eager to plunge their snouts into my body and drink of my substance and suck me dry. I tried to stand up and fell over. I was as weak as a woflo.

I was ripe game for these Khirrs. They would enjoy spitting at me, weak, feeble, barely able to crawl. With an idiot's fumble I dropped the crystal rectangle before my face, and the world described whorls of distorted circular dizziness. The nausea had to be fought back, pushed away. The bow was useless, for I had but one arm. The sword, a solid, single-edged cut and thruster, somewhat too long for the balance, would have to serve—somehow. My scrabbling fingers fastened on the stirrup. Heaving and grunting I hauled myself up alongside the zorca. He was a fine animal, a fleet runner, strong, well-built. He shivered now and I could smell the sweat of fear.

That broad back of mine would have to be wedged against a support. I could not use the zorca, for the acid spit would burn into his hide. They'd spit their poison at his eyes and if he was done for then so was I. His tether twanged and he twisted and turned; but he remained steady as I pulled myself up, speaking to him, croaking.

"Hold on, my lad, my bonny zorca. Hold on and we'll deal with these cramphs."

I spoke as my father was wont to speak to his horses as he so patiently and skillfully doctored their hurts. The zorca quieted at the sound of my voice. But I lied to him, I lied . . .

Zorcas are animals of splendid intelligence. He was denied his usual method of dealing with foes. If he swung that magnificent head with the silky mane flying toward them and charged down with the spiral horn lancing to skewer and degut them, he would expose his eyes. And he knew that, he knew. . . .

Holding to his saddle I slid the sword out awkwardly. Peering back owlishly through the crystal at the hideous advancing shapes, seeing their black hairy bodies, the crafty black beady eyes, the goggle effect of the protective rings of horn, the protrusions of the ridged snouts, I lifted the sword. Unsteadily, I slapped the zorca with the hilt and slashed on to cut through the tether. He sprang away.

"I lifted the sword and faced the advancing Khirrs."

I fell against the tree stump. The fierce effort of turning about and wedging my back against the stump taxed me. I was gasping. But I stood up, shivering, plastered against the stump, and I lifted the sword and faced the shuffling advance of the Spitballs of Antares.

The ridged snouts quivered. They spat. The crystal smeared and blurred and a foul reek stank into the clearing. I felt the deep acid burn of the amber drops on my neck.

Alone, shaking, almost spent, I struggled to stand and face the loathesome menace advancing toward me, these Khirrs, all black and hairy and spitting, Spitballs of Antares, fit food for dogs.

Around their small brilliant eyes each one had a horny ring, a protective circle of bone, filmed with a membrane, for all the world like those heavy horn-rimmed spectacles that were once so fashionable on Earth.

The sword wavered. I tried to swash it menacingly and nearly dropped it. I, a Krozair Brother, to drop a sword! The spit hit the crystal square and splashed against the rags tattered about me and bit excruciatingly into the remnants of my arm and side. The reek bit into my throat like acid. That muck must be washed off the naked skin soon, or it would eat and fume away the flesh itself.

I shouted. I bellowed. I croaked. "Stupid rasts! Foul kleeshes! Come on! Come on to your deaths!"

I almost slipped, then, and wedged back against the mouldering stump, harsh against my back. The sword glittered as I hefted it. If the Khirrs were puzzled their spit did not blind me, if they were aware of the power of the sword—these things are imponderables. I did not expect to win free; but gradually as they shuffled and spat and did not approach any nearer, I began to think these Khirrs were cowardly at heart. They hesitated. I swung the sword so that it caught the opaline glitter of the suns and shot sharding reflections across the glade.

In all the world of Kregen I could expect no help. I was done for, truly done for, then, as I believed, as the Spitballs of Antares, scavengers, vermin, crept forward again, more cautiously, sending their spurting globs of spitting poison before them. I had to stand on my own two feet. Had to. Had to show them I was not defenseless. I stood. I swung the sword.

Their scarlet claws raked the air before them; vision was almost totally obscured by the streaming mass of amber poison smearing the crystal square. They could see I was weak and trembling and they advanced—cautiously, hesitantly—but with very deadly intent for the last time.

One and one only of the Khirrs ventured within reach of the sword.

Him, I clove down the middle.

A sewer stench burst upward. His insides, all black and vile, glistening, spewed forth. He burst and shrank. The others drew back. Again I shouted, wheezing, taunting them with boastful words and lurid promises of their fate if they tried to molest me further. They drew back. They drew back and skittled away on their spindly legs, and their black hair draggled on their plump frames.

The respite was only momentary. I could barely see for the spit streaming on the crystal square. I had a chance, a bare chance, a last chance to escape from being done for finally.

If I fell over now I was done for. I peered about, dazedly choking, the ruin of a man. The zorca, his silky black coat very splendid in the lights, trotted back to me. He flung his head up, the spiral horn glinting. I took hold of the saddle. I was seated in the saddle. Do not ask me how. The sword, all smeared and foul, dangled beside the scabbard from the sword knot. The stirrups dangled until I thrust my bare toes into them.

I dangled, limp and broken, dangled as a strung collection of bones dangles, jangling. The zorca was superb. He broke into a canter. Then a lunging gallop that took us away from the sullen, cowardly contemptuous ring of Khirrs.

Nowadays I give thanks for that deliverance. Then I merely hunched on the zorca's back and slumped, my head dangling on my breast, and went away without a coherent thought in my skull.

Agony gripped my body. My arm was a mere scarlet branch of fire. And in my skull those famous old bells of Beng Kishi rang and resonated, clanging in time to the thudding to the zorca's hooves.

# *Chapter Sixteen*

## A Draught to Mother Zinzu the Blessed

That cheerfully rubicund spirit of luck and good fortune, Five-handed Eos-Bakchi of Vallia, must have smiled on me, a mortal sinner. It was all my own fault, my own doing, and there was no one else to blame but myself. No blame could attach to the Krozairs of Zy, for their Disciplines might demand a Krozair Brother hurtle down to the defense of the weak and helpless; but they were chivalrous enough to weigh need against need. They understood when the odds were too great, the cost too high, the game not worth the candle. To throw one's life away selflessly in the name of honor is all very well; but when a higher honor demands a different course the mad act of devoted courage is seen for what it is—vainglorious selfishness.

My Delia, the fate of Vallia, set against an eloping lion-lad, a pretty Fristle fifi—no, never!

Of course, remembering so little of that horrific journey, I can only surmise what happened. No doubt I greatly exaggerated my own importance.

After all, why should the fate of all Vallia hang on me? So what if I had been nearly killed and had my arm just about ripped off? That would affect me and my family—but Vallia? I detest affectation. So I guessed with a somber foreboding that no matter how much I sought to evade the future I did not want and responsibilities that would be thrust upon me, the weight of Vallia would be mine. Only a foolish notion would uphold me. For Valka and Stromber and Djanduin and Azby and my Clansmen—and also to a lesser degree Paline Valley—I not only admit my responsibility and indebtedness, I struggle to prove myself at least half worthy of the trust of my own people.

Some of these thoughts must have collided in my aching

head along with the infernal never-ending clanging of the Bells of Beng Kishi as I found a pool and washed myself as thoroughly as I could. The zorca washed, also. Frequently, bouts of emptiness closed in when the enveloping cloak of Notor Zan dropped over me with the silent rush of black wings.

But, in the fullness of time, with the dawning of whatever day it was—for all track of time had flown along with much else in that dreadful journey across the hostile face of Savage Kregen—I found myself riding alongside the river. I seemed to have awoken from a bad dream. I must have found rabbits and edible shoots and roots, and the blessed palines were always there to comfort the ailing. I must have crossed a high pass of the mountains—a vague memory stirred of cold and snow and of hard riding, the frosty breath glittering. But, on this day—which could have been any of the named days out of any moon, any sennight, all with their own different names and attributes—I saw the river and the gorge and heard the titanic uproar of masses of water falling bodily through thin air to crash into the stone basin beneath. Blearily, I peered around.

If I was where I thought I was, where I ought to be, then I'd struck into the River Zelph. I'd avoided many dangers. The last time I'd been here I'd been clad in russet hunting leathers, bearing a Savanti sword, in full health and strength, helping along the beautiful crippled girl who was to become everything that mattered in two worlds.

But all that had been a long time ago.

Delirious, off my head, with a mangled side and a skeletal thing that might have been a bit of arm dangling all green and black, I knew that if I was not where I wanted to be I wouldn't be anywhere else anymore, save the Ice Floes of Sicce.

The sight of spider-beasts dangling from the rocks, the clicking of beetle-beasts as they crowded close, reassured me. Aye! By Zair! These monsters seeking to shred me, to scatter me in pieces, to devour me, these ravening furies reassured me and gave me a fresh confidence.

I was here! The waterfall dropped into the stony basin and bubbled all plum-colored from the sandy amphitheater. As the beasts descended on me I looked for the overhang of crystal rock and the dark entrance to the cave which led to the pool. I staggered and held onto the zorca.

He responded nobly, a proud stallion, full of fire and spirit.

The first spider-beast was dispatched with a straight cutting slash. A beetle-beast was hacked so that he stumbled back, his legs clashing, and fell into the river. Forging on, I led the zorca without holding his reins and he followed because he trusted me and stayed with me. The narrow stony path curved around the last bend and with the thunder of the falls beating up, the mouth of the cave formed a welcoming darkness ahead. The fuzzy pink radiance all about blurred as I remembered.

Yes, the remembrances of that journey are vague and phantasmal, patchy, illuminated by the cutting shafts of recollected horror, misted by things I am thankful to forget.

This path must have led into the amphitheater among the rocks along the narrow way avoiding the majority of the guardian monsters. The route for the candidates and their Savanti tutors lay up from the river. I suppose I must have cut and hacked my way through and swung the sword one-handed, for I arrived; but it is all misty and dim and dream like.

The zorca followed me into the cave and without ado walked daintily over to the far side and beyond a ledge out of sight began to crop gently at fronds that grew there. The wet, fragrant herbs would not hurt him if he ate a few; but I would not allow him too many for the safety of his insides.

Odd thoughts kept spurting through my brain. My arm hung twisted and shredded and horrible, my side bit numbly, the rips and claw-gouges there certain death for anyone without the protection afforded by the balm of the place. The Bells of Beng Kishi clamoring in my head continued and I guessed I had been injured there, also, in the battle with the leem. If I did not drop into the pool and bathe in the milky liquid very very soon I, too, would be dead.

And then—noises, the clatter of disturbed rock, voices, cheerful and excited now the danger of the trail was passed, relieved and yet tensely expectant voices—the noises and the voices echoed from the cave entrance.

So close to victory I was not prepared to be beaten.

There was no time to dive into the water. I sank down painfully behind a screen of rocks and, truthfully, that small respite felt wonderful.

Men and women entered the cave. They did not see either the zorca or myself. They were absorbed in the reasons why they had ventured here through perils that were to them novel and ghastly and out of all the previous experience of their worlds.

Events jerked ahead, I heard and saw in snatches; what I record is far too continuous a narrative. The single searing lump of agony that was me suffered there in hiding among the rocks.

There were eight people—as customary. Four tutors and four aspirants, four fine young people who would one day be Savapims and work for the great plan of improvement for Kregen.

There were two women and two men. They wore the Savanti hunting leathers and carried Savanti swords and they were upstanding, stalwart, brilliant people, picked, chosen, of the elite to be.

One of the tutors was Maspero. Maspero, he who had been my own tutor; from the concealment of the rocks I watched and I longed to reach out the hand of friendship, to hear him greet me, to hear again "Happy Swinging!" But I remained dumb and silent, hidden in my rocks, for I was not the Dray Prescot that Maspero had known. Too much had passed and I had learned more, even, I think, than Maspero could teach.

The four aspirants stripped off their clothes and waded down the stone steps. They remained submerged for the time they could hold their breaths, and when they emerged they were transformed, irradiated, made glorious in the name of the Savanti nal Aphrasöe.

I swallowed down hard. The scene kept flickering and blurring, the stone walls swooping sickeningly. I heard what they said, their awed exclamations, the expression of the realization that they were each possessed of a thousand years of life. They talked animatedly donning their clothes for the journey back down the River Zelph to the Swinging City.

Listening I picked out the scraps of conversation that held meaning for me and I wished them away. My life was ebbing. The leem had worked cruelly upon me. I have fought leems; this time I had been unlucky as well as stupid. So I listened, hearing some things clearly, and one said: "And they were all dispatched, Harding?"

"Yes," agreed the tutor called Harding, a lean, competent man who looked as hard as his name. "They all profaned the Sacred Pool. Vanti, as is his duty, banished them all back to the places from whence they came."

"Why did they risk so much?" The fair-haired girl had been merely pretty before her immersion. "They say a Wizard of Loh was among their number. Yet the Wizards, you teach us, fear the Savanti—"

"They have cause." Maspero smiled, gesturing. He looked exactly the same as I remembered him, the same dark curly hair, the same air of vivacity, the sense of completeness as a person. "As to why they came, it is always the same story. They hear of a miracle cure. But, this time, they did not even seek our permission." He looked about at the ribboned reflections of the cave, the milky-white liquid shooting shards of colored light against the groined arches. He took a sharp breath. "There is an old story you will be told concerning a man you must know of. A man who—I had an affection for him—a man who failed the tests."

"He would have been a Savapim?" The aspirant questioned, hanging on Maspero's words.

"Yes. But in his nature were darker depths—yet my affection for him remained. He was ejected."

"Vanti. . . ?" said the dark full-faced man with the features of a Roman emperor.

"Yes." Maspero gestured for them to descend from the lip of the Pool and make their way to the exit. The only sound I could hear for a space was my own hoarse breathing and the spurting clicking of their sandals on the rocks. All that I saw jumped and leaped, like a reflection in a racing stream, and the bands of fire about my head, constricting about my body, searing that shattered arm, crushed in, agonizing, choking, deadly. "Yes. Vanti ejected him as was his duty. But he was not with these people who so recently profaned this shrine, as I had expected, knowing him, to be. They were banished. They left their airboats and all their belongings. We have them now. Safely. Soon I believe, we shall find out more about them, for this is a serious business, unique. As to where they came from—" He stopped there, and laughed in that old wry manner.

Harding drew his sword in preparation for the return. "Yes. Wherever it was, they are back there now." And he, too laughed with the others.

"And this man," asked an aspirant. "This man of whom you speak and who failed."

"I often wonder," said Maspero. "far more often than I should, just what has become of him on Kregen."

The remark sounded strange.

"If we fail," said the aspirant with the close-cropped hair and the fighter's face. "If we are ejected..."

They walked toward the cave entrance. I understood that of the aspirants one was Italian, one French, one German, and one, the hard-looking girl with straight dark hair bound with a fillet and a lean muscular body, might not be from Earth or Kregen at all.

The last I heard was Maspero saying, not lightly but with a grave resonance of meaning in his voice: "I do not think you will be called on to face the temptation that destroyed the man—the man for whom I cherish still an affection—the man of whom I speak."

When they had gone I tried to rouse myself to crawl out and drop into the water. I imagined myself crawling. I did not move. I could not move. My muscles locked. Sweat started out on my forehead and along my limbs—all three of them. I strained. If I did not reach the pool. . . . Every last ounce of will power left must be summoned. Sheer muscular power was long since passed. Only by a last enormous effort of will could I drag myself over the harsh stones to the water's edge.

I moved.

Creaking like unoiled leather, my body answered the savage commands I imposed. I moved. Like a half-crushed beetle I crawled out of the rocks. A smear of blood followed in a trail where wounds opened. The whole world of Kregen revolved, inside and outside my skull. If I were to go staggering down to the Black Spider Caves of Gratz I would go down, as ever, clawing and fighting and struggling like a maniac every last inch of the way.

Slowly, laboriously, agonizingly, the water came nearer.

The liquid moved gently with spiraling wisps of vapor rising from the surface, like heating milk. The refulgent blueness of the place pressed down more strongly. I gasped. I do not know what my face looked like; and I am glad I do not know.

The rocky edge scraped under my chest. I leaned over the Sacred Pool of Baptism and I drew a deep shuddery breath and gave thanks I had at last reached its miraculous healing powers.

My friends had reached here and the emperor had been cured. Maspero had said so. The tutors had laughed—why had they laughed? If I have given some semblance of a continuous narrative to my experiences here then that is purely illusory. Everything reached me in chopped-up segments, distracting, dazzling, obscure. My head expanded and contracted with pain. My arm—no, I prefer to forget that, for all the numbing effects of the journey wore off as I trembled on the edge of the pool, trying to find the energy for one last agonized dragging of my body over the stone lip to topple over and into a blessed surcease from agony.

Why did I hesitate? Why did I not make that final effort and plunge to resurrection?

And then—and then! For, of course, I realized almost too late why I hesitated, why those tutors had laughed. My friends had all bathed here with the emperor and they had all been banished, every last one, back to whence they came.

They had been ejected and returned to their homes on Kregen.

If I dropped into the Sacred Pool as I so ardently wished, then I, Dray Prescot, of Kregen and of *Earth*—I would—as I had been once before, so I would inevitably be again—I would be ejected and sent hurtling across the dark spaces between the stars back to Earth where I had been born.

If I achieved the healing and surcease I craved I would be flung headlong back to Earth.

But, if I did not recuperate, if I were not healed, I would die.

To go back to Earth, flung there by the agent of the Savanti, this Vanti whose monstrous bulk moved in the pool, must mean a banishment that might last a thousand years. For in that case the Star Lords would not have banished me and therefore in their distant way might have no further interest in me. So cruelly beset by pain and indecision and torment was I that the thought seemed natural; later I questioned that assumption.

There were two evils, and I must make a decision. The decision was made for me, of course. I dare not allow myself to die. Delia—I would be of no use to Delia if I were dead and wandering like a wraith through the echoing vastnesses of Caottmer's Caverns.

So I must live to fight another day and take my chances of ever returning to Kregen.

Perhaps, I thought, maundering, raging with fever, delirious, out of my head—I remember it all in flashes and spurts and jolting savage impressions of pain and horror and urgency—perhaps it would be better for me just to die, after all, just to let slip rather than live out a thousand years of meaningless life on Earth.

But, as it was in the nature of the scorpion to sting the frog, so it is in my nature to struggle and never give in, however foolish that makes me. There had to be a way around this. I tried to grasp onto my whirling thoughts— confusion, a roaring in my head, a drugged empty feeling as though the evil concoctions of the black lotus-flowers of Hodan-Set wafted through my brain—desperately, near despair, I tried to think and reason this out, trying to act in the puffed-up character of the cunning old leem-hunter so many people credit me with being. I am just an ordinary man—oh, yes, I am blessed or cursed with a thousand years of life and I have seen and done much; but I am no superman.

If I—I remember turning and rolling, slowly, agonizingly, over onto my stomach alongside the stone lip of the pool. First things first. If I—cautiously I plucked at the ghastly bundle that wrapped all that was left of my arm. If I—I did not want to disturb that mess. I may have a strong stomach; I do not think I could have withstood the impact of the horror of my own body that must have been revealed. Slowly, cautiously, I inched out over the water, and let the thing dangle down.

The milky fluid closed around my arm. I felt—well, I wondered if I did feel anything through the bite of agony. Then the warm comforting sensation as of a soft mouth kissing me, a million tiny needles pricking my skin, rather, pricking the shreds of skin and fragments of bone. The rags would all be melted away. I waited, feeling the warm glowing sensation increase and expand. I managed to shift around so my shoulder dipped.

If I ventured any more I would fall in. Then it would be Earth for me. . . .

Weird, to think I thus hung over a drop of four hundred light years. . . .

Presently, in due time, I withdrew my arm.

The arm was whole.

I flexed the muscles. I gripped that iron hand of mine into a fist.

Well!

So I pushed out over the water, gripping the stone lip of

the rim with two strong hands, and dipped my head. I dunked my head in and held my breath and all the pains of Kregen flowed and dissolved and washed away as the snows of the Heart Heights of Valka vanish when the full glory of the Suns of Scorpio pours upon them.

When I withdrew, a vast shape moving slowly in the milky waters drew back at the far end of the pool. Vanti...

It was not bravado, not pride, not foolishness, that made me stand up and walk away without dipping my side. I knew enough of the powers of the milky liquid in the pool. My side, which was ripped and torn and poking crushed ribs through in a bloody crust, would heal of itself.

Over at the far side the Guardian grew restless. A vast smooth bulk humped beneath the water. Waves of the liquid flowed outwards in smooth rolling rings to luminous reflections. I walked away, a whole man once again, and I will not attempt to speak of my feelings, for they poured in a hot jumbled tide, irrational, thanksgiving, angry, shamed, glorious. I had sinned grievously and I had been reprieved. Now, there was work to be done.

A voice whispered through the still air.

"Oh, unfortunate is the city—"

"You have no powers over me, Vanti!" I bellowed back. "Return to your hole, hide away from me—for I warned you I would return." Then, I added: "I return in friendship."

The powers of the Guardian of Pool could hurl me four hundred light years through space back to Earth. Had done so.

I must be an old vosk-skull, for I turned and cupped my hands and splashed the liquid over me, letting it run down over my body and legs.

Yes, an old onker—for as Zair is my witness, I knelt down and took a long swigging drink.

Foolhardy? Of course! But then, that is me, Dray Prescot, Lord of Strombor, Krozair of Zy...

I stood up, tall and straight once more, a fighting man, ready to face what must come on the wild and beautiful, savage and horrendous world of Kregen.

I licked the last moisture from my lips.

"By Mother Zinzu the Blessed," I said, wiping my mouth. "I needed that!"

# *Chapter Seventeen*

# Gifts from a Savanti nal Aphrasöe

The magnificent black zorca trotted along the path above the waterfall. Proud, high-tempered, a stallion, this zorca was a mount fit for a king. I had formed the impression that he had not been well treated by his Kataki owner. This is no novel thing. Some races on Kregen, as on Earth, care nothing for the suffering of animals, as other races care nothing for the suffering of women and children. For me, the stallion responded nobly, and I think he understood very quickly the difference in attitude between his old master and his new rider.

Mind you, Katakis have no feelings for the suffering of animals, women, children or men. They enslave them all.

Once again back to full health and strength, for my side healed with wonderful alacrity after I had taken the swigging, impudent drink, I jogged along on Shadow. I had decided to call this muscular and elegant steed Shadow because he moved like a ghosting shadow across the land. What lay ahead of me I did not know; but the broad outlines of what I had to do remained clear. What was I going to do. The light-headed exultant feeling persisted.

But, of course, Kregen would always come up with frustrations, and plans gang aft agley under Savage Scorpio.

The way opened out and I stared across a plain of brownish grasses studded by a few wilting trees here and there. My eye was caught by a scrap of white high in the firmament. I stared up, eyes narrowed against the glare, and cursed.

Certainly, surely, the white dove of the Savanti flew down and circled, eyeing my zorca with quick intelligence manifested in every movement, an intelligence far past that of any mortal bird.

So, feeling truculent as well as foolish, I shook my fist at the white dove.

"What d'you want?" I bellowed up. "Sink me! I'm not going to the Swinging City, much as I'd like to. I have work to see to that will not wait."

The Gdoinye, the gold and scarlet raptor of the Star Lords, had spoken to me before, as had the Scorpion—I wondered if the representative of the Savanti would deign to open his beak and speak in human terms using a human voice.

He did not. He swung about and then dipped away, going at right angles to my track.

He flew on, with my watchful gaze on him, swung back with a beautiful lift of white wings, soared high again. Again he circled my head and flew off at right angles. Three times he did this before I understood he wanted me to follow him. I had never observed this conduct in the dove before.

I pondered.

The plain remained bare. No purely human enemies threatened. If the Savanti wanted to take me they had powers to snatch me up no matter where I was—so I thought.

Gently easing Shadow around and jogging along after the bird we followed as he circled and rose and fell, pacing his eager flight to our more sedate progress. That after all these years on Kregen I had phlegmatically turned my back on Aphrasöe struck me not so much as odd as highly practical and a sensible course of action. Opaz knew what might happen in Aphrasöe. And Vallia called.

I knew now where the island of Aphrasöe was situated. When my affairs in the Outer Oceans had been settled, why, then, it might be time to return to the Swinging City. I hoped I might return as a friend.

So I followed the beckoning white dove. In for a zorca in for a vove, as my Clansmen say. Soon a little copse came into view half hidden in a field in the ground. The dove fluttered and settled on a branch. He cocked his eager head. I halted Shadow and stared.

Around the dove's neck a thin brilliant scarlet ribbon glowed against the white feathers.

I had never seen that before.

The dove fluffed around and then dived off the branch, almost striking the ground where dried leaves were heaped into a pile before zooming up. Three times he dived. So I dismounted, with a quiet affectionate pat to Shadow's neck, and walked across and kicked the dead leaves away.

Well. Looking down I stood for a few moments and did not move.

Neatly wrapped in a length of scarlet cloth lay my own Krozair longsword with the plain strong strappings, the short sword in the lesten hide and golden scabbard given me by the Clansmen of Viktrik, the greenwood longbow of Erthyrdrin made by Seg and a full quiver of clothyard shafts, each fletched with the glowing blue feathers of the crested korf of the Blue Mountains. In its worn old sheath snugged my sailor knife. The lesten hide belt with the dulled silver buckle was drawn up around the bundle. Well, indeed. . . .

These things had been left by me in the stateroom of Delia's voller. There could be one and only one explanation of how they had come to be here pointed out by a dove wearing a scarlet ribbon. So Maspero had known I was in the cave! I remembered his words—he would not wonder what had happened to me on Kregen. He had a dove to send to spy on me. I surmised that perhaps each Savanti tutor operated his own individual dove.

Also there was a filled water bottle and a satchel containing bread and meats, fruit and nuts. Eating, I realized I was hungry; but that formed a tithe of the burden of my thoughts. I had not touched the water bottle I had filled with the milky liquid from the pool. Did Maspero know I had that?

Laid among the weapons and glinting up was a neatly fitting transparent face piece, which I handled with some awe. It was not glass. Now I know it was made of plastic. It strapped about the head and covered the whole face without obstructing vision.

Evidently Maspero had experience of the Spitballs. . . .

After I had eaten I picked up the length of scarlet cloth, and not without a twinge or two, as you may well imagine. It was far finer than humespack, and Delia had been at pains to secure it at some cost. Although silk and sensil are regarded as superior they do have this infuriating tendency to slip. So I wrapped the brave old scarlet around and drew it up between my legs and tucked the end in and cinched it all tight with the broad lesten hide belt. My old knife snugged at my right hip. The quiver went over my shoulder. I hesitated and then, philosophically, slung the Krozair brand there, also. The short sword buckled up scabbarded at my right side. The longbow, unstrung, could slip into the harness at my left side, leaving my hands free, and the case of strings and the satchel could fasten at my belt.

There were no sandals, or shoes or boots.

The spaces for a rapier and a left-hand dagger were left bare.

Just about then a pack of lurfings showed up, lean-flanked, low-bellied, grey-furred scavengers of the plains. Their probing snout-like faces reminded me unpleasantly of the Khirrs.

It was time to mount up and ride.

The Savanti dove had vanished. I took a good look around for the Gdoinye. Evidently, the Star Lords had no interest in me at the moment.

There was no real reason for it; but I said, aloud, looking up and scowling: "By the disgusting diseased tripes of Makki-Grodno, Star Lords! There is a settlement overdue between us!"

That the settlement would come I had no doubt. If I welcomed or dreaded it I did not know. But, in Zair's good time, it would come. . . .

And, now, there was Zena Iztar to add to the reckoning.

Cantering off and feeling extraordinarily wonderful, clad once more in the brave old scarlet, weapons about me, a superb zorca between my knees, I felt the whole of Savage Kregen might take up arms against me and I would win through. Ah, my Delia. Soon, now, I would find my way back to Vallia and Valka.

Maspero, as I was sure it must have been Maspero, had included in the bundle beautiful Savanti leather hunting gloves and arm-guard, and these I donned, with pleasure.

There was, of course, no shield.

Like the Dray Prescot of yore, I rode on, singing lustily through the streaming mingled suns shine of Zim and Genodras.

I sang *The Bowmen of Loh*, and I sang every verse, every last stanza of that rousing song, and I thought of Seg, and I roared. Then, with a different emotion, I yodelled out *The Daisies of Delphond*. I knew the Delphondian Daisy I coveted. Mind you, the Princess Majestrix might not favor being called a Daisy. . . . I decided it was high time I found out.

The journey progressed in grand style. I suppose, looking back, I was drunk on physical fitness. The horror of my experience in crawling like a half-crushed beetle across this savage land had profoundly affected me. By Vox! I'd been as near death and the Black Spider Caves of Gratz as I care to come—although I was to come closer, as you shall hear, and more than once—and so this ride in the brave old scarlet astride a magnificent zorca, well, it turned my head a little.

Shadow carried me surely and safely across the land of Ba-Domek and we avoided habitations and took the back ways and we did not tangle with the Khirrs, save for a little fracas in which three or four of them burst in black slime, and my face mask was smeared, and I washed us all and my longsword most carefully afterwards. For a space the longsword was carried swinging cleanly in the bright air, for I was reluctant to return it to the scabbard Delia had made for me until it was purified, for all I had scrubbed the glittering blade clean with sand and spittle.

Vomanus of Vindelka, with his slapdash ways with weapons, would have to smarten himself up if he tangled with the Spitballs of Antares, that was for sure. Assuming he won free of the hairy black horrors, of course. All along the way expectations of what I would say to all my comrades enlivened my thoughts.

So, on a day with some cloud rolling up to haze over the glory of the suns, I rode out of the last of the foothills beyond the mountains and down through pleasant shallow valleys and along winding river courses and so found myself faced, at last, with the final long haul to the coast. Although I had used Seg's bow I still carried a full quiver; an old paktun always retrieves his shafts when he can.

If I dwell with what must seem a fey fondness on that journey I think you will understand. I felt reborn. I could taste the glory of Kregen's air and smell the sweetness of the grasses and revel in the warmth of the suns.

On and on we trotted and the plains widened and the sky lifted high above and the clouds rolled and dissipated and I lifted up my head and sang. Silly songs, bawdy songs, stirring war ballads and battle chants, songs of the swods. Vast herds of animals grazed everywhere and the lean forms of the carnivores passed between them, mutually indifferent until the time of hunting. At that time I saw to my weapons and kept a sharp lookout. A massive herd of chunkrah grazed and I gazed at them with the sharp knowing eye of a Clansman, built from wild skirling days on the Great Plains of Segesthes. The chunkrah is perhaps the most superb cattle animal of Paz, deep-chested, horned, fierce, impressive, and his russet coat gleams splendidly. I would not slay one of those magnificent beasts for my supper for that would be wanton waste. Each night I camped and made a fire and slept well away, so that I might espy whoever or whatever sought me by the fireglow.

A sennight later, along with herds of ordel and other cattle, another prairie-darkening herd of chunkrah came in sight, clear proof of the fecundity of the land. Rain fell in due season and the grasses thrived. I skirted the herd, admiring the craggy strength of the chunkrah, giving them no cause to take alarm.

With my old sailorman's knack I had been steering by the suns and the stars and I'd kept on a course that I hoped would be the reciprocal of any vollers out scouting for me toward Aphrasöe. I just accepted with thankfulness the fact—for it is an undeniable fact—that when I am lost and wandering on the face of Savage Kregen my Delia will find ways and means of searching for me. No beautiful idol in a niche, lit by a golden lamp, Delia of Vallia. By Vox, no! She is vibrant and energetic and confoundedly cunning and femininely shrewd. Delia is no stay-at-home dowdy, nor is she a hard and bitter would-be-male chauvinist. She is a woman, and glorious in her womanhood. Also, she casts a too-perceptive eye on me, from time to time, seeing straight through my most artful wiles. So I knew there was a good chance I'd spot an airboat.

Thinking decidedly hot thoughts, I trotted gently over the brow of a hill, a long rolling swaying of the land, and automatically looked for a voller, and all around for potential foes.

A wheeling cloud of Katakis—away in the distance around a scattering of broken rocks beside a broad river Katakis were spurring their zorcas with fiendish cruelty. I stopped at once and pulled Shadow around and rode smartly back over the brow of the hill.

Dismounting and with a pat to Shadow I dropped on all fours and crept up the hill low to the ground and stuck my head out alongside a small chansi bush, its tiny round bottle-green leaves rustling musically in the little breeze. I trusted at the distance that to any sharp eye among the Katakis my shaggy head would look merely like another chansi bush. The wild animals of the plains like the

"The stranded vessel was surrounded by an army of shrilling Katakis."

chansi, for it moistens their mouths and chews for a long time, like cham.

The grey rocks out there had fallen in long ago. They lay scattered and broken, weather-beaten. The muddy river humped along and many wildfowl scattered and squawked and commotioned there, a myriad wings against the brightness.

A glint among the rocks took my attention. A careful look, a scrutiny through narrowed eyes—and I let out a sigh of exasperation.

A voller—stuck down among the rocks. She had come down hard. Fastened to a twisted scrap of her prow, upflung, a flag flew bravely—a flag of orange and grey.

Well, it made sense.

Djanduin was the land nearest here to which any of the trespassers at the pool would have been flung. So it would naturally be Kytun and his fellow four-armed tearaways who would reach Ba-Domek first in search of me.

And their voller had crashed, as vollers did on Kregen.

No thought entered my head of rushing down and getting into the fight. Although I will not be pedantic or intractable on the subject, in my view there is no finer fighting man than a Djang, except a Clansman. But—but, again, that must wait. As I stared down I had no concern for the safety of my Djangs man to man with the Katakis.

Katakis are fierce and vicious with their two powerful arms and steel-bladed whiptails. They are excellent if dirty fighters. But Djangs have four arms, and they are better—and dirtier—fighters, when it behooves them to be.

As now, I saw, peering carefully. For there were not above ten Djangs, and the Katakis numbered over a hundred, shrilling around on their zorcas, shooting arrows into the rocks, charging in only to haul around and pull back, taunting the ferocious Djangs to follow them out to be chopped.

On the ring of plain between the Katakis and the rocks lay many bodies. Most were Kataki. There were Djang bodies there, whereat my face grew grim and I ceased from my careless pleasure in once more seeing my Djangs.

I do not forget I am the King of Djanduin.

The simple brainless course would be to mount up and send Shadow flying down there, to burst through the ring, and to join my people in mutual defiance. Then we could fight it out to the end. Oh, yes, there would be joy in that, perhaps some of the tinsel glory that appeals to the bone-heads among military men of two worlds, as among berserker warriors. But I was Dray Prescot, not a stupid thick-headed nincompoop, not a simpleton in these things, even if I am an onker in others. The picture of the leem, stalking the two young elopers, stayed with me. But even the old Dray Prescot, he who had struggled so intemperately in his early days on Kregen, might have thought on before charging down there to the last great fight.

Although I could not tell how long the fight had been going on, by certain signs I judged my Djangs had been cooped up in that rat trap for longer than most men would have survived. The Katakis had set up a camp nearby, and that told much. The actions of the four-armed warriors bespoke tired arms. Unless I did something positive, and soon, my people down there, brave fighting men who looked to me as their king, would be either killed or enslaved.

Wriggling back from the crest I stood up and put a foot in the stirrup.

"Now we work, Shadow," I said. He tossed that superb head, the horn gleaming and sharp. "By the Black Chunkrah! You and me, together. We must do those Katakis a most diabolical mischief."

And I mounted up, foursquare in the saddle, and trotted out.

## Chapter Eighteen

### The King of Djanduin Flies to Vallia

The russet backs of the chunkrah herd heaved and shimmered and rippled in long sinuous lines like a cornfield in the sun. In the sun Zim. I trotted to the rear of the herd and sat looking at them, weighing their configurations and the lay of the land and selecting those specimens who might be trusted to do my work for me. What I purported was neither new or clever; but it would have to serve now.

Maybe it was not new and not clever; but it would be damned tricky to carry through with just one man.

My Clansmen can perform wonders with chunkrahs. They can wheel them about like flying spindrift, they can form them into raging torrents of pounding hooves and tossing horns and fiery eyes, they can split them into neat parcels, and catch and tame one to quietness. In my time as a Clansman I had learned many of these skills; but I was still far more of a simple warrior than a skilled Chunkrah Clanner, although I could get at least a part of this herd moving. Not for me the spiteful bark of a forty-four, and I had no wideawake to wave, howling. But I shouted and riding up boldly to the specimens I had selected I nudged them into action, yelling, striking them with the flat of my blade. There are tricks. Soon I had a wedge moving sullenly, the mass beginning to pick up speed. I rode around their rear and flanks, herding them with increasing confidence, and Shadow, although unused to chunkrah work, responded nobly.

Then—if it was Zena Iztar I would try to remember to thank her at a suitable time—a leem prowled over. He was hungry. I had never liked leems. After my ordeal, I liked them even less. But the slinking ochre devil served me for the herd picked him up instantly. Any sensible chunkrah will run when a leem hunts. I have seen chunkrah fight leem, and highly horrible it is, to be sure. A leem will not always win, not by any means. But, with my worrying and the stink of the leem, these chunkrahs chose to be sensible. They ran.

"Hai!" I shouted. "Move along! Hai! Run!"

We roared over the brow of the hill and down the long slope like an avalanche of doom.

I took the larboard side of the pack, for the river was over on the starboard and I knew I'd have to exert every effort to keep the herd running close to the bluffs over the water. Chunkrah are not idiots among animals. So we went smoking down the hill toward the rocks.

The Katakis saw us. They spurred their zorcas about. They do not do honest work, Katakis, and probably had no idea how to halt that wild stampede. A Clansman of Segesthes would have known what to do—after he'd gotten himself and his mount out of the way.

Waving and shouting I drove the larboard flank of the

herd in so that the whole enormous mass continued straight on for the rocks. The Katakis hovered, uncertain . . . Some, with sense, set spurs to their steeds and bolted.

Others tried to hide among the rocks, and four-armed demons of destruction rose, raging.

The chunkrah herd opened to pass each side of the rocks and I let the larboard side spill out, for my work with the russet-clad beauties was done.

"Hai!" I shouted, and stuffed the sword away and ripped out the longbow.

Seg knows how to shoot from the back of a zorca. So do I.

The blue-fletched shafts soared sweetly. Katakis began to drop from their zorcas. One or two tried to shoot back; but their bows were puny things, mere flat staves, not rounded longbows, and the arrows dropped plummeting along the river of russet backs.

So the chunkrahs smashed alongside the rocks and a mess of Katakis was scraped up, trodden down, utterly squashed into the ground. Swerving away from the river the front of the herd broadened: the chunkrah pounded on, dust spurting, horns tossing. I saw a Kataki impaled and flung high, ripped and torn and trailing greasy green and red banners of blood. Another slaver was carried along, the long horn clear through him, wriggling like an insect on a pin. But most were simply trodden down.

The booming stentorian bellowings of the herd clamored away, echoing from the rocks. The hammering thunder of the eight-hooved chunkrahs battered away like the long-running drumming of Balintolian droombooms. Thundering in power and might and sheer irresistible energy, the chunkrah herd hammered the Katakis flat and on and away across the plain.

Cantering up to the rocks I saw a few remaining slaving whiptails being dealt with summarily, and I turned in the saddle and looked back, and, by Krun! I hoped to see the leem. But the beast must have had the sense not to follow. So, gently, I dismounted and sauntered over to the rocks and the crashed flier.

A titanic figure, all blazing blood and energy, bounded up, four arms windmilling. I was seized by the upper right and lower left arms, bear-hugged. The upper left hand clapped me on the back, while the lower right fist gut-punched me in an abandonment of joyous welcome.

I gut-punched back with my fifty percent of his equipment, that, so recently, had been twenty-five percent.

"Kytun! You old devil! Having fun again!"

"King! Notor Prescot!" And thump, thump against my ribs he tattooed. "Dray! What a sight!"

Yes, you see. My Djangs are never surprised when their king turns up to rescue them from a tight spot. It is infuriating, I suppose, the way they just take it for granted that their king will be around in times of trouble; but I am used to it. And, anyway, it gives me a warm delicious feeling, I admit.

The sad truth is I am so often away from Djanduin. But all the sorcery of the Wizards of Loh, all the magical powers of the Savanti, cannot place me in different spots on Kregen at the same time. When a time loop operates, of course, *I have been* ...

The others crowded up, the remaining nine. They had lost six of their number in the crash and the fight.

"Katakis!" said Felder Kholin Mindner, dismissively.

"Aye," said Kytun Kholin Dorn. "It was a bonny fight. And only ten to one. The whiptails didn't stand a chance."

Mind you, he did not boast. I vouch for that.

Then followed the greetings and the handclasps and the joyous shouted insults, the horseplay. We made a camp and ate, for the voller was well-provisioned. If any Katakis remained alive they dared not show their ugly faces. Katakis, these bladed whiptails, fear very few races—Chuliks, Pachaks who share a racial hostility; perhaps most of all they fear Djangs, when they meet them, which is not often. As for my Clansmen—well, again, that is for another time.

Kytun broke open an amphora of best Jholaix he had been keeping against our meeting. The wine had been a present from me; we eleven drank it down, and right royally it served its purpose.

"And the emperor—?"

"Aye, Dray! The queen, may Mother Diocaster smile forever upon her, went first into the pool, walking at the side of her father down the stairs. And he moved and sat up on the litter—before, by Zodjuin of the Silver Stux, before it dissolved away—and spoke rationally. He was cured, Dray. Perfectly cured. And then, why then—" And here Kytun scratched his head with his upper left hand and his other hands busied themselves in eating and drinking. "Why, there was blueness and coldness in the pool, and we were in Djanguraj and I was shouting for a new voller. It was not Drig's business. We were there, and then we were home. But, as Djan is my witness, it was a mighty strange affair. Mighty strange, by Zodjuin of the Stormclouds."

Afterwards the dead Djangs were prepared for burial, an extempore, battlefield ritual, with due feeling and solemnity. I watched, taking my part, for I was king.

As to my own story, the wonder of their experiences tended to help and, anyway, as I say, my Djangs perfectly accepted that I would turn up to help them out in any little spot of bother if I could manage it. When troubles hit a party of them they couldn't handle and I did not turn up they would swing those four arms of theirs, and say, so I was told, that, by Zodjuin, the king could not be everywhere at once.

Talking to Kytun, I could not stop my own overriding concerns from showing.

"You are our king, Dray. But it is Vallia that demands, at the moment." He worked his oiled rag over his djangir, setting up the polish. "Of course, they only see you as a prince. One day—"

"Djanduin," I said harshly. "Djanduin means more to me than Vallia. Perhaps Valka—" I had no need to go on. "One day, Kytun, the whole of Paz will be one, united."

He was a good comrade and so he could insult me with a jest; also, I was his king, so he refrained from any comment on so patently absurd a notion.

During the siege among the rocks there had been no time to work on the flier with any consistency; now we went at it to straighten out the linkages controlling the silver boxes that upheld and powered the voller in flight. After some hot and toiling work, mixed with profanities that encompassed the Pantheon of the Warrior Gods of Djanduin, we had the thing fixed, and the voller was once more operational.

Kytun cocked an eyebrow at me.

"Djanguraj," I told him. "We will take this wonderful zorca, Shadow, with us. There is room. In Djanguraj I shall take a small fast roller for Vondium—"

I got no farther.

"King!" bellowed Kytun. The djangir gleamed brilliantly. "We follow you to chop the cramphs who poisoned the queen's father! By Djondalar of the Twisted Staff! This is our duty—aye, and our pleasure."

I was tempted.

Zair knew, with a rascally gang of ferocious Djangs at my back I could do the business speedily enough. But caution supervened. I explained it patiently.

"Suppose a great crowd of Vallian nobles came barging into Djanduin to punish Djangs? Would you—"

"I would rip their guts out!—Oh. . . ."

"Pride, Kytun, is very foolish at times, as at others it is very necessary in a man. I must go alone. To do otherwise would alienate those who—" I paused, annoyed with myself. I had been about to say, those who did not think things through, and, by Djan! that applies to four-armed Dwadiangs, without a doubt. But I love them, for they are bonny fighters. So I said, firmly: "The pride of Vallians would be insulted. Anyway, the emperor has probably sorted things out by now."

"I trust so, by Zodjuin of the Storm Clouds."

Just whereabouts in their home parts of Kregen Vanti would have dispatched my friends I did not know. That depended on how good a shot he was. He'd dumped me down on the coast of Africa somewhere near where I'd been when the Scorpion first took me up to Kregen. But the emperor, Delia, Drak and Jaidur could all be scattered over the whole of Vallia. They could have been shot cleanly into the throne room of the palace in Vondium. I did not know. As to my other friends—well, they'd been scattered halfway around Kregen, as you shall hear.

Perhaps, looking back, I made a mistake in not there and then deciding to load as many fighting Djangs as possible into airboats and going vengefully back to Vallia to settle affairs finally. But, remember, I was still attempting to be the conciliatory Dray Prescot I fancied I must be to attain my goals on Kregen. So, instead, we flew to Djanguraj, I stayed for the shortest possible time decency would allow, and then, with Shadow, took off for Vallia in a small, fleet craft that should see me safely all the way there.

The journey north along the South Lohvian Sea and across the western section of the Southern Ocean—which lies north of Havilfar—and so skirting close to the Koroles, and away up with a great swing to the west of north around the tip of Pandahem, a place remarkably dear to many men, being called Jholiax, passed uneventfully. Uneventfully, save that twice the scarlet and golden raptor appeared high in the blue, circling, watching, and twice the white dove of the Savanti flew down to take a look at my craft.

I say the white dove—maybe, I wondered, it might be better to say a white dove. The idea that each tutor operated his own individual dove did make sense.

So, at last, the southern coastline of Vallia hove in sight over the horizon. The breakers thundered against the shore, the broad bay of the Great River of Vallia, She of the Fecundity, passed below and away up the shining reaches of the river the enormous fantastical skyline of Vondium came in sight. I slanted down.

There was to be no fooling about with attempts to pass guards this time. No secret passages. From the wardrobe kept up in the Palazzo of the Four Winds in Djanguraj I had selected a suit of decent Vallian bluff, so I was dressed as a Vallian as I brought the voller down to the emperor's own landing platform and leaped out. The patrolling airboats of the Vallian Air Service had been late—I frowned at that—and I started off across the broad paved space toward the porticoed entrance.

Shadow looked at me a little reproachfully from the stall built for him in the aft body of the voller, and I flung him a few words of comfort.

Around me the pinnacles of the higher towers reached for the sky. The wind whispered across the open space where airboats were parked, with men working on them in the shadows of their hangars. Chulik guards ran out toward me, angry, intent, ready to do me a mischief. Up here there were usually the Crimson Bowmen on guard.

"Stand, cramph, for the emperor's guards!" yelled their Deldar, a Chulik of mean aspect, with a golden tip to his portside tusk.

"Out of the way!"

I bundled into them, took the first three-grained staff that came handy, knocked three or four of the fellows over and went on, running, into the shadows under the portico.

Only two arrows splintered against the marble. The Chuliks had compound reflex bows of some power; but any skill I may possess at arrow-dodging was not required.

I knew the way.

Past a few slaves I hurried, along the sumptuous corridors well-lit by tall windows where the brocaded drapes barely stirred in the breeze, ignoring a party of Fristle guards who went stepping past smartly across an intersection. Their uniforms might be considered to indicate they were in the emperor's service; but there was altogether too much green and brown about them, and not enough of the red and yellow.

Various doors were guarded by various guards.

If they did not let me through I sent them to sleep without regret. After all, time was wasting.

My calculations told me there would be time for me to reach the penultimate corridor before the guards rallied sufficiently to come in a body to check this madman who had stormed into the palace. The front door, the front aerial door, had been easier than all the other ways. I went on, ignored a group of pretty girls in silks and bangles who shrank away, chattering, angled around the last ornate doorway.

Only four Chuliks stood there.

I gave them no chance to speak.

Only one had a chance to shriek out, and then he, too, slumbered. I kicked a silly ornate golden helmet away and bashed the balass and silver door open. Straight ahead of me down a long and brilliantly lit corridor, filled with people waiting, talking, arguing, drinking, lay the folded doors of the emperor's throne room. He was there. I knew that. These people were waiting audience of him.

I walked on.

Someone yelled: "Hey, fambly! Wait your turn."

I walked on.

A man, he was a kov, a high colored, fleshy man—I knew him—took my arm with anger. I shook him off. I stalked on, and now I was recognized. The whisper ran around the tall room.

"The Prince Majister!"

At the folded doors I came at last to the time when the guards would confront me in real earnest. From a narrow side door they boiled out, Chuliks, tusked, blankly fierce, not reasoning, ready instantly to kill to earn their hire. So far I had not drawn a weapon.

A voice lifted from the waiting brilliantly attired throng.

"He is the Prince Majister! Treat him well—"

The Jiktar at the head of the Chuliks said: "I do not know him. No man enters here without leave of Kov Layco Jhansi. Seize him up!"

I kicked the Jiktar betwixt wind and water, slid the rapid succession of blows, got a sword blade between my elbow and side and wrenched it away from its startled owner, belted a few more, toppling them over. They crashed into their fellows. I was at the doors. The fastenings were immense. I gripped the handles as big as spear blades, dragged the folding doors inward. The oiled panels picked up speed. I had to put my foot into one wight's face to stop his head from being crushed. The massive doors thudded shut.

The bar fell almost of its own accord.

The dinning sound dimmed and faded from outside. The hush fell oddly, menacingly.

Slowly, with the closed doors at my back, I turned around.

The floor of polished marble glimmered in the lights from many samphron oil lamps and from the sparkling rays striking through the wide latticed windows in the curved roof. The distance down to the multiple dais was not great, for this was the third throne room, used for more personal requests. The crimson carpet and the zhantil pelt seatings were familiar, the gold ornaments, the idols, the trophies of battle, the small sacrificial fire and the altar. Beautiful girls waited to bring refreshments when bidden. The room was almost empty.

I started on down the marble floor, my Vallian boots clacking loudly.

The figure in the throne under the ritual canopy sat up. The people standing on the dais, lower down, but not on the floor, went rigid.

"So you return bearing words, son-in-law?"

"Not so, emperor!" I bellowed back. "See—I come empty-handed."

And I held up my hands, palms outwards, as I marched.

A small quick gesture from the emperor halted the reflex action of the bodyguard lining out each side of the throne. These guards, too, were Chuliks. I did not like the look of this at all. I have employed Chuliks as mercenaries, for they are powerful fighters; but the numbers of them, the positions they occupied, argued some calamity had befallen the Crimson Bowmen, or some other deviltry was at work.

"You are banished from Vondium, son-in-law. Tell me why I should not order you cast down to the deepest dungeons?"

"Because you know that will not serve you." I looked about, for the moment ignoring the few men and women in attendance on him, looking for certain faces I hungered to see.

"Where is Delia? Where are Drak and Jaidur?"

"Well may you ask, Dray Prescot. Since I am well again I have seen nothing of—"

I held onto my roaring senses. Didn't the buffoon know what had happened? Probably not. He'd been on the point of death in his imperial bed, and then he'd been dumped down in his palace full of life. Probably he had no memory of what had intervened, or of that moment of lucidity in the Pool.

"You remember your request to your daughter?"

"I have made many requests of her. She usually refuses."

"And damned sensible, too! So you don't remember."

"Enough of this—" he started to say, getting his temper up, which with him was deplorably easy.

"I want to see Delia and the children!" I stopped at the foot of the dais and my left hand rested on the hilt of the Krozair longsword, which I wore angled out almost parallel with the ground, jutting, arrogant, I confess, very boastfully. The rapier hanging from its baldric looked thin and puny in contrast.

"And I would like to see some of these people you tell me are my friends. I was near unto death—and what happened to you and your friends?"

"I was banished—or have you forgotten?"

His dark, heavy face flushed. He was back to full health, all right. Why, the old devil had never felt better in his life.

"This Seg Segutorio, this Inch of the Black Mountains, kovs, both of them, because I gave you the gifting. I have my loyal men about me now." His powerful face showed an intensity of belief. "I have made a winnowing of my enemies. Now I have loyal friends and an impregnable bodyguard of Chuliks—"

I laughed. I, Dray Prescot, laughed. The laugh was filled with scorn, contemptuous.

"Impregnable?"

He swallowed down bile for a space. But he was not beaten by mere words; he was emperor. "I let you live. One word from me and you die."

"And your daughter?"

That nettled him sorely.

It did more than that. I fancied I knew what had happened. No matter where Delia had landed back in Vallia, she had swiftly organized fliers, men and weapons, supplies. Then she had gone haring off back to the forbidden island of Ba-Domek. She had gone to find me. And, no doubt, everyone else of our company she could find had gone with her.

That was an eventuality I had hoped to forestall. But I was too late. So, since the emperor was safe, I had no more business with him.

One more fact remained to be established.

"Of these people you stigmatize by calling them my friends." I named the people I meant, the brave company who had flown with me to Aphrasöe carrying the dying body of this emperor with us. He knew them and of their loyalty to me. "Are there any in Vondium now?"

"No, son-in-law. Not one. Not a single person of those you champion so loudly. I tell you, I have friends, and I know where to look for succor."

He started to shake with anger, working himself up. A further thought occurred to me. I was aware of a small side door opening and of the guards springing to assist the people who entered; but I wanted to ask the emperor one last question before I retired.

"You were nearly dying, emperor. Now you are well. Do you know how that was accomplished?"

"Of course. Need you ask?"

His reply astonished me. He was looking off to the side, to the group of people who had entered and who now came up to the foot of the dais, bowing with the air of those who had power and authority at the emperor's hand.

"Here, Dray Prescot, are those who saved me. Loyal subjects all. To them, I owe my life and Vallia. They should be the lesson you so sorely need."

He gestured, raising them up from their postures of reverence. I looked.

Oh, I looked, like an idiot, like an onker, like the stupid simpleton I am.

These were the people Delia's father put his trust in, these the folk he had given power, and chief among them Doctor Charboi, and hard, bright, cutting, Ashti Melekhi, the Vadnicha of Venga.

# Chapter Nineteen

## "There Stands the Notorious Dray Prescot!"

"Why is this man allowed to wear swords in the presence of the emperor? Disarm him, instantly!"

The vicious words of Ashti Melekhi spattered into the bright radiance of the throne room.

The guard Chulik—he was an ord-Jiktar and therefore very high in the guard, probably the third in command—stepped down from the dais heading for me, and he half-drew his rapier.

"Wait, wait, my dear Ashti!" called the emperor.

I felt nausea at his way of addressing her.

Down in Djanduin my warrior Djangs would feel naked and dishonored to appear in the presence of their king without a ceremonial djangir buckled up to their harness. But this was Vallia, and only on special occasions would the court wear anything other than fancy smallswords for decorative purposes. Vallia was a civilized country.

"This man, Ashti, is the Prince Majister." He relished his power. "There stands the notorious Dray Prescot! He is my son-in-law, I am afraid. I do not care for him overmuch; but he has served me well on occasion. He is a man of swords, a man of blood, a man of violence."

I felt the outrage. "I am not a man of blood!" I bellowed. "I am a man of peace!"

"That is as may be. But you may keep your swords."

The Chulik Jiktar slapped his rapier back. He looked annoyed, as though denied a pleasure. But the emperor knew me better than this yellow-faced, tusked, malevolent Chulik.

The emperor knew I was more malevolent on occasion than any Chulik born—and this, too, was for my sins.

Melekhi stared at me. Charboi had the grace to shuffle

away, eyes cast down, and stand nervously some distance off. Ashti Melekhi! A long cool gown of green she wore, with golden motifs, and the strigicaw seizing the korf, her badge, emblazoned upon breast and arm and thigh. She stared challengingly at me and I sensed she had an inkling that I had taken the emperor away, following his gasped instructions, and was not yet prepared to take up that particular challenge. The emperor believed she and Charboi had cured him. To challenge me now, openly, would raise awkward questions, and she wanted to choose her time and place for the confrontation.

I said: "Twelve friends of yours paid me a call. I hope they spoke well of me."

She started, and controlled herself, her thin cheeks pinching in. I noticed she wore a small sword that was, in reality, a strong and cunning dagger, emblazoned with gems.

"Oh," she says, very sure of herself. "No doubt you will meet some more of my—friends—very soon."

"I welcome it. Let them come swiftly. The canals are cooling in the hot weather."

The emperor made a sign and a beautiful girl ran across to give him a drink of parclear. He drank, thirstily. "I don't know what foolery this is; but anyone knows the canals of Vallia are deadly to those not of the canalfolk. Now, Dray Prescot, say what you have to say and go."

"The banishment upon me is lifted?"

Melekhi gasped at this; but the emperor, after another insolent drink, and having his mouth wiped by a Fristle fifi, nodded. "Yes. But if you err again, son-in-law—"

"Only time will tell that. For there are things you must know. And you will not relish the telling of them."

"And will the word onker come into it?"

"Only if an onker listens, instead of an emperor."

His face swelled up again, and he thundered out: "You try my patience sorely! Have a care. You had best go while your head is still on your shoulders."

Considering it redundant once more to point out what that order had come to in the past, I nodded stiffly to him. I faced Ashti Melekhi. I did not smile, as is my wont, and I kept my face as naturally molded into its ugly old lineamants as I could. All the same, something showed, for her eyes narrowed and the tip of a red tongue flicked her lips.

Nath the Iarvin started at this, and stilled. All the time

his bulky form towered at Ashti Melekhi's shoulder, silent, unspeaking, his small dark eyes watchful. He still wore the brown leather tunic and buff breeches, with the wide, black, silver-studded belt girt up around his gut. The lockets for his rapier swung empty; but he carried a twin to the dagger worn by Melekhi. The sheer ferocity of that lowering face impressed me once again. This man had been bought body and soul by Melekhi, he would fight and kill and die for her and joy in the doing of it.

I walked out with my shoulders held braced, my boots clacking on the polished marble floor. At the door where Womoxes hoisted up the bar and swung it away, folding the panels open, I turned back. The emperor sat forward on his throne, watching, and the others remained still in the postures I had left them.

"I give you Remberee, emperor. We shall meet again—"

"Not if Opaz wills it," he shouted after me.

So I went out and took myself off. This time I was allowed through. But the looks I took from some of the Chuliks heartened me. They hadn't seen the half of it, yet.

The voller lifted off smartly and I turned in the direction of the Great Northern Cut and Bargom's *Rose of Valka*—and then my hands clicked the control levers over. No. No, I did not wish just yet to become embroiled with stikitches. The assassins Melekhi would send must wait. Business before pleasure.

Information was vital, information I needed but that could not have been asked for from any of those in the throne room. Although I have an ugly old figurehead and a pair of shoulders that are somewhat on the wide side, it is possible for me on a world like Kregen to disguise myself adequately. A large hat, perhaps a false beard, a long cloak, the cunning application of makeup and a different walk, these things work wonders.

The voller was dropped at our Delphondian villa, a piece of work rapid in the extreme, for Melekhi would probably send her assassins to all my villas as well as *The Rose of Valka*. With Shadow safely stabled in a public livery, for I might need him in a hurry, I could stroll into *The Savage Woflo*, a riotous tavern where soldiers and guards gathered, and fling a few silver stivers across the table and roar for good Vallian ale.

The sight of my father-in-law's face glinting upon the stivers, a variety of propaganda slogans and pictures on the reverses, did not altogether please me; but the money fetched ale, and company, and I could settle down before the singing began. Here in *The Savage Woflo* information could be come by. Because of the many lords in Vondium the tavern was crowded with their guards. Colors blazed in the mineral-oil lamps. Soon I was being filled in with all the latest gossip.

A few Crimson Bowmen sat drinking, and most of them looked glum. There were few Pachaks. The Chuliks outnumbered all. This, I owned to myself, was passing strange. Vondium had recovered from the dread spell of impending doom that hung over the city like a pall when the emperor lay dying. Now he was back in his palace, hale and well, Vondium could go back to the usual round of commerce and industry, secure that all was well with Vallia. By careful talk, by intimating I knew more than I did, I got out the story.

Briefly: all the Crimson Bowmen and the Chuliks who had guarded the emperor's door that night had been discharged. I was amazed they had not been slaughtered out of hand. But that would have entailed stringent inquiries. Melekhi stood in a position of great power, that was undeniable. She was being used by an even more shadowy figure of greater power; and for an instant I trembled, thinking it might be Phu-Si-Yantong. There was nothing to link him with this plot against the emperor personally; this was a palace intrigue, and Yantong had worked through his Black Feathers of the Great Chyyan against the whole of Vallia.

Her mentor might be this Kov Layco. He was an astute man, holding the empire together for the emperor, guiding with ruthless and clever hands the destinies of all, trusted. Yes, he might cherish ambitions; it could be him. I tended to doubt it would be any Racter, for they attempted, for all their evil, to work through legal means. And for the Panvals the same held. There were many parties and factions ready to strike if the emperor died; now they were muzzled; but any one of them could own and instruct Ashti Melekhi in her evil designs.

The emperor insisted these days on guards hired from the Chulik mercenaries. The Crimson Bowmen, like the Archer Guard of Valka assigned to duty around the emperor, had been sent off on distant expeditions into the country.

Naghan Vanki, who, I knew, or thought I knew, was the emperor's spymaster, had recently, after his good work with the chyyanists, been rewarded by being made Vad of Nav-Sorfall. The province was lush, rich with ponsho pastures, situated just east of Vomansoir. Because of this addition to his estates Naghan Vanki, the new vad, was off in Nav-Sorfall busily at work consolidating his position. I could not turn to him for immediate information on the plots and intrigues surrounding the emperor.

To think, the woman who had bribed a doctor to poison the emperor was now held in great esteem by her intended victim! She would strike again, and soon. I stirred myself. The singing would begin soon; but because there were so many Chuliks, the singing promised to be half-hearted and short if the yellow-tuskers did not remove themselves, as they usually did when there were not many of them.

The last piece of information amused me. Queen Lushfymi, the Queen of Lome, whom men still called Queen Lush, despite the emperor's strict injunctions against the loss of dignity, was rumored to be hot on her way to the emperor's side.

If the old devil married her, I'd heave a sigh of relief. That would take a deal of weight off Delia's and my shoulders.

The Maiden with the Many Smiles shone down brilliantly as I wrapped my cloak about myself, pulling it up to my eyes, and set off for the palace. The first moon of Kregen showed those mysterious markings that had so often tantalized the astronomers of Kregen. Up there, on that world floating in space, were continents and islands and seas, and an atmosphere. The ever-changing radiance gave her her name. In that soft and fuzzy roseate moonlight I strode swiftly through the pink-tinged shadows.

Vondium went about the usual pursuits of the great city after the suns had set and the moons ruled the skies. I avoided all entanglements. This time there was another Rapa guard at the Jasmine Tower beyond the Canal of Contentment. He went to sleep peacefully and I opened the plastered niche and, pulling the revolving stone free, passed swiftly down the slimed stairs.

The lantern showed nitered walls, dripping thick with green slime, and the darkly patterned stairs. That first Rapa guard had recovered, all right, and said nothing, greeting his relief with a hearty: "All's well!" So do mortal men's sins find them out and aid hairy old villains like me.

Reaching the secret panel that led onto the emperor's

chamber, I paused. He had plenty of bedrooms to choose from. Maybe he wouldn't relish sleeping again in the room in which he had so nearly died. I'd find him, though, if I had to roam all through the palace.

What I really wanted to do was take voller and fly as swiftly as I could after Delia, on toward Ba-Domek and Aphrasöe. But I conceived I had a duty to the emperor; the old devil owed me, and I suppose, really, I owed him. He was Delia's father. I could not let him be killed. I could not abandon him to his fate.

I pushed the panel in soundlessly.

Anyway, I did not want the forces controlling Ashti Melekhi to slay the emperor and gain their coveted powers—I did not want them to win.

Intrigue, dark plots, the shadows of night, the hushed footfall—these were games I would play, I decided, as I padded into the chamber. The room stood empty, a few faintly glimmering lamps reflecting from the old polished furniture. The wide bed lay with its covers turned back. A golden tray rested on a low table at the side. Miscils, palines, purple wine of Wenhartdrin in a golden vessel with two golden cups—the old devil was all set up for the night, then.

A noise at the door, the oiled creak of its opening, light splashing sharply across the rugs of Walfarg weave. I moved back into the shadows of the overhanging draperies. He walked in with a few handmaids and servants, scolding them, full of good humor. Eventually, when he was dressed in a long crimson brocaded gown he shooed them out. As the door closed he shouted out jovially past them to the corridor; "And mind you stand a good watch, my bonny Chuliks."

They were bonny all right, working for anyone who paid them. If someone else had crossed their yellow palms with more gold than the emperor, they'd as lief slit his throat as stand a good guard.

He started up when I stepped out into the lamplight. His face worked with shock. His hand darted to the golden bell.

I put my hand over his and the bell hung mute.

"Ha!" he cried. "Murder, is it?"

"No." I held him gently. "I mean you no harm, as I have told you often enough. I wish to talk to you. For the sake of your daughter and your grandchildren, will you hear me out?"

The bell must be removed from his clutching fingers, for I would not trust him, as I trust no one save a very few on Kregen and Earth.

"Talk? You talk big, son-in-law. But you desert me when danger—"

"You banished me. Forget that. You remember nothing of your illness?"

He shook his head. For a space, so long as I offered him no violence, he would humor me and listen. . . . "No. I remember nothing. I was ill. Ashti cured me."

I let him go but I did not step back. I stared at him. "Listen to me, emperor, and mark me well. You were poisoned." He started up angrily at this, but I went on doggedly. "The name of the poison was solkien concentrate—"

"I know it! Cottmer's work!"

"Aye. And you were fed it, lovingly, spoonful by spoonful."

"I do not believe—how could I? I was cared for, nursed, no one—Ashti would not have allowed it—you lie!"

"I do not lie. I pass over your intemperate words. I tell you the truth."

For a moment he stood there, tall and bluff and robust, filling his crimson gown with the golden cords. His face showed a sudden crafty intelligence. "I know of solkien concentrate. Once it gets a hold on the system its evil results cannot be averted. I was ill, very ill. Ashti told me. If you speak sooth then I could not have been cured."

"Not by normal men. I agree."

He looked bewildered. "But—"

I bore down on him. "You called out in your delirium. You asked your daughter, you begged Delia to take you to those who could cure you, as they had cured her."

His eyes widened.

"Yes—yes—I do not remember—but I would—I did! The Todalpheme of Hamal."

"Your daughter Delia took you there. You were cured. If you do not remember then that is probably better. Now you are back in your palace, fit and well. Delia did that."

"Solkien concentrate." He wet his lips and took up the golden vessel, poured wine. He did not pour for me. I let him drink. Then I said: "Suppose that wine is poisoned, also?"

He choked and spat and the purple wine sprayed all over the white linen of the bed.

He swung to face me. He was trembling. "If I believed you, your story, if I did—you have not told me who did this thing."

"Ah," I said. I used the old formula out of spite, watching him squirm. "I wondered when you'd come to that."

"Tell me! I can find out if you speak truth. I can seek and find the answers to my questions—"

"Oh, aye. You can have folk tortured to your heart's content."

"Tell me, you insolent cramph!"

"I wonder, sometimes," I told him. "Why I suffer myself to bother with you. Only for Delia's sake. Otherwise, I really think I would let you go your own way to damnation."

His face shook with his rage, cunning and powerful, used to absolute obedience. "Tell me!"

"Ashti Melekhi."

He gaped at me.

Then he laughed and sneered, all in one, and sank back in the ornate brocaded chair at the bedside. The golden tassels shook with his sarcastic mirth. He brayed at me.

"You onker! Your sorry story is a pack of lies. The woman cut you down to size and you resent that. Ashti—why, Ashti nursed me devotedly. She found Doctor Charboi. Your story of solkien concentrate must be untrue, this leem's nest of a story about going for the miracle cure—lies, all lies. I shall call the guard instantly—"

"There is no need for that. I have warned you. The woman is deadly. She will try again. What I would like to know is whom she is working for."

"She works for me. She is devoted."

"And Queen Lush?"

He glared, choking with rage, trying to rise from the chair and being held down by my hand. "She is Queen Lushfymi and she has nothing to do with this. Ashti knows she can never become empress. That is not to be thought of."

"I wasn't thinking of that, either. But it would give you a reason to understand. Myself, I believe there are other stronger forces at work here to destroy not only you but the whole of our family."

"Our family?"

"I know how you regard me, a wild clansman; but your grandchildren are Delia's children. You must believe me."

"I cannot. I must think on what you have said and think best how to deal with you."

You see? You see how the powerful of the land think?

I said to him, speaking pretty savagely: "Very well, emperor. You think on. I have warned you and I shall try to protect you. If I leave now I expect no trouble from your Opaz-forsaken Chulik guards. Or you'll have a slew of death bonuses to pay out."

He panted, heaving up as I stepped back into the shadows of the bed. "Sometimes, Dray Prescot, sometimes I think I would gladly pay all my treasury in death bonuses if one of them was yours."

"Oh, aye. You're not the only one."

The door creaked on its oiled hinges and fresh light spurted through the opening gap. No one had knocked. The emperor stood up from the chair, half turned away from where I stood shrouded in the bed hangings. He looked relieved and glad.

"Here is Ashti now. Now we will test the lies you spew!"

So that explained the second cup. The purple wine would be safe, then. I licked my lips, thirstily.

Ashti Melekhi entered the emperor's bed chamber, walking like a neemu, all feline undulation and grace. Her thin mannish figure was clad in the green hunting leathers. At this the emperor's face fell. He took a half-step forward.

"Ashti? You are welcome, welcome—but why this costume?"

She flashed that brilliant scything white smile at him.

"Because there is hunting to do tonight, majister."

"Hunting?" The buffoon was bemused.

Following Melekhi the hulking form of Nath the Iarvin shouldered through the door. With him came six Chuliks. They were officers, Hikdars and Jiktars, and at their head strode the Chulik Chuktar of the guard. Their weapons glittered naked in their fists.

The emperor fell back.

"Ashti!" he screeched.

"Yes, emperor. We cannot wait. Your interfering son-in-law has returned, and he knows the truth. So you must die tonight, now!"

# Chapter Twenty

## Savage Kregen

"Slay him, you fools, and have done!"

Ashti Melekhi pointed scornfully at the emperor, who fell back over his chair, twisting, knocking the golden cups of wine to the priceless carpets.

I stepped out into the light. The long dark cloak covered my face in shadow.

"Whoever he is, slay him also!" cried Melekhi.

The Chuliks advanced with grim purpose.

"You see, emperor," I said. "There's no telling an old onker the truth even if it's staring him in the face."

The emperor choked. He tried to struggle up. "Guards!" he got out in a strangled voice. "Guards! To me! To me!"

"What!" said I. "D'you want more of 'em to do your business for you? This bitch has bought them all."

Ashti Melekhi drew in a sharp breath. Her face glowed with pleasure, her grey-green eyes bright, her pursed red mouth moist.

"The Prince Majister! Two with but a single cast! Now the gods smile on me."

"It depends on which gods," I said as I threw off the swathing cloak. "Some of that fraternity are not too reliable."

"Slay them both," screeched Melekhi. She held her hands pressed to her thin breast. She craned to watch.

The rapier came out smoothly enough, and the left-hand dagger. These Chuliks were past masters at their art, trained from birth. I was in for a strenuous few murs—or however long the fight lasted. The problem would be to keep the emperor from being killed.

I never forgot he was an emperor. Now he struggled up

and the look on his face would have quelled an ordinary rabble. He grabbed for the bedhead table. He kept a sword ready to hand there as do all sensible folk on Kregen.

"I am the emperor!" he shouted. "Foresworn traitoress!"

"Now, emperor," I said. "Remember. Remember the fight with the third party outside your very own palace grounds?" As I said this I crossed swords with the first of the Chuliks, who came on with great panache. I twinkled his blade about; but he knew that one, and I had a quick little spot of nimble parry and duck with his left hand companion before the rapier went into his guts and I could withdraw, skip aside and so kick another Chulik betwixt wind and water. He staggered; but I gave him no time to fall, by reason of the dagger that skewered into his eye. Bits of fluid gristle and blood spurted.

"I remember that fight, Dray Prescot!"

"Aye. Well, I'll pull your hair again if you get in the way."

Two Chuliks were down. The four remaining came on, violently, rapidly, and I had a deal of ducking and parrying to do, using the full of the blade, feeling the solid power of their blows ring and chingle along the steel.

"Get past him, you fools!" screeched Melehki. "Get at the emperor."

"You stay behind me, emperor!" I yelled, and shoved him back with my shoulder, as cursing and swashing his blade, he struggled to get past the bed and the table.

Because of that wide, ornate, draped bed the Chuliks could not get around me on one side, or leap at my back. They had to come at me from the front and the right. This, I fancy, put them at a disadvantage. There were four of them. Nath the Iarvin stood, blocky, solid, immense, at the side of his mistress, watching it all with those cold piggy eyes.

And I saw, instantly, that the Chuliks would be cut down when they had done their work.

This Nath was good with a blade. Everyone knew that.

A third Chulik staggered back, most surprised. He had thought I would thrust with the rapier, having feinted for that purpose, and he had dropped into line ready for the riposte. But my rapier held down the blades of two of his companions, beating them back. My main gauche whipped across, very fast, horizontal, very nastily.

The Chulik looked surprised because his throat was cut

from ear to ear. He grinned at me with a blood-bubbling mouth where his throat should be.

The fourth Chulik, for the moment disengaged, shoved his dying comrade aside to get at me, and as he came on so I dropped and gut-thrust him before he even settled, and sent him toppling over on the last long journey to the Ice Foes of Sicce.

The other two stepped back, their blades snaking up, free of mine, and so for a space we looked at one another.

"What do you wait for!" Melekhi stamped her foot—a futile, stupid gesture. "Slay them both!"

And Nath the Iarvin spoke.

"He is a great swordsman, my lady."

"And so are you—better, by all accounts."

"Then let me—"

"Wait!"

The Chuliks were filled with the blood lust and the purport of this exchange passed them by. They leaped in, still deadly, still ferociously anxious to spill my tripes.

Well aware that this brooding Nath was watching my play I tried to play the next one cleverly and foin a little and a Chulik blade sliced down my face. I cursed and jumped aside and my brand scorched across his face, not where I had intended and I felt the steel jar against a tusk. He screamed.

This was turning from a pleasant little passage at arms into the bloody and squalid fight it truly was.

There was no jikai here, I surmised.

Blood ran down my chin.

The two were heartened at this and came on. The emperor was still thrashing and swashing about, and he near-nicked me a couple of times.

"Keep you back, you great onker!" I said. "By Zair! I don't want your nose sliced off for my Delia to see!"

"Let me at 'em!" he was yelling, kicking the chair, the table, the bed, foaming.

My blade licked in and out, and the Chuliks, who can handle weapons, played me, one against the other; but I had them in the end, although not as I had expected.

The right hand one stepped back. He stepped away from the struggle of his comrade. Swiftly he thrust his rapier under his left arm and whipped out a throwing knife. It was not a terchick, being altogether heavier and not so finely balanced; but it would do the emperor's business for him.

Fight fire with fire. There was no time. I lifted the left-hand dagger. I hurled it as my Clansmen hurl the ter-chicks, riding the backs of their voves. Left-handed, right-handed, it makes little difference to a Clansman.

At the same time I slid the point of the last Chulik and presented my point to his throat.

The main gauche flew true. It smashed into the Chulik's face, staggering him, bringing a great splashing spurt of dark blood. And the rapier point slid, cutting through the windpipe and the jugular of the Chulik before me. The distant yellow-tusk screeched, flailing about, spraying gobbets of blood, screaming. The one before me glared madly, trying to wrench the blade from his throat, and that damned fool the emperor came up—well, not between my legs, but close by them—surged up to take a juicy whack with his blade at the wriggling Chulik.

The mercenary flailed over backwards taking my rapier with him.

I stood there, glaring myself, furiously angry.

"Get back out of it, you fambly!" I roared.

And Ashti Melekhi, in a voice like steel, said: "Now, Nath. Now."

Nath the Iarvin drew his rapier and main gauche with the single fluid motion that told of a master fencer. He advanced on me and the look on his dark powerful features meant only one thing in the whole wide world of Kregen.

I stood before him, my hands empty.

"Dray!" screeched the emperor, squirming about between bed and table. "A sword—here—take mine!"

"Too late for that, rast," said this Nath, speaking up, very jovial, very purring-pleased now he had been unleashed.

"True," I said, brightly. "True."

Nath leaped in with that smooth skilful poised motion of the bladesman.

So, with a sigh, I, Dray Prescot, Krozair of Zy, unlimbered the deadly Krozair brand, and with spread fists, met that headlong charge.

His first swift passage aimed at sliding past the long blade was met and repulsed. He dodged back, the main gauche fending. He blinked.

"You'd best put up that old bar of iron, dom. Make it easy on yourself. Just relax and, by the Blade of Kurin, I swear to make it quick and painless."

And, as he spoke, cunning bladesman, he leaped again

and so twinkled his blades before my eyes. Cunning, cunning! Oh, yes, he was very good as a bladesman, this Nath the Iarvin. But I have been a bladesman in my time—still am, I suppose. He had not met a Krozair brand before. All that old agony of indecision of mine about a Krozair brand facing a rapier—well, that has been settled. The beautiful blade, perfectly balanced, rotated smoothly, oiled, flaming with power, scorched in past his darting blades, sank in over his silver-studded black belt, sank in and in and burst on through.

I withdrew.

He stood, gaping, bewildered. Even as he began to shake and topple and the weapons fall from his hands, the door opened.

A man stepped through, very alert, intense, filled with an eagerness of spirit I could recognize. My gaze switched back to Nath as the blood bubbled out over his brown tunic. His outspread arms with the brown and green banded sleeves quivered; his hands gripped and relaxed, gripped and relaxed, and they would never more grasp rapier or main gauche. The irony was not lost on me. By the rapier he had lived, and by the longsword he had died.

"What!" I cried. "Another ponsho for the slaughter."

The man who had entered stopped stock still.

He wore Vallian evening clothes, a deep crimson robe, embroidered with silver risslacas, circled by a jewelled belt, very thin, from which swung on gemmed lockets a long dagger. Around his neck a chain formed of gold links and rubies and laybrites caught the samphron oil lamp's gleam and winked and shone magnificently, the red and yellow gems blinding.

"Layco!" cried Ashti Melekhi, and she lifted her arms imploringly.

"Majister!" said this newcomer, this man I now knew to be Kov Layco Jhansi. "You are unharmed?"

"Never better," growled the emperor. "And these rasts are dead, and that she-leem is the blackest traitor this side of Cottmer's Caverns."

"Layco!" shrieked Melekhi again. Her white scornful face caught up all the agony in her, and she screamed. She ripped the dagger from her belt and crouched, ready to spring.

Layco Jhansi appeared to be in the prime of life, short, with closely cropped brown hair. His face was regular, unmarked by suffering, his eyes large and luminous. He carried within himself a shining spirit that marked him out as a man who would adorn any walk of life he chose to inhabit.

Ashti Melekhi poised, the slim dagger held high. In a heartbeat she would hurl it straight at the emperor—it was written clearly on that white and twisted face.

No one there could know the Krozair brand would flick the flying dagger away. The moment hung with menace. Then Jhansi stepped in close to Ashti Melekhi. He whipped his own needle-slim dagger out. She saw him from the corner of her eye.

She screamed and fell back as the dagger plunged into her bosom. The green leathers punctured and as Kov Layco withdrew the blade blood welled.

"No! No—Layco!" she screamed. "Please—please—" The dagger in the Chief Pallan's hand lifted again. This time it would finish her. "Please, Layco! I could not help it!"

"You could not, Ashti," said Jhansi. "But you are a traitoress. Foresworn. The life of the emperor is not to be taken lightly or without punishment."

And his dagger flashed down and buried itself in her heart.

Thus died Ashti Melekhi, the Vadnicha of Venga.

"A just retribution for a foul traitoress, majister," said Jhansi. He calmly left his blade where it jutted from the bosom of the corpse. He walked across to the emperor and bowed.

"You are unharmed, majister?"

"I'm perfectly all right. This great hairy graint of a Clansman stopped me from having any fun again—it's always the same."

I held down my disgust. What did he know of the actual hurly-burly of battle? What fun was there in that? He did not even inhabit the same kind of world my Djangs or my Clansmen did when they spoke of fun.

"I shall have everything seen to, majister." He eyed me with a lively glance. He hesitated, which I fancied was an odd thing for him to do. He glanced toward the door, and opened his mouth; then he closed that firm-lipped mouth and nodded. "By morning the culprits, if there are any left, will have been rooted out. And I shall start with the guards at your door. They must have heard the commotion, and yet they did nothing."

"Bought," I said. "Bought and paid for."

"Aye, prince," He said. Even without the pappattu and the Lahals, he knew who I was. "But who?"

"We'll find out."

"And the quicker the better," said the emperor. "I must give you thanks, Layco, for saving my life. That she-leem would have skewered me with that dagger. But it means she cannot testify."

"I shall do all I can, majister."

"Yes, Layco. On you I rely. You never fail me."

I remained silent.

"You honor me, as always, majister."

"I shall never forget your loyalty for as long as I live." The emperor looked around on the shambles, on the dead, the six Chuliks, the bladesman, the vadnicha. He shook his head. "Indeed, it is a terrible thing to be an emperor."

And I felt the stupid giggle starting deep within me.

The emperor's enemies had attempted to poison him and get him out of the way of their schemes, remove him at the first from the palace revolution. My wonderful Delia and our friends had foiled that plot and cured the emperor. The guilty had been punished. The traitors would be paid off, and the loyal guards return. Layco Jhansi would see to that.

But—but! We had given the emperor a thousand years of life.

Never before had he been seated so thoroughly upon the throne. It was a joke. His enemies would fade away and vanish like Drig's Lanterns. The emperor of Vallia would remain the emperor of Vallia for a thousand years.

I felt the relief like wine bubbles rising and bursting.

It was marvelous!

And my Delia—how we would laugh, together, back with our family in Esser Rarioch.

The emperor was staring at me. Layco Jhansi was staring at me. The stench of blood rose dizzyingly in the room. I glared back at them. I could feel the unleashing of emotions bursting in me, rising like the wine bubbles, forcing their way out.

A thousand years and not a care in the whole wild world of Savage Kregen beneath the Suns of Scorpio!

And I laughed. I, Dray Prescot, Lord of Strombor and Krozair of Zy, I laughed and laughed and laughed.

## ALAN BURT AKERS—

## the great novels of Dray Prescot

### The Delian Cycle

| | | |
|---|---|---|
| ☐ | TRANSIT TO SCORPIO | #UY1169—$1.25 |
| ☐ | THE SUNS OF SCORPIO | #UY1191—$1.25 |
| ☐ | WARRIOR OF SCORPIO | #UY1212—$1.25 |
| ☐ | SWORDSHIPS OF SCORPIO | #UY1231—$1.25 |
| ☐ | PRINCE OF SCORPIO | #UY1251—$1.25 |

### The Krozair Cycle

| | | |
|---|---|---|
| ☐ | THE TIDES OF KREGEN | #UY1247—$1.25 |
| ☐ | RENEGADE OF KREGEN | #UY1271—$1.25 |
| ☐ | KROZAIR OF KREGEN | #UW1288—$1.50 |

### The Vallian Cycle

| | | |
|---|---|---|
| ☐ | SECRET SCORPIO | #UW1344—$1.50 |
| ☐ | SAVAGE SCORPIO | #UW1372—$1.50 |

---

**DAW BOOKS are represented by the publishers of Signet and Mentor Books, THE NEW AMERICAN LIBRARY, INC.**

---

**THE NEW AMERICAN LIBRARY, INC.,**
P.O. Box 999, Bergenfield, New Jersey 07621

Please send me the DAW BOOKS I have checked above. I am enclosing $_____(check or money order—no currency or C.O.D.'s). Please include the list price plus 35¢ per copy to cover mailing costs.

Name_____

Address_____

City_____ State_____ Zip Code_____
Please allow at least 4 weeks for delivery